HERE
LIES

TO DOROTHY PARKER

Edited by
David Gilbert and Karl Roeseler

HERE
LIES

Printed on acid-free paper
Printed in the United States of America

A complete list of acknowledgments appears on pp. 247-248.

ISBN 0-9639192-5-3

First Edition. 2001

Book design by Clare Rhinelander
Printed by McNaughton & Gunn, Inc.

Trip Street Press books are distributed by
Small Press Distribution
1341 Seventh Street, Berkeley, CA 94710
Telephone: 1.800.869.7553 or 510.524.1668
www.spdbooks.org

Trip Street Press | P. O. Box 190201 | San Francisco, CA 94119

TABLE OF CONTENTS

INTRODUCTION

The premise of *Here Lies* is that every story either features the telling of a lie or the presence of a liar.

The premise raises the question of what is and what is not a lie. The lie, as a theme, is unwieldly, perhaps dated, and certainly not as glamourous as the ubiquitous ambiguity. Lies are harder to find than one might imagine. Dorothy Parker gave us the title. Another writer, who became a contributor, gave us the theme. As for the stories themselves, at least one editor is an enthusiastic advocate for each story's inclusion, and, in most cases, both of us are.

We also applied a criterion in our selection process of which the contributors were not aware: each story we chose had to hold up to a second or third reading so strongly that we felt even more compelled to include it than we did after our initial reading. In order to allow us this last luxury, we had to allow ourselves the luxury of time. And so we did: we spent nearly four years in the editing of this book. We use the word luxury because it has been exactly that: something beyond what is required by necessity.

— THE EDITORS

DRINKING COFFEE ELSEWHERE

by ZZ Packer

Orientation games began the day I arrived at Yale from Baltimore. In my group we played heady, frustrating games for smart people. One game appeared to be charades reinterpreted by existentialists; another involved listening to rocks. Then a freshman counselor made everyone play Trust. The idea was that if you had the faith to fall backward and wait for four scrawny former high-school geniuses to catch you, just before your head cracked on the slate sidewalk, then you might learn to trust your fellow-students. Russian roulette sounded like a better game.

"No way," I said. The white boys were waiting for me to fall, holding their arms out for me, sincerely, gallantly. "No fucking way."

"It's all cool, it's all cool," the counselor said. Her hair was a shade of blond I'd seen only on *Playboy* covers, and she raised her hands as though backing away from a growling dog. "Sister," she said, in an I'm-down-with-the-struggle voice, "you don't have to play this game. As a person of color, you shouldn't have to fit into any white, patriarchal system."

I said, "It's a bit too late for that."

In the next game, all I had to do was wait in a circle until it was my turn to say what inanimate object I wanted to be. One guy said he'd like to be a gadfly, like Socrates. "Stop me if I wax Platonic," he said. The girl next to him was eating a rice cake. She wanted to be the Earth, she said. Earth with a capital "E."

There was one other black person in the circle. He wore an Exeter T-shirt and his overly elastic expressions resembled a series of facial exercises. At the end of each person's turn, he smiled and bobbed his head with unfettered enthusiasm. "Oh, that was good," he said, as if the game were an experiment he'd set up and the results were turning out better than he'd expected. "Good, good, good!"

When it was my turn I said, "My name is Dina, and if I had to be any object, I guess I'd be a revolver." The sunlight dulled as if on cue. Clouds passed rapidly overhead, presaging rain. I don't know why I said it. Until that moment I'd been good in all the ways that were meant to matter. I was an honor-roll student—though I'd learned long ago not to mention it in the part of Baltimore where I lived. Suddenly I was hard-bitten and recalcitrant, the kind of kid who took pleasure in stick-ing pins into cats; the kind who chased down smart kids to spray them with mace.

"A revolver," a counselor said, stroking his chin, as if it had grown a rabbinical beard. "Could you please elaborate?"

The black guy cocked his head and frowned, as if the beakers and Erlenmeyer flasks of his experiment had grown legs and scurried off.

"You were just kidding," the dean said, "about wiping out all of man-kind. That, I suppose, was a joke." She squinted at me. One of her hands curved atop the other to form a pink, freckled molehill on her desk.

"Well," I said, "maybe I meant it at the time." I quickly saw that that was not the answer she wanted. "I don't know. I think it's the architecture."

Through the dimming light of the dean's-office window, I could see the fortress of the old campus. On my ride from the bus station to the campus, I'd barely glimpsed New Haven—a flash of crumpled build-ing here, a trio of straggly kids there. A lot like Baltimore. But every-thing had changed when we reached those streets hooded by the Gothic buildings. I imagined how the college must have looked when it was founded, when most of the students owned slaves. I pictured men wearing tights and knickers, smoking pipes.

"The architecture," the dean repeated. She bit her lip and seemed to be making a calculation of some sort. I noticed that she blinked less often than most people. I sat there, waiting to see how long it would be before she blinked again.

My revolver comment won me a year's worth of psychiatric counseling, weekly meetings with Dean Guest, and—since the parents of the roommate I'd never met weren't too hip on the idea of their Amy sharing a bunk bed with a budding homicidal loony—my very own room.

Shortly after getting my first D, I also received the first knock on my door. The female counselors never knocked. The dean had spoken to them; I was a priority. Every other day, right before dinnertime, they'd look in on me, unannounced. "Just checking up," a counselor would say. It was the voice of a suburban mother in training. By the second week, I had made a point of sitting in a chair in front of the door, just when I expected a counselor to pop her head around. This was intended to startle them. I also made a point of being naked. The unannounced visits ended.

The knocking persisted. Through the peephole I saw a white face, distorted and balloonish.

"Let me in." The person looked like a boy but sounded like a girl. "Let me in," the voice repeated.

"Not a chance," I said.

Then the person began to sob, and I heard a back slump against the door. If I hadn't known the person was white from the peephole, I'd have known it from a display like this. Black people didn't knock on strangers' doors, crying. Not that I understood the black people at Yale. There was something pitiful in how cool they were. Occasionally one would reach out to me with missionary zeal, but I'd rebuff that person with haughty silence.

"I don't have anyone to talk to!" the person on the other side of the door cried.

"That is correct."

"When I was a child," the person said, "I played by myself in a corner of the schoolyard all alone. I hated dolls and I hated games, animals were not friendly and birds flew away. If anyone was looking for me I hid behind a tree and cried out 'I am an orphan—'"

I opened the door. It was a she.

"Plagiarist!" I yelled. She had just recited a Frank O'Hara poem as though she'd thought it up herself. I knew the poem because it was one of the few things I'd been forced to read that I wished I'd written myself.

The girl turned to face me, smiling weakly, as though her triumph were not in getting me to open the door but in the fact that she was able to smile at all when she was so accustomed to crying. She was large but not obese, and crying had turned her face the color of raw chicken. She blew her nose into the waist end of her T-shirt, revealing a pale belly.

"How do you know that poem?"

She sniffed. "I'm in your Contemporary Poetry class."

She was Canadian and her name was Heidi, although she said she wanted people to call her Henrik. "That's a guy's name," I said. "What do you want? A sex change?"

She looked at me with so little surprise that I suspected she hadn't discounted this as an option. Then her story came out in teary, hiccup-like bursts. She had sucked some "cute guy's dick" and he'd told everybody and now people thought she was "a slut."

"Why'd you suck his dick? Aren't you a lesbian?"

She fit the bill. Short hair, hard, roach-stomping shoes. Dressed like an aspiring plumber. The lesbians I'd seen on TV were wiry, thin strips of muscle, but Heidi was round and soft and had a moonlike face. Drab mud-colored hair. And lesbians had cats. "Do you have a cat?" I asked.

Her eyes turned glossy with new tears. "No," she said, her voice wavering, "and I'm not a lesbian. Are you?"

"Do I look like one?" I said.

She didn't answer.

"O.K." I said. "I could suck a guy's dick, too, if I wanted. But I don't. The human penis is one of the most germ-ridden objects there is." Heidi looked at me, unconvinced. "What I meant to say," I began again, "is that I don't like anybody. Period. Guys or girls. I'm a misanthrope."

"I am, too."

"No," I said, guiding her back through my door and out into the hallway. "You're not."

"Have you had dinner?" she asked. "Let's go to Commons."

I pointed to a pyramid of ramen-noodle packages on my windowsill. "See that? That means I never have to go to Commons. Aside from class, I have contact with no one."

"I hate it here, too," she said. "I should have gone to McGill, eh."

"The way to feel better," I said, "is to get some ramen and lock yourself in your room. Everyone will forget about you and that guy's dick and you won't have to see anyone ever again. If anyone looks for you—"

"I'll hide behind a tree."

"A revolver?" Dr. Raeburn said, flipping through a manila folder. He looked up at me as if to ask another question, but he didn't.

Dr. Raeburn was the psychiatrist. He had the gray hair and whiskers of a Civil War general. He was also a chain smoker with beige teeth and a navy wool jacket smeared with ash. He asked about the revolver at the beginning of my first visit. When I was unable to explain myself he smiled, as if this were perfectly respectable.

"Tell me about your parents."

I wondered what he already had on file. The folder was thick, though I hadn't said a thing of significance since Day One.

"My father was a dick and my mother seemed to like him."

He patted his pockets for his cigarettes. "That's some heavy stuff," he said. "How do you feel about Dad?" The man couldn't say the word "father." "Is Dad someone you see often?"

"I hate my father almost as much as I hate the word 'Dad.'"

He started tapping his cigarette.

"You can't smoke in here."

"That's right," he said, and slipped the cigarette back into the packet. He smiled, widening his eyes brightly. "Don't ever start."

I thought that that first encounter would be the last of Heidi, but then her head appeared in a window of Linsly-Chit during my Chaucer class. Next, she swooped down a flight of stairs in Harkness. She hailed me from across Elm Street and found me in the Sterling Library stacks. After one of my meetings with Dr. Raeburn, she was waiting for me outside Health Services, legs crossed, cleaning her fingernails.

"You know," she said, as we walked through Old Campus, "you've got to stop eating ramen. Not only does it lack a single nutrient but it's full of MSG."

"I like eating chemicals," I said. "It keeps the skin radiant."

"There's also hepatitis." She already knew how to get my attention—mention a disease.

"You get hepatitis from unwashed lettuce," I said. "If there's anything safe from the perils of the food chain, it's ramen."

"But you refrigerate what you don't eat. Each time you reheat it, you're killing good bacteria, which then can't keep the bad bacteria in check. A guy got sick from reheating Chinese noodles, and his son died from it. I read it in the *Times*." With this, she put a jovial arm around my neck. I continued walking, a little stunned. Then, just as quickly, she dropped her arm and stopped walking. I stopped, too.

"Did you notice that I put my arm around you?"

"Yes," I said. "Next time, I'll have to chop it off."

"I don't want you to get sick," she said. "Let's eat at Commons."

In the cold air, her arm had felt good.

The problem with Commons was that it was too big; its ceiling was as high as a cathedral's, but below it there were no awestruck worshippers, only eighteen-year-olds at heavy wooden tables, chatting over veal patties and Jell-O.

We got our food, tacos stuffed with meat substitute, and made our way through the maze of tables. The Koreans had a table. Each singing group had a table. The crew team sat at a long table of its own. We passed the black table. The sheer quantity of Heidi's flesh accentuated just how white she was.

"How you doing, sista?" a guy asked, his voice full of accusation, eyeballing me as though I were clad in a Klansman's sheet and hood. "I guess we won't see you till graduation."

"If," I said, "you graduate."

The remark was not well received. As I walked past, I heard protests, angry and loud, as if they'd discovered a cheat at their poker game. Heidi and I found an unoccupied table along the periphery, which was isolated and dark. We sat down. Heidi prayed over her tacos.

"I thought you didn't believe in God," I said.

"Not in the God depicted in the Judeo-Christian Bible, but I do believe that nature's essence is a spirit that—"

"All right," I said. I had begun to eat, and cubes of diced tomato fell from my mouth when I spoke. "Stop right there. Tacos and spirits don't mix."

"You've always got to be so flip," she said. "I'm going to apply for another friend."

"There's always Mr. Dick," I said. "Slurp, slurp."

"You are so lame. So unbelievably lame. I'm going out with Mr. Dick. Thursday night at Atticus. His name is Keith."

Heidi hadn't mentioned Mr. Dick since the day I'd met her. That was more than a month ago and we'd spent a lot of that time together. I checked for signs that she was lying, her habit of smiling too much, her eyes bright and cheeks full, so that she looked like a chipmunk. But she looked normal. Pleased, even, to see me so flustered.

"You're insane! What are you going to do this time?" I asked. "Sleep with him? Then when he makes fun of you, what? Come pound your head on my door reciting the *Collected Poems of Sylvia Plath*?"

"He's going to apologize for before. And don't call me insane. You're the one going to the psychiatrist."

"Well, I'm not going to suck his dick, that's for sure."

She put her arm around me in mock comfort, but I pushed it off, and ignored her. She touched my shoulder again, and I turned, annoyed, but it wasn't Heidi after all; a sepia-toned boy dressed in khakis and a crisp plaid shirt was standing behind me. He handed me a hot-pink square of paper without a word, then briskly made his way toward the other end of Commons, where the crowds blossomed. Heidi leaned over and read it: "Wear Black Leather—the Less, the Better."

"It's a gay party," I said, crumpling the card. "He thinks we're fucking gay."

Heidi and I signed on to work at the Saybrook Dining Hall as dishwashers. The job consisted of dumping food from plates and trays into a vat of rushing water. It seemed straightforward, but then I learned better. You wouldn't believe what people could do with food until you worked in a dish room. Lettuce and crackers and soup would be bullied into a pulp in the bowl of some bored anorexic; ziti would be mixed with honey and granola; trays would appear heaped with mashed-potato snow women with melted chocolate ice cream for hair. Frat boys arrived at the dish-room window, en masse. They liked to fill glasses with food, then seal them, airtight, onto their trays. If you tried to prize them off, milk, Worcestershire sauce, peas, chunks of bread vomited onto your dish-room uniform.

When this happened one day in the middle of the lunch rush, for what seemed like the hundredth time, I tipped the tray toward one of the frat boys, popping the glasses off so that the mess spurted onto his Shetland sweater.

He looked down at his sweater. "Lesbo bitch!"

"No," I said, "that would be your mother."

Heidi, next to me, clenched my arm in support, but I remained motionless, waiting to see what the frat boy would do. He glared at me for a minute, then walked away.

"Let's take a smoke break," Heidi said.

I didn't smoke, but Heidi had begun to, because she thought it would help her lose weight. As I hefted a stack of glasses through the steamer, she lit up.

"Soft packs remind me of you," she said. "Just when you've smoked them all and you think there's none left, there's always one more, hiding in that little crushed corner." Before I could respond she said, "Oh, God. Not another mouse. You know whose job that is."

By the end of the rush, the floor mats got full and slippery with food. This was when mice tended to appear, scurrying over our shoes; more often than not, a mouse got caught in the grating that covered the drains in the floor. Sometimes the mouse was already dead by the time we noticed it. This one was alive.

"No way," I said. "This time you're going to help. Get some gloves and a trash bag."

"That's all I'm getting. I'm not getting that mouse out of there."

"Put on the gloves," I ordered. She winced, but put them on. "Reach down," I said. "At an angle, so you get at its middle. Otherwise, if you try to get it by its tail, the tail will break off."

"This is filthy, eh."

"That's why we're here," I said. "To clean up filth. Eh."

She reached down, but would not touch the mouse. I put my hand around her arm and pushed it till her hand made contact. The cries from the mouse were soft, songlike. "Oh, my God," she said. "Oh, my God, ohmigod." She wrestled it out of the grating and turned her head away.

"Don't you let it go," I said.

"Where's the food bag? It'll smother itself if I drop it in the food bag. Quick," she said, her head still turned away, her eyes closed. "Lead me to it."

"No. We are not going to smother this mouse. We've got to break its neck."

"You're one heartless bitch."

I wondered how to explain that if death is unavoidable it should be quick and painless. My mother had died slowly. At the hospital, they'd said it was kidney failure, but I knew that, in the end, it was my father. He made her scared to live in her own home, until she was finally driven away from it in an ambulance.

"Breaking its neck will save it the pain of smothering," I said. "Breaking its neck is more humane. Take the trash bag and cover it so you won't get any blood on you, then crush."

The loud jets of the steamer had shut off automatically and the dish room grew quiet. Heidi breathed in deeply, then crushed the mouse. She shuddered, disgusted. "Now what?"

"What do you mean, 'Now what?' Throw the little bastard in the trash."

At our third session, I told Dr. Raeburn I didn't mind if he smoked. He sat on the sill of his open window, smoking behind a jungle screen of office plants.

We spent the first ten minutes discussing the *Iliad*, and whether or not the text actually states that Achilles had been dipped in the River Styx. He said it did, and I said it didn't. After we'd finished with the *Iliad*, and with my new job in what he called "the scullery," he asked more questions about my parents. I told him nothing. It was none of his business. Instead, I talked about Heidi. I told him about that day in Commons, Heidi's plan to go on a date with Mr. Dick, and the invitation we'd been given to the gay party.

"You seem preoccupied by this soirée." He arched his eyebrows at the word 'soirée.'

"Wouldn't you be?"

"Dina," he said slowly, in a way that made my name seem like a song title, "have you ever had a romantic interest?"

"You want to know if I've ever had a boyfriend?" I said. "Just go ahead and ask if I've ever fucked anybody."

This appeared to surprise him. "I think that you are having a crisis of identity," he said.

"Oh, is that what this is?"

His profession had taught him not to roll his eyes. Instead, his exasperation revealed itself with a tiny pursing of his lips, as though he'd just tasted something awful and were trying very hard not to offend the cook.

"It doesn't have to be, as you say, someone you've fucked, it doesn't have to be a boyfriend," he said.

"Well, what are you trying to say? If it's not a boy, then you're saying it's a girl—"

"Calm down. It could be a crush, Dina." He lit one cigarette off another. "A crush on a male teacher, a crush on a dog, for heaven's sake. An interest. Not necessarily a relationship."

It was sacrifice time. If I could spend the next half hour talking about some boy, then I'd have given him what he wanted.

So I told him about the boy with the nice shoes.

I was sixteen and had spent the last few coins in my pocket on bus fare to buy groceries. I didn't like going to the Super Fresh two blocks away from my house, plunking government food stamps into the hands of the cashiers.

"There she go reading," one of them once said, even though I was only carrying a book. "Don't your eyes get tired?"

On Greenmount Avenue you could read schoolbooks—that was understandable. The government and your teachers forced you to read them. But anything else was anti-social. It meant you'd rather submit to the words of some white dude than shoot the breeze with your neighbors.

I hated those cashiers, and I hated them seeing me with food stamps, so I took the bus and shopped elsewhere. That day, I got off the bus at Govans, and though the neighborhood was black like my own—hair salon after hair salon of airbrushed signs promising arabesque hair styles and inch-long fingernails—the houses were neat and orderly, nothing at all like Greenmount, where every other house had at least one shattered window. The store was well swept, and people quietly checked long grocery lists—no screaming kids, no loud cashier-customer altercations. I got the groceries and left the store.

I decided to walk back. It was a fall day, and I walked for blocks. Then I sensed someone following me. I walked more quickly, my arms around the sack, the leafy lettuce tickling my nose. I didn't want to hold the sack so close that it would break the eggs or squash the hamburger buns, but it was slipping, and as I looked behind a boy my age, maybe older, rushed toward me.

"Let me help you," he said.

"That's all right." I set the bag on the sidewalk. Maybe I saw his face, maybe it was handsome enough, but what I noticed first, splayed on either side of the bag, were his shoes. They were nice shoes, real leather, a stitched design like a widow's peak on each one, or like birds' wings, and for the first time in my life I understood what people meant when they said "wing-tip shoes."

"I watched you carry them groceries out that store, then you look around, like you're lost, but like you liked being lost, then you walk down the sidewalk for blocks and blocks. Rearranging that bag, it almost gone to slip, then hefting it back up again."

"Huh, huh," I said.

"And then I passed my own house and was still following you. And then your bag really look like it was gone crash and everything. So I just thought I'd help." He sucked in his bottom lip, as if to keep it from making a smile. "What's your name?" When I told him, he said, "Dina, my name is Cecil." Then he said, "'D' comes right after 'C.'"

"Yes," I said, "it does, doesn't it."

Then, half question, half statement, he said, "I could carry your groceries for you? And walk you home?"

I stopped the story there. Dr. Raeburn kept looking at me. "Then what happened?"

I couldn't tell him the rest: that I had not wanted the boy to walk me home, that I didn't want someone with such nice shoes to see where I lived.

Dr. Raeburn would only have pitied me if I'd told him that I ran down the sidewalk after I told the boy no, that I fell, the bag slipped, and the eggs cracked, their yolks running all over the lettuce. Clear amniotic fluid coated the can of cinnamon rolls. I left the bag there on the sidewalk, the groceries spilled out randomly like cards loosed from a deck. When I returned home, I told my mother that I'd lost the food stamps.

"Lost?" she said. I'd expected her to get angry, I'd wanted her to get angry, but she hadn't. "Lost?" she repeated. Why had I been so clumsy and nervous around a harmless boy? I could have brought the groceries home and washed off the egg yolk, but, instead, I'd just left them there. "Come on," Mama said, snuffing her tears, pulling my arm, trying to get me to join her and start yanking cushions off the couch. "We'll find enough change here. We got to get something for dinner before your father gets back."

We'd already searched the couch for money the previous week, and I knew there'd be nothing now, but I began to push my fingers into the couch's boniest corners, pretending that it was only a matter of time before I'd find some change or a lost watch or an earring. Something pawnable, perhaps.

"What happened next?" Dr. Raeburn asked again. "Did you let the boy walk you home?"

"My house was far, so we went to his house instead." Though I was sure Dr. Raeburn knew that I was making this part up, I continued. "We made out on his sofa. He kissed me."

Dr. Raeburn lit his next cigarette like a detective. Cool, suspicious. "How did it feel?"

"You know," I said. "Like a kiss feels. It felt nice. The kiss felt very, very nice."

Raeburn smiled gently, though he seemed unconvinced. When he called time on our session his cigarette had become one long pole of ash. I left his office, walking quickly down the corridor, afraid to look back.

It would be like him to trot after me, his navy blazer flapping, just to eke the truth out of me. *You never kissed anyone.* The words slid from my brain, and knotted in my stomach.

When I reached my dorm, I found an old record player blocking my door and a Charles Mingus LP propped beside it. I carried them inside and then, lying on the floor, I played the Mingus over and over again until I fell asleep. I slept feeling as though Dr. Raeburn had attached electrodes to my head, willing into my mind a dream about my mother. I saw the lemon meringue of her skin, the long bone of her arm as she reached down to clip her toenails. I'd come home from a school trip to an aquarium, and I was explaining the differences between baleen and sperm whales according to the size of their heads, the range of their habitats, their feeding patterns.

I awoke remembering the expression on her face after I'd finished my dizzying whale lecture. She looked like a tourist who'd asked for directions to a place she thought was simple enough to get to only to hear a series of hypothetical turns, alleys, one-way streets. Her response was to nod politely at the perilous elaborateness of it all; to nod in the knowledge that she would never be able to get where she wanted to go.

The dishwashers always closed down the dining hall. One night, after everyone else had punched out, Heidi and I took a break, and though I wasn't a smoker, we set two milk crates upside down on the floor and smoked cigarettes.

The dishwashing machines were off, but steam still rose from them like a jungle mist. Outside in the winter air, students were singing carols in their groomed and tailored singing-group voices. The Whiffenpoofs were back in New Haven after a tour around the world, and I guess their return was a huge deal. Heidi and I craned our necks to watch the year's first snow through an open window.

"What are you going to do when you're finished?" Heidi asked. Sexy question marks of smoke drifted up to the windows before vanishing.

"Take a bath."

She swatted me with her free hand. "No, silly. Three years from now. When you leave Yale."

"I don't know. Open up a library. Somewhere where no one comes in for books. A library in a desert."

She looked at me as though she'd expected this sort of answer and didn't know why she'd asked in the first place.

"What are you going to do?" I asked her.

"Open up a psych clinic. In a desert. And my only patient will be some wacko who runs a library."

"Ha," I said. "Whatever you do, don't work in a dish room ever again. You're no good." I got up from the crate. "C'mon. Let's hose the place down."

We put out our cigarettes on the floor, since it was our job to clean it, anyway. We held squirt guns in one hand and used the other to douse the floors with the standard-issue, eye-burning cleaning solution. We hosed the dish room, the kitchen, the serving line, sending the water and crud and suds into the drains. Then we hosed them again so the solution wouldn't eat holes in our shoes as we left. Then I had an idea. I unbuckled my belt.

"What the hell are you doing?" Heidi said.

"Listen, it's too cold to go outside with our uniforms all wet. We could just take a shower right here. There's nobody but us."

"What the fuck, eh?"

I let my pants drop, then took off my shirt and panties. I didn't wear a bra, since I didn't have much to fill one. I took off my shoes and hung my clothes on the stepladder.

"You've flipped," Heidi said. "I mean, really, psych-ward flipped."

I soaped up with the liquid hand soap until I felt as glazed as a ham. "Stand back and spray me."

"Oh, my God," she said. I didn't know whether she was confused or delighted, but she picked up the squirt gun and sprayed me. She was laughing. Then she got too close and the water started to sting.

"'God damn it!" I said. "That hurt!"

"I was wondering what it would take to make you say that."

When all the soap had been rinsed off, I put on my regular clothes and said, "O.K. You're up next."

"No way," she said.

"Yes way."

She started to take off her uniform shirt, then stopped.

"What?"

"I'm too fat."

"You goddam right." She always said she was fat. One time, I'd told her that she should shut up about it, that large black women wore their fat like mink coats. "You're big as a house," I said now. "Frozen yogurt may be low in calories but not if you eat five tubs of it. Take your clothes off. I want to get out of here."

She began taking off her uniform, then stood there, hands cupped over her breasts, crouching at the pubic bone.

"Open up," I said, "or we'll never get done."

Her hands remained where they were. I threw the bottle of liquid soap at her, and she had to catch it, revealing herself as she did.

I turned on the squirt gun, and she stood there, stiff, arms at her sides, eyes closed, as though awaiting mummification. I began with the water on low, and she turned around in a full circle, hesitantly, letting the droplets from the spray fall on her as if she were submitting to a death by stoning.

When I increased the water pressure, she slipped and fell on the sudsy floor. She stood up and then slipped again. This time she laughed and remained on the floor, rolling around on it as I sprayed.

I think I began to love Heidi that night in the dish room, but who is to say that I hadn't begun to love her the first time I met her? I sprayed her and sprayed her, and she turned over and over like a large beautiful dolphin, lolling about in the sun.

Heidi started sleeping at my place. Sometimes she slept on the floor; sometimes we slept sardinelike, my feet at her head, until she complained that my feet were "taunting" her. When we finally slept head to head, she said, "Much better." She was so close I could smell her toothpaste. "I like your hair," she told me, touching it through the darkness. "You should wear it out more often."

"White people always say that about black people's hair. The worse it looks, the more they say they like it."

I'd expected her to disagree, but she kept touching my hair, her hands passing through it till my scalp tingled. When she began to touch the hair around the edge of my face, I felt myself quake. Her fingertips stopped for a moment, as if checking my pulse, then resumed.

"I like how it feels right here. See, mine just starts with the same old texture as the rest of my hair." She found my hand under the blanket and brought it to her hairline. "See," she said.

It was dark. As I touched her hair, it seemed as though I could smell it, too. Not a shampoo smell. Something richer, murkier. A bit dead, but sweet, like the decaying wood of a ship. She guided my hand.

"I see," I said. The record she'd given me was playing in my mind, and I kept trying to shut it off. I could also hear my mother saying that this is what happens when you've been around white people: things get weird. So weird I could hear the stylus etching its way into the flat vinyl of the record. "Listen," I said finally, when the bass and saxes started up. I heard Heidi breathe deeply, but she said nothing.

We spent the winter and some of the spring in my room—never hers— missing tests, listening to music, looking out my window to comment on people who wouldn't have given us a second thought. We read books related to none of our classes. I got riled up by *The Autobiography of Malcolm X* and *The Chomsky Reader*; Heidi read aloud passages from *The Anxiety of Influence*. We guiltily read mysteries and *Clan of the Cave Bear*, then immediately threw them away. Once, we looked up from our books at exactly the same moment, as though trapped at a dinner table with nothing to say. A pleasant trap of silence.

Then one weekend I went back to Baltimore. When I returned, to a sleepy, tree-scented spring, a group of students were holding what was called "Coming Out Day." I watched it from my room.

The MC was the sepia boy who'd invited us to that party months back. His speech was strident but still smooth, and peppered with jokes. There was a speech about AIDS, with lots of statistics: nothing that seemed to make "coming out" worth it. Then the women spoke. One girl pronounced herself "out" as casually as if she'd announced the time. Another said nothing at all: she appeared at the microphone accompanied by a woman who began cutting off her waist-length, bleached-blond hair. The woman doing the cutting tossed the shorn hair in every direction as she cut. People were clapping and cheering and catching the locks of hair.

And then there was Heidi. She was proud that she liked girls, she said when she reached the microphone. She loved them, wanted to sleep with them. She was a dyke, she said repeatedly, stabbing her finger to her chest in case anyone was unsure to whom she was referring. She could not have seen me. I was across the street, three stories up. And yet, when everyone clapped for her, she seemed to be looking straight at me.

Heidi knocked. "Let me in."

It was like the first time I met her. The tears, the raw pink of her face.

We hadn't spoken in weeks. Outside, pink-and-white blossoms hung from the Old Campus trees. Students played hackeysack in T-shirts and shorts. Though I was the one who'd broken away after she went up to that podium, I still half expected her to poke her head out a window in Linsly-Chit, or tap on my back in Harkness, or even join me in the Commons dining hall, where I'd asked for my dish-room shift to be transferred. She did none of these.

"Well," I said, "what is it?"

She looked at me. "My mother," she said.

She continued to cry, but it seemed to have grown so silent in my room I wondered if I could hear the numbers change on my digital clock.

"When my parents were getting divorced," she said, "my mother bought a car. A used one. An El Dorado. It was filthy. It looked like a huge crushed can coming up the street. She kept trying to clean it out. I mean—"

I nodded and tried to think what to say in the pause she left behind. Finally I said, "We had one of those," though I was sure ours was an Impala.

She looked at me, eyes steely from trying not to cry. "Anyway, she'd drive me around in it and although she didn't like me to eat in it, I always did. One day, I was eating cantaloupe slices, spitting the seeds on the floor. Maybe a month later, I saw this little sprout, growing right up from the car floor. I just started laughing and she kept saying what, what? I was laughing and then I saw she was so—"

She didn't finish. So what? So sad? So awful? Heidi looked at me with what seemed to be a renewed vigor. "We could have gotten a better car, eh?"

"It's all right. It's not a big deal," I said.

Of course, that was the wrong thing to say. And I really didn't mean it to sound the way it had come out.

I told Dr. Raeburn about Heidi's mother having cancer and how I'd said it wasn't a big deal, though I'd wanted to say exactly the opposite. I meant that I knew what it was like to have a parent die. My mother had died. I knew how eventually one accustoms oneself to the physical world's lack of sympathy: the buses that still run on time, the kids who still play in the street, the clocks that won't stop ticking for the person who's gone.

"You're pretending," Dr. Raeburn said, not sage or professional but a little shocked by the discovery, as if I'd been trying to hide a pack of his cigarettes behind my back.

"I'm pretending?" I shook my head. "All those years of psych grad,"

I said. "And to tell me *that*?"

"You construct stories about yourself and dish them out—one for you, one for you—" Here he reënacted the process, showing me handing out lies as if they were apples.

"Pretending. I believe the professional name for it might be denial," I said. "Are you calling me gay?"

He pursed his lips noncommittally "No, Dina. I don't think you're gay."

I checked his eyes. I couldn't read them.

"No. Not at all," he said, sounding as if he were telling a subtle joke. "But maybe you'll finally understand."

"Understand what?"

"That constantly saying what one doesn't mean accustoms the mouth to meaningless phrases." His eyes narrowed. "Maybe you'll understand that when you need to express something truly significant, your mouth will revert to the insignificant nonsense it knows so well." He looked at me, his hands sputtering in the air in a gesture of defeat. "Who knows?" he asked, with a glib, psychiatric smile I'd never seen before. "Maybe it's your survival mechanism. Black living in a white world."

I heard him, but only vaguely. I'd hooked on to that one word, pretending. What Dr. Raeburn would never understand was that pretending was what had got me this far. I remembered the morning of my mother's funeral. I'd been given milk to settle my stomach; I'd pretended it was coffee. I imagined I was drinking coffee elsewhere. Some Arabic-speaking country where the thick coffee served in little cups was so strong it could keep you awake for days. Some Arabic country where I'd sit in a tented café and be more than happy to don a veil.

Heidi wanted me to go with her to the funeral. She'd sent this message through the dean. "We'll pay for your ticket to Vancouver," the dean said.

"What about my ticket back?" I asked. "'Maybe the shrink will pay for that."

The dean looked at me as though I were an insect she'd like to squash. "We'll pay for the whole thing. We might even pay for some lessons in manners."

So I packed my suitcase and walked from my suicide-single dorm to Heidi's room. A thin wispy girl in ragged cutoffs and a shirt that read "LSBN!" answered the door. A group of short-haired girls in thick black leather jackets, bundled up despite the summer heat, encircled Heidi in a protective fairy ring. They looked at me critically, clearly wondering if Heidi was too fragile for my company.

"You've got our numbers," one said, holding onto Heidi's shoulder. "And Vancouver's got a great gay community."

"Oh God," I said. "She's going to a funeral, not a 'Save the Dykes' rally."

One of the girls stepped in front of me.

"It's O.K., Cynthia," Heidi said. Then she ushered me into her bedroom and closed the door. A suitcase was on her bed, half packed. She folded a polkadotted T-shirt that was wrong for any occasion. "Why haven't you talked to me?" she said. "Why haven't you talked to me in two months?"

"I don't know," I said.

"You don't know," she said, each syllable seeped in sarcasm. "You don't know. Well, I know. You thought I was going to try to sleep with you."

"Try to? We slept together all winter!"

"Smelling your feet is not 'sleeping together.' You've got a lot to learn." She seemed thinner and meaner.

"So tell me," I said. "What can you show me that I need to learn?" But as soon as I said it I somehow knew that she still hadn't slept with anyone.

"Am I supposed to come over there and sweep your enraged self into my arms?" I said. "Like in the movies? Is this the part where we're both so mad we kiss each other?"

She shook her head and smiled weakly. "You don't get it," she said.

"My mother is dead." She closed her suitcase, clicking shut the old-fashioned locks. "My mother is dead," she said again, this time reminding herself. She set the suitcase upright on the floor and sat on it. She looked like someone waiting for a train.

"Fine," I said. "And she's going to be dead for a long time." Though it sounded stupid, I felt good saying it. As though I had my own locks to click shut.

Heidi went to Vancouver for her mother's funeral. I didn't go. Instead, I went back to Baltimore and moved in with an aunt I barely knew. Every day was the same: I read and smoked outside my aunt's apartment, studying the row of hair salons across the street, where girls in denim cutoffs and tank tops would troop in and come out hours later, a flash of neon nails, coifs the color and sheen of patent leather. And every day I imagined visiting Heidi in Vancouver. Her house would not be large, but it would be clean. Flowery shrubs would line the walks. The Canadian wind would whip us about like pennants. I'd be visiting her at some vague time in the future, deliberately vague, for people like me, who realign past events to suit themselves. In that future time, you always have a chance to catch the groceries before they fall, your words can always be rewound and erased, rewritten and revised.

But once I imagined Heidi visiting me. There would be no psychiatrists or deans. No boys with nice shoes or flip cashiers. Just me in my single room. She would knock on the door and say, "Open up."

THE BLOCK

by James Kelman

The body landed at my feet. A short man with stumpy legs. He was staring up at me but though so wide open those eyes were seeing things from which I was excluded, not only excluded from but irrelevant to; things to which I was nonexistent. He had no knowledge of me, had never had occasion to be aware of me. He did not see me although I was staring at him through his eyeballs. I was possibly seeking some sort of reflection. What the hell was he seeing with his eyelids so widely parted. He was seeing nothing. Blood issued from his mouth. He was dead. A dead man on the pavement beneath me—with stumpy legs; a short man with a longish body. I felt his pulse: there was no pulse. I wasnt feeling his pulse at all. I was grasping the wrist of a short man. No longer a wrist. I was grasping an extension, the extension to the left of a block of matter. This block of matter was a man's body several moments earlier. Unless he had been dead on leaving the window upstairs, in which case a block of matter landed at my feet and I could scarcely even be referred to in connection with 'it', with a block of matter describable as 'it'—never mind being nonexistent of, or to. And two policemen had arrived. O Jesus, said one, is he dead?

I was looking at them. The other policeman had knelt to examine the block and was saying: No pulse. Dead. No doubt about it poor bastard.

What happened? he addressed me.

A block of matter landed at my feet.

What was that?

The block of matter, it was a man's body previous to impact unless of course he was out the game prior to that, in which case, in which case a block of matter landed at my feet.

What happened?

This, I said and gestured at the block. This; it was suddenly by my feet. I stared into the objects that had formerly been eyes before doing as you did, I grasped the left extension there to... see.

What?

The pulse. You were saying there was no pulse, but in a sense— well, right enough I suppose you were quite correct to say there was no pulse. I had grasped what I took to be a wrist to find I was grasping the left extension of a block of matter. Just before you arrived. I found that what was a man's body was in fact a block and...

... do you live around here?

What, aye, yes. Along the road a bit.

Did you see him falling?

An impossibility.

He was here when you got here?

No. He may have been. He might well have been alive, it I mean. No—he... unless of course the... I had taken it for granted that it landed when I arrived but it might possibly... no, definitely not. I heard the thump. The impact. Of the impact.

Jesus Christ.

The other policeman glanced at him and then at me: What's your name?

McLeish, Michael. I live along the road a bit.

Where exactly?

Number 3.

And where might you be going at this time of the morning?

Work, I'm going to work. I'm a milkman.

The other policeman began rifling through the garments covering the block. And he brought out a wallet and peered into its contents. Robert McKillop, he said, I think his name's Robert McKillop. I better go up to his house Geordie, you stay here with... He indicated me in a vaguely surreptitious manner.

I'm going to my work, I said.

Whereabouts?

Partick.

The milk depot?

Aye, yes.

I know it well. But you better just wait here a minute.

The policeman named Geordie leaned against the tenement wall while his mate walked into the close. When he had reappeared he said, Mrs McKillop's upset—I'll stay with her meantime Geordie, you better report right away.

What about this yin here? I mean we know where he works and that.

Aye... the other one nodded at me: On your way. You'll be hearing from us shortly.

At the milk depot I was involved in the stacking of crates of milk onto my lorry. One of the crates fell. Broken glass and milk sloshing about on the floor. The gaffer swore at me. You ya useless bastard: he shouted. Get your lorry loaded and get out of my sight.

I wiped my hands and handed in my notice. Right now, I said, I'm leaving right now.

What d'you mean you're leaving! Get that fucking wagon loaded and get on your way.

No, I'm not here now. I'm no longer... I cannot be said to be here as a driver of milk lorries any more. I've handed in my notice and wiped my hands off the whole carry on. Morning.

I walked to the exit. The gaffer coming after me. McArra the check-erman had stopped singing and was gazing at us from behind a row of crates but I could see the cavity between his lips. The gaffer's hand had

grasped my elbow. Listen McLeish, he was saying. You've got a job to
do. A week's notice you have to give. Dont think you can just say
you're leaving and then walk out the fucking door.

I am not here now. I am presently walking out the fucking door.

Stop when I'm talking to you!

No. A block of matter landed at my feet an hour ago. I have to be
elsewhere. I have to be going now to be elsewhere. Morning.

Fuck you then. Aye, and dont ever show your face back in this depot
again. McArra you're a witness to this! he's walking off the job.

Cheerio McArra. I called: I am, to be going.

Cheerio McLeish, said the checkerman.

Outside in the street I had to stop. This was not an ordinary kind
of carry on. I had to lean against the wall. I closed my eyelids but it
was worse. Spinning into a hundred miles of a distance, this speck.
Speck. This big cavity I was inside of and also enclosing and when the
eyelids had opened something had been presupposed by something.
Thank Christ for that, I said, for that, the something.

Are you alright son?

Me... I... I was... I glanced to the side and there was this middle-
aged woman standing in a dark colored raincoat, in a pair of white
shoes; a striped headscarf wrapped about her head. And a big pair of
glasses, spectacles. She was squinting at me. Dizzy, I said to her, a bit
dizzy Mrs—I'm no a drunk man or anything.

O I didnt think you were son I didnt think you were, else I wouldnt've
stopped. I'm out for my messages.

I looked at her. I said: Too early for messages, no shops open for
another couple of hours.

Aye son. But I cant do without a drop of milk in my tea and there
was none left when I looked in the cupboard, so here I am. I sometimes
get a pint of milk straight from the depot if I'm up early. And I couldnt
sleep last night.

First thing this morning you could've called me a milk man, I said
while easing myself up from the wall.

O aye.

I nodded.

Will you manage alright now?

Aye, thanks, cheerio Mrs.

Cheerio son.

I was home in my room. A tremendous thumping. I was lying face down on the bed. The thumping was happening to the door. McLeish. McLeish. Michael McLeish! A voice calling the name of me from outside of my room. And this tremendous thumping for the door and calling me by name McLeish! Jesus God.

Right you are, I shouted. And I pulled the pillow out from under my chin and pulled it down on the top of the back of my head. The thumping had stopped. I closed my eyelids. I got up after a second of that and opened the door.

We went to the depot, said one, but you'd left by then.

The second policeman was looking at my eyes. I shut the lids on him. I opened my mouth and said something to which neither answered. I repeated it but still no reply.

I told your gaffer what'd happened earlier on, said one. He said to tell you to give him a ring and things would be okay. No wonder you were upset. I told him that, the gaffer. Can we come in?

Can we come in? the other said.

Aye.

Can we come in a minute Michael? said the other.

I opened the door wider and returned to bed. They were standing at the foot of it with their hats in their hands. Then they were lighting cigarettes. A smoke, asked one. Want a smoke?

Aye. I'm not getting things out properly. I'm just not getting out it all the way. The block as well... it wasnt really the block.

Here... The other handed me an already burning cigarette.

I had it in my mouth. I was smoking. Fine as the smoke was entering my insides. The manner in which smoke enters an empty milk bottle and curls round the inner walls almost making this kind of shinnying noise while it is doing the curling. The other was saying: Nice place this. You've got some good pictures on the wall. I like the one with the big circles. Is it an original?

Aye, yes. I painted it. I painted it in paint, the ordinary paint. Dulux, I mean—that emulsion stuff.

Christ that's really good. I didnt know you were a painter.

It is good right enough, the other said.

Fingers. I used my pinkies; right and left for the adjacents. You know that way of touching the emulsion. That was what I was doing with the... I was... and the milk bottle, the milk bottle I suppose.

But dont let it get you down because the gaffer definitely did say you were to get in touch with him and it would be okay, about the job and that.

Aye, the other said. The thing is we'll need to go to the station. Our serjeant wants to hear how it happened with Mr McKillop this morning. How you saw it yourself—witnessed it Michael. We can get a refreshment down there, tea or coffee. Okay?—just shove on your clothes and we'll get going.

In the back seat of the patrol car one of them said: I'm not kidding but that painting of yours Michael, it was really good. Were the rest of them yours as well?

Aye, yes. I was doing painting. I was painting a lot sometimes. On the broo and that, before I started this job. In a sense though...

The policeman was looking at me, between my eyes; onto the bridge of my nose. I closed the eyelids: reddish grey. I could guess what would be going on. The whole of it. The description. A block of matter wasnt it. It would be no good for them—the serjeant, the details of it, the thump of impact. What I was doing and the rest of it. Jesus God. I was painting a lot sometimes, I said to him.

What's up?

Nothing. I'm just not getting the things, a hold... sploshing about.

It had to upset you—dont worry about that.

Not just the block but. Not just the block that I was... Ach.

I stopped and I was shaking my head. The words werent coming. Nothing at all to come and why the words were never. They cannot come by themselves. They can come by themselves. Without, not without. The anything. They can do it but only with it, the anything. What the fuck is the anything; that something. A particular set of things maybe.

Open the window a bit, the other said. Give him a breath of fresh air. Gets hell of a stuffy in here. And refreshments when we get there.

A wee room inside the station I was walked into. A policeman and a serjeant following. I was to sit at a table with the serjeant to be facing me. And he saying: I just want you to tell me what it was happened earlier on. In your own words Mr McLeish.

A block of matter, it was at my feet. I was... I glanced at the serjeant to add, I couldnt be said to be there in a sense. A thump of impact and the block of matter.

A block of matter, he replied after a moment. Yes I know what you're meaning about that. Mr McKillop was dead and so you didnt see him that way; you just saw him as a kind of shape—is that right, is that what you're meaning?

You could—I mean I could, be said to—no. No, I was walking and the thump, the block.

You were walking to work?

Aye, yes.

And the next thing, wham? the body lands at your feet?

No. In a sense though you... No, though; I was walking, thump, the block of matter. And yet—he was a short man, stumpy legs, longish body. And less then—less than, less than immediately a block of matter. Eyes. The objects that had been eyes. Jesus no. Not had been eyes at all. They were never eyes. Never ever had been eyes for the block. McKillop's eyes those objects had been part of. Part of the eyes. And I looked into them and they were not eyes. Just bits—bits of the block.

Look son I'm sorry, I know you're... The serjeant was glancing at the policeman. And his eyes!

Your gaze is quizzical: I said.

Ho. Quizzical is it!

Aye, yes.

And what is my gaze now then?

He was looking at me then I was looking out at him. He began looking at the policeman. Without words, both talking away. I said, It doesnt matter anyhow.

What doesnt matter?

Nothing, the anything.

The serjeant stood up: I'll be back in a minute. He went out and came back in again carrying 3 cartons of tea and a folder under his arm. Tea Mr McLeish, he said, breaking and entering 1968, '69. But you said nothing about that though eh!

I grasped the carton of tea.

So, he continued while being seated. Out walking at the crack of dawn and wham, a block called McKillop lands at your feet.

That'll do, I said.

What'll do?

The serjeant was staring at my nose. I could have put an index finger inside. He was speaking to me. It's okay son breaking and entering has nothing to do with it, I just thought I'd mention it. We're not thinking you were doing anything apart from going to your work. A bit early right enough but that's when milk men go about. Mrs McKillop told us her end and you're fine.

Serjeant?

What?

Nothing.

After a moment he nodded: Away you go home. It's our job to know you were done in '68 '69. A boy then but and I can see you've changed. A long time ago and Geordie tells me you've a steady job now driving the milk lorries and you've a good hobby into the bargain so—you're fine. And I dont think we'll need to see you again. But if we do I'll send somebody round. Number 3 it is eh? Aye, right you are. The serjeant stood up again and said to the policeman: Let him finish his tea.

Okay serj.

Fine. Cheerio then son, he said to me.

ALVIN THE TYPESETTER

by Lydia Davis

Alvin and I worked together typesetting for a weekly newspaper in Brooklyn. We came in every Friday. This was the autumn that Reagan was elected President, and everyone at the newspaper suffered from a sense of foreboding and depression.

The old gray typesetting machines, with their scratches and scars, were set back to back in a tiny room next to the toilet. People raced in and out of the toilet all day long and the sound of flushing was always in our ears. Pinned to the corkboard walls around us as we bent over our keyboards was an ever-thickening forest of paper strips. The damp paper strips were covered with type, and when they had dried, they were taken away by the paste-up people to become columns on the newspaper page.

The work we had to do was not hard, but it required patience and care, and we were under constant pressure to work faster. I typed straight copy, and Alvin set ads. If the machines stopped rumbling for more than a few minutes, the boss would come downstairs to see what was holding us up. And so Alvin and I continued to type while we ate our lunch, and when we talked to each other, as we did from time to time, we talked surreptitiously, sticking our eyes up over the tops of the machines.

We were blue-collar workers. Every time I thought about how we were blue-collar workers, it surprised me, because we were also, with any luck, performing artists. I played the violin. As for Alvin, he was a standup comedian. Every Friday Alvin told me about his career and his life.

For seven months he had auditioned over and over again without success at a well-known club. At last the manager had relented and given him a spot. Every week now he came on in the dead early hours of Sunday morning for five minutes to close the show. Sometimes the audience liked him and sometimes it did not respond at all. If the manager occasionally left him on-stage for ten minutes or gave him a spot earlier in the evening, at 9:30, Alvin felt this was an important advance in his career.

Alvin could not describe his art except to say that he had no script, no routine, that he never knew just what would happen on stage, and that this lack of preparation was part of his act. From the snatches of monologue he spoke for me, however, I could see that some of his patter was about sex—he made jokes about cream and sperm—and that some of his patter was about politics, and that he also liked to do impersonations.

He usually worked without any props. In the week of Election Day, in November, he carried to the nightclub a special patriotic kerchief covered with red, white and blue American symbols to wear over his head. Most often, though, what he took out onstage was only himself, as though his long, solemn face were a mask, or his body a marionette that he controlled with strings from above, slim, loose-jointed, floating over the floor. He had his stance, his silences, his bald head, and his clothes. He wore the same clothes on stage that he wore to work: dark formal pants and often a shirt of cheap synthetic material covered with palm trees or pine trees on a white background.

When I arrived at the office, Alvin would be typing at his machine in his stocking feet and his long narrow shoes would be sitting next to my machine. If Alvin was glum, neither of us said much. If he was elated, he could not help standing up from his machine and talking.

And on some days I would speak to him and he would look at me blankly. He would later admit that he had been smoking hash for days on end.

Over the clicking of the machines Alvin told me that he lived apart from his wife and son. His son did not like Alvin's friends or the food Alvin ate, and made the same excuse over and over again not to see him. He told me about his circle of friends—a group of Brooklyn vegetarians. He was planning to eat Thanksgiving dinner with these vegetarians and he was planning to spend the Christmas holiday sleeping at the YMCA. He told me about his travels—to Boston and places in New Jersey. He asked me many times to go out on a date with him. We went once to a circus.

He told me about the typesetters' agency that never found him any work. "Don't I seem ambitious to you?" he asked. He complained to me about the lack of order in our office, and about the poor writing in the pieces we were given to typeset. He said how it was not part of his job to correct spelling and grammar. He told me with indignation that he would not do more than should be expected of him. He and I had a sense of our superiority to those in charge of us, and this was only aggravated by the fact that we were so often treated as though we had no education.

Because Alvin was good-natured and presented himself to the rest of the newspaper staff without reservation, because his whole art consisted of isolating and exposing himself as a figure of fun, he was well liked by many of them but also became a natural victim of some: the manager of the production department, for instance, kept pushing him to work faster and often asked him to do his ads over again, and talked against Alvin behind his back. Alvin responded to this goading with injured pride. But worse than the production manager was the owner of the paper, who worked most of the week upstairs in his office but on press day came down to the production department and sat on a stool alongside the others.

He was a little man with a red mustache and glasses who wore his flannel shirts tucked into his bluejeans and smelled of deodorant when he became excited. He never walked slowly and he was in and out of the toilet faster than anyone else: no sooner had the door shut behind him than we would hear the thunderous flush from the tank overhead and he would spring out the door again. For much of the week he talked to his employees with good humor, though not to us, the typesetters, and tolerated the caricatures of his face posted all over the room and the remarks about him written on the toilet wall. On press day, however, and when things were going badly at the paper, his sense of catastrophe would drive him to turn on us one by one and dress us down publicly in a way that was humiliating and surrounded by silence. What made this treatment especially hard to accept was that our pay was low and our paychecks bounced regularly. The accountant upstairs could not keep track of where the newspaper's money was, and she added on her fingers.

Alvin received the worst of it and hardly defended himself at all: "I thought you said... I thought they told me to... I thought I was supposed to..." Any answer he made provoked another outburst from the boss, until Alvin retired in silence. I was embarrassed by his lack of pride. He was afraid of losing his job. But after Christmas his attitude changed.

Over the holidays, Alvin and I both performed. I played the violin in a concert of excerpts from *The Messiah*. Alvin's performance was to be an entire evening of monologues and songs at a local club run by a friend. Before the event Alvin handed out a xeroxed flyer with crooked lettering and a picture of himself wearing a beret. In his text he called himself "the widely acclaimed." The tickets were five dollars. Our newspaper ran an ad for his performance and everyone who worked with us there showed great interest in the event, though when the evening came, no one from the newspaper actually went to see him.

When Alvin came in to work on the Friday following his performance, he was the center of attention for a few minutes and an aura of celebrity floated around him. But Alvin told a sad tale. There were only five people in the audience at his performance. Four were fellow come-dians, and the fifth was Alvin's friend Ira, who talked throughout his monologues.

Alvin was eloquent about his failure. He described the room, his friend the owner, his friend Ira. He talked for five minutes. The boss, who had been listening with the others, grew restless and distracted and told Alvin there was work waiting for him. Alvin raised a hand in concession and went into the typesetting room. The production people returned to their stools and bent over their pages. Our machines began rumbling. The boss hurried upstairs.

Then Alvin stopped typing. His pupils were dilated and he looked peculiarly remote. He stood up and walked out. He said to the produc-tion room at large: "Listen: I have work to do. But I haven't started yet. I would like to perform for you first."

Most of the production people smiled because they liked Alvin.

"Now I'm going to impersonate a chicken," he said.

He climbed up on a stool and started flapping his arms and cluck-ing. The room was quiet. The production people perched on their long-legged stools like a flock of resting egrets and stared at this bald chicken. When there was no applause, Alvin shrugged and climbed down and said, "Now I'm going to impersonate a duck," and waddled across the room with his knees bent and toes turned in. The produc-tion people glanced around the room at one another. Their looks darted and hopped like sparrows. They gave Alvin a smattering of applause. Then he said, "Now I'm going to do a pigeon." He shook his shoulders and jerked his head forward and back as he strutted in the circular patterns of a courting pigeon. He managed to convey some-thing of the ostentation of a male pigeon. Abruptly he stopped and said to his audience, "Well, don't you have any work to do? What are you sitting around for? All this should have been done yesterday!" The little hair he had was poking straight out from his head as though he were full of electricity. He swallowed his saliva. "That's all we are," he said. "A bunch of dumb birds."

The smiles faded from the faces of his audience. All the weariness of that leafless late December in Brooklyn, our fear of our weakened government, our dread of its repressive spirit fell over our faces again like a gray curtain.

Into the abrupt silence came the chiming of a church-bell across the street. The production manager by reflex checked his watch. Alvin's body sagged. He turned and walked into our tiny room. The back of his head had its own expression of defeat.

For a moment everyone stared at him in amazement. He sat slumped over his machine, solitary, flooded by fluorescent light, exhausted by his performance. He had not been very funny, in fact he was a poor actor, and yet something about his act had been impressive: his grim determination, the violence of his feelings. One by one the production people went back to work: paper rustled, scissors clattered on the stone tabletop, murmurs passed back and forth over the sound of the radio. I sat down at my machine and Alvin looked up at me from under his heavy lids. His look carried all the hurt, the humiliation, the mockery of the past few months. He said without smiling, "They think I'm nothing. They can think what they like. I have my plans."

ADVERT FOR LOVE

by David Lynn

My Minda returned home from her first day at Shri Krishna College
and discovered that Subji-Auntie had spent the day with the newspapers, with *The Times of India*, *The Hindustan Times*, even *The Delhi Times*,
scouring matrimonial ads. She had snipped them, Subji-Auntie did, the
ones she found most promising, and arranged them in a delicate jigsaw
on the dining table for Minda's parents to review.

The puzzle puzzled my Minda as she entered from the street,
flushed with the excitement of her initiation into college life, and went
to the kitchen for a glass of water. The little scraps of newsprint made
a pattern on the table. She bent over and discovered what they contained and understood at once. She was surprised only that there were
so many eligible ones—not ideal, not really possible, many of them,
but *eligible*.

By that evening the puzzle had disappeared, but Minda's mother
looked at her over the dinner table, worried and silent. Subji-Auntie
did not look at Minda at all during the meal, but she ate a great deal
and purred at her fingers, licking them clean like a satisfied cat.

Every day for two years Minda returned home to discover a fresh
puzzle spread accusingly across the table. "Some very nice boys are
looking for young brides," Subji-Auntie says, not every day and not to

Minda, but to Minda's mother. "*Young* brides."

"I am a writer," I say to Minda, "and you are a historian. Together we can make the solution." I have a plan. My older brother Alok suggested it. Even so, it is a brilliant plan.

Minda and I met at a poetry reading of the south branch of the university—students from different colleges together. What matters is not that we talked and we had coffee, that we walked together and met, when we could, when we dared, every week for more than a year. It does not matter that we fell in love, or it matters only to us. What matters is that her family are Brahmin, Maithili Brahmin, not terribly wealthy or ambitious, but Brahmin nonetheless and they will marry her only to an auspicious candidate.

I am that candidate. My family is also from Mithila. We are Brahmin as well. My family has known her family for generations; our family name, Misra, is the same name; we are even related, cousins, but not for seven generations and that is all that matters. It is not chance that Minda and I met at the poetry reading; it is chance that we did not know each other all our lives. *I* am the auspicious candidate. Even so, we must make it seem not a love match, but a match arranged in the stars. And so it is—our parents would have made the match if it had occurred to them. But, but. If we approach through a matchmaker now it will be impossible. There is another way. Subji-Auntie's way.

```
Alliance  invited  for  educated  young  man
with  great  prospects  as  writer.  Age  21,
5'7", 60 kg. Looking for educated girl with
creative  abilities,  modern  views.  No dowry.
Must be Maithil Brahmin. Write Box 4777.
```

Minda shakes her head, bites her lip. She is already ahead of me, knows at once what I am suggesting. No pleasure allowed me: no surprise, delight, admiration for my craft. "Educated girl," she says.

"That's all? My family will be offended—it must be more. Beautiful. Definitely must include *beautiful*."

"Sure," I say. "Naturally."

"And you don't seem much of a catch. 'Great prospects.' Hmph— what are they? They mean nothing. What about the salary you must have? And you don't want to tell them you're a writer—that'll kill it right off, Misra or no Misra." She gives a quick, dismissive shake of her head.

"Great—see what a team we are? You're just helping me be more creative. Easy."

But she isn't through yet. "And you've got to be bigger to impress them. Make it five-eleven and seventy kilos."

"Let's make him a real dream boat, why not?"

She snaps me a quick look, blushes.

```
Alliance  invited  for  educated,  affluent
young  man  with  career.  Age 24, 5'11", 70
kg.  Looking  for  beautiful,  educated  tal-
ented  girl.  No  dowry.  Must  be  Maithil
Brahmin.  Contact Box 4777.
```

Even so, it doesn't happen right away. Hawk-like Subji-Auntie, Subji-Auntie who doesn't miss anything, she misses the ad. Three days in a row Minda comes home and studies the puzzle-of-the-day and it isn't there. Her third year of college, and to make Mummy and Daddy happy, to keep Subji-Auntie at bay, she pretends closer attention. She considers the puzzle as if everything is now possible. They are waiting, her family. I am waiting too. The stars must come together.

What I have not anticipated is that other letters will arrive. The box I gave—here was I thinking?—this Alok's idea too, it is my parents' post box. Every day now, beginning with one, then two or three, each day more, the letters arrive. Mama is puzzled. "Alok—what is this about?" she asks my brother.

He shrugs. "Must be wrong box, wrong advert, Mama. You don't find me putting ad in paper."

But Babu, he has been searching and now he finds it in the paper. "Look at this ad. If it isn't you, it seems to be you. Right size, right box, right caste even. Alok, what are you not telling us?"

Again my smooth brother shrugs innocently. "Maybe you placed ad for me, Babuji? Trying to trap me at last, are you?" He laughs.

So many Maithili girls. I had no idea. Even so many Misras, cousins beyond cousins I never heard of. They must think I'm the Maharaja of Darbhanga, they're so many, they're so eager.

On the seventh day Subji-Auntie breaks down and presents the ad, one among an extra-plentiful puzzle. Minda studies, oh no, not giving anything away. She doesn't hurry. Maybe, she thinks, she will not even notice today. The ad if we are patient will surely show up again. It will throw Auntie off the scent of scandal. But no, Minda finally taps her finger on the grey little scrap. "Hmm," she says, tapping. "This one is interesting. What do you think, Mummy?"

One father writes to the other. A photo of my Minda is included. Yes, she is beautiful. She had no need to remind *me*.

Her ears are not quite in alignment, it is true, and her chin is sharp in this photo. But Babu studies it seriously, one among several, and asks Alok what he thinks.

"Bit of a dog, seems to me," he says with a bite of toast. He is heading out the door to his new scooter dealership. "But we're being so choosy already, we cannot be more so."

I hate my brother.

I have spent my life invisible, my brother's shadow. No, too small even to be his shadow—it would fit him only at mid-day. Cricket he played and soccer. So fast, such a star, so stupid—in school he did nothing. No, not true—he smoked, he smuggled bottles of beer with his friends.

School I could make my own. The life of the mind! The life of a writer—someday!

Babu arranges the meeting for Thursday. Minda will come with her father for inspection. My mother spends the day cooking and cleaning, harassing our servant. She will work herself up, exhaust herself, annoy herself at universal imperfection, all the better to be severe and critical of the girl. "Vijay, you come too," she says.

Astonished, I manage not to snort through my nose. Then I do not want to laugh at all.

I grab Alok when he comes home for lunch, greasy with smugness at selling his scooters. "For *you* they are matchmaking. You don't want a wife, Brother. You always say so. Tell them the match is for me," I demand angrily. "Tell them it was your idea. My Minda is coming."

"But this *isn't* you, Vijay Brother. Read the ad you wrote. Twenty-four it says. Five-foot-eleven, yes? Who is this if not me? It is your ad, you wrote it, but this is me you describe. Her father will be furious to find deceit. He will cancel everything. No, we must carry through a little farther."

Minda arrives with her father. She is all shyness and blushes. I signal her but she does not see.

A match made by the stars they all agree. Mama is put out only that she cannot find more fault. Alok is casual, condescending. He sits on a cushion and smokes, gazing in appraisal at Minda through haze and half-closed eyes. Minda squirms self-consciously and says nothing.

I am invisible again. I tear at my hair. I stomp along the walls of the room and no one sees. "This is impossible," I say aloud—I think I say aloud—but no one hears.

Outside her classroom at Shri Krishna I catch Minda by the arm. Other students look on in alarm as she snatches herself free. "Stop it," she cries.

"But Minda—this is crazy. All of it. Crazy."

"What can I do?" she pleads with a stubborn shake of her head. "There is nothing for me to do. It is arranged. Settled. For after my graduation."

"But this is all craziness," I cry. "This was to be for us, for you and me."

She shrugs. Nothing to be done, she says without saying.

"Did *he* do this? Was this arranged all along with his idea? And you? You and Alok?"

She is looking over my shoulder. "It was all in the stars," she says firmly and turns away.

BUSBOY

by Philip Terry

1. Maddy says she's not interested unless you stop smoking. No buts. Maddy used to smoke like a Turk. Now she's stopped and she wants you to stop as well. She wants you to choose between her and smoking. She wants you to choose *her*. Can't we talk about it, you say. Maddy puts the phone down.

2. You undress a fresh pack of Gitanes, tap the box until one of the line of cigarettes pokes its head above the level of the others. You slip it out, light up, inhale.

3. Nothing could be clearer. Either you give up the fags for Maddy, or you give up Maddy for the fags. The problem is you want both; you want to be *spoilt*. You want Maddy *and* the fags.

4. You take out another cigarette. Light it. Inhale.

5. At the café they ask if you've seen Maddy. You say no, that she's playing hard to get. You clear the tables from lunch in readiness for the next set of customers.

6. There are two ways out of the dilemma as you see it. You either travel back in time looking for Maddy-who-still-smokes-like-a-Turk (difficult); or you persuade Maddy to re-start (also difficult, but less so). Other ways out you will consider later.

7. "A cigarette is the perfect type of perfect pleasure. It is delicious, and it leaves one unsatisfied. What more can one want?"
    —*Oscar Wilde.*

8. From a call box you phone the Smokers' Helpline. You ask them how you should go about preventing a friend from stopping. As soon as they have understood your demand they hang up.

9. That evening you take a long meditative bath. You smoke a joint, then suture the remaining Gitanes. Before going to bed you drink a large tumbler of whisky accompanied by a Havana cigar. You dream of Maddy, smoking.

10. At the café there are workmen installing a waterwheel propelled by an artificial waterfall. The dust and noise created by their goings on keeps most customers at bay, despite the BUSINESS AS USUAL sign in the window. You sit in a corner reading the daily papers, nursing your sore head with a glass of tonic water.

11. You phone Maddy. There is nobody at home. When the ansaphone whirrs into action you speak calmly: *call me*.

12. Later, you check out the smoking section at the local library: predictably, there is a great deal on stopping, nothing on starting up. The only book holding any promise, Richard Klein's *Cigarettes Are Sublime*, you read in one sitting, without stopping for a cigarette. You are particularly impressed by his chapter on *Carmen*, which describes the seductive powers attributed to tobacco in the opera. You resolve to take Maddy to see it.

13. Outside you light up, taking a profound drag on your cigarette, letting its toxic smoke caress the cilia of your lungs.

14. You phone Maddy. Still the ansaphone. When it whirrs into action you speak calmly once again: *please*. You flirt with the idea of paying her an impromptu visit. Think better of it. Light up.

15. Sweet talk, sweet talk of lovers
      it's all smoke!
   Their raptures, their raptures, and their vows,
      it's all smoke!
   Drifting away into the air, we watch
      the smoke
      the smoke
      the smoke
      the smoke!
   —*Georges Bizet*, CARMEN.

16. In the park two small boys are playing on the slides. Behind them, on a bench, sits their young mother, smoking. You ask her for a light.

17. Your ideal lover.
   She would smoke *all the time*.

18. Maddy phones. She asks if you've given up. You say you've bought two tickets for *Carmen*.

   Have you given up?
   Will you come, then?
   If you've given up.

   You lie, say yes, you have. She blows you a kiss down the phone.

19. You spend an evening in front of the television, smoking Old Holborn. Before turning in you flirt with your pipe over a small port. You dream that someone has stuck pins into your cigarette box, so that when you go for a smoke the cigarettes emerge tattered, flayed.

20. At the café they ask after Maddy. You say you're meeting her in the evening. That you're going to a show. You clean out the coffee grinders, sweep the floor.

21. A down-and-out stops you in the street. Asks you for a light. You reach into your pocket and pull out your lighter. Offer it to him. He takes it, pockets it. Then asks you for a cigarette.

22. In the park three fit-looking men in tracksuits are jogging round the outer path. Sitting on your bench, cigarette in hand, you follow their fictional movements with your gaze. Where are they going?

23. Your Top Ten:
    Gitanes
    Gauloises
    Lucky Strike ("It's toasted!")
    Marlboro
    Camel
    Benson and Hedges
    Rothmans
    Navy Cut
    JPS
    MS

24. "The healthy are not real. They have everything except being— which is only confirmed by uncertain health."—*E.M. Cioran.*

25. You weigh up your chances of converting Maddy. Low. Nevertheless, you purchase a packet of Silk Cut, just in case she rises to the bait.

26. You light a Gitane. Inhale. You exhale slowly, through the nose, the smoke descending in swirling eddies over your lips and chin, enveloping your head in its dizzying cloud.

27. Maddy arrives late at the opera, and you are shuffled ungraciously into two pillar seats. The production is set on the planet Argon, in the 21st century. Carmen works in a microchip factory. None of the cast smoke, and the songs have been altered accordingly. Nevertheless, after the performance, you offer Maddy a cigarette. I knew you were lying, she says.

28. You smoke your last cigarette of the day, accompanied by a tumblerful of whisky. When you stub out the cigarette a fair amount of whisky remains. You top it up, smoke another last cigarette of the day.

29. At the café they ask you about the show. You say it was great, that Maddy loved it too. A fetching young woman with dark hair and prominent breasts asks you for a coffee. You take her order, pass it on, without bothering to explain you're not one of the waiters yourself.

30. Already, you are beginning to lose hope of converting Maddy. She's a tough nut to crack, and you haven't the necessary stratagems. As a last resort you decide to try getting her pissed.

31. Your *bête noire*.
    NO SMOKING signs.

32. You telephone Maddy: no reply.

33. In a bar you find yourself eyeing up the women customers. One girl in particular, wearing pink tights and a tartan mini-skirt, smoking roll-ups, attracts your attention. Before you leave your eyes meet: the look in hers is hostile.

34. A friend tells you he's seen Maddy with another man. You remark that she's not your property. That she's often to be seen in the company of other men.

35. "The cigarette is the prayer of our time."—*Annie Leclerc*.

36. It occurs to you there might be another way out of your dilemma. Rather than having *Maddy* and the fags, you could have *another woman* and the fags. Even *another-woman-who-smokes-like-a-Turk* and the fags. A compromise, for sure: but better than Maddy plus no fags. An improvement too on fags plus no Maddy.

37. In bed you toss yourself off, thinking alternately of Maddy and the woman with prominent breasts.

38. In the café you empty an ashtray full of lipstick-stained cigarettes. You read the Lonely Hearts.

    ```
    Fit 31yo, brunette. Virgo, hedonist,
    seeks 24-30yo Gemini man, GSOH, for
    partying etc. NS.—ML 25066.

    Woman, WLTM warm, wickedly funny man
    for walks, talks and corks. When will I
    get my cuddle? NS.—ML 13072.
    ```

    NS could only mean one of two things: NO SEX or NO SMOKING.

39. You telephone Maddy. There is nobody at home. When the ansaphone comes on you put down the receiver.

40. In the park two small boys are playing on the slides. On a bench behind them sits their young mother. You sit down beside her, ask her for a light. She says she's given up.

41. "The cigarette, which is the most imperious, the most engaging, the most demanding, the most loving, the most refined of mistresses, tolerates nothing which is not her, and compromises with nothing."—*Théodore de Banville.*

42. You light a cigarette. The smoke pierces your lungs, then emerges slowly, softly enfolding your body in its mist, at once extending and dissolving the body's limits, erasing the boundary marking inside and outside.

43. You phone Maddy. No answer.

44. You wander from bar to bar in the hope of picking someone up. It's so long since you did this sort of thing that you forget how to read the signs. You get as far as asking for a light three times, but even when the response is encouraging you fail to follow up your first move, retreat to your own table to enjoy the cigarette, your only true mistress. Late in the evening, when you're fairly drunk, you manage to share a few drinks with a student taking a year out. Even though you don't fancy her, at least she smokes. When the bar closes you invite her back to your place. She says no.

45. You stumble clumsily into bed, hit the light. You dream you are in a forest. At the forest's edge you find a path leading up into the mountains. You climb to the top, where you find a lake. You are about to strip off and go for a swim when, suddenly, snow

begins to fall, fast and hard.

46. At the café you cut the stems off some gladioli with a blunt pair of scissors before placing them in vases on the dining tables. Again, you leaf through the Lonely Hearts. Again, NS everywhere.

47. A friend tells you you're looking rough. You're *feeling* rough, you say.

48. You phone Maddy. She picks up the receiver.

> Hello?
> Hello, Maddy it's me.
> Oh!
> I'm sorry, we've got to talk.
> About?
> Maddy, please, why don't you come round for a drink?
> No thanks.
> Then can we meet?

Eventually, she agrees. Insists on her place. You assent, not too enthusiastically.

49. Your worst nightmare.
Finding the 24 hour garage shut.

50. You buy a packet of Marlboro. Smoke half of them on the trot.

51. "If Prometheus had stolen fire from heaven in order to light his cigarette, they would have let him do it."—*Mme de Girardin.*

52. When you arrive at Maddy's flat she's watching *Casablanca* on TV. You make an ironic remark about allowing Humphrey Bogart to chain-smoke in her sitting room. Regret it. During the meal you

keep topping up her wine glass. Every time you do so she smiles at you, in her enchanting, disapproving way. When you've finished eating you casually roll a joint, offer it to Maddy. She refuses, says she has a headache, is going to bed.

53. You catch the last bus home. Finish off the evening with your remaining cigarettes and a can of beer. You dream you are attacked by an oversized pair of scissors.

54. You wake up wanting Maddy more than ever. You are mad about her all over again.

55. Running full tilt in the face of your most powerful instincts, you resolve to STOP.

56. You telephone Maddy. There is no answer.

57. At the café you busy yourself placing small brightly colored paper parasols into slices of melon. You empty an ashtray full of lipstick-stained cigarettes, holding it at arm's length.

58. In the park you stroll round the outer path, soon becoming breathless. You need a cigarette.

59. You telephone Maddy. Still no answer.

60. Your favorite color.
    Blue.

61. Increasingly in need of a cigarette you visit the local library again to solicit the aid of its literature. *Stop Now!* advises you to begin by disgusting yourself with cigarettes, suggests smoking a *whole* packet. You follow its advice. Then smoke another.

62. A friend tells you he succeeded with nicotine patches. I'm a new man, he says.

63. In the evening you smoke your last cigarette. Ever. Four times. You dream someone's fist-fucking your lungs.

64. You wake with a sore throat, drink a glass of orange juice and chew a clove of garlic. Following the course of action prescribed by *Stop Now!* you free-associate, writing out a list of all that is bad about cigarettes.

    THEY KILL YOU
    THEY STOP YOU SLEEPING WITH MADDY
    THEY KILL YOU
    THEY ARE EXPENSIVE
    THEY STOP YOU SLEEPING WITH MADDY
    THEY KILL YOU
    THEY CAUSE BRONCHITIS AND OTHER DISEASES
    THEY STOP YOU SLEEPING WITH MADDY
    THEY STOP YOU SLEEPING WITH MADDY

65. In the park there is a juggler practicing. You watch him trying to light his cigarette while maintaining his three batons in the air. He drops one, but is able to scoop it up again with his foot.

66. From a call box you phone Maddy. There is nobody at home. When the ansaphone whirrs into action you speak forcibly: *call me.*

67. At the café they ask after Maddy. You shrug. You distribute ashtrays in the smoking area. Breathing in deeply, hugging the margins of the occupied tables, you gather as many fumes into your lungs as passive smoking allows.

68. A friend offers you a cigarette. You refuse, saying you have stopped.

69. Life is a cigarette,
    Cinder, ash, and fire,
    Some smoke it in a hurry,
    Others savor it.
    —*Manuel Machado.*

70. At home you find yourself biting your nails. You tell yourself to stop. You find your hand reaching out for a cigarette. What the hell, you think. A last last cigarette. You light it, inhale.

71. Maddy phones. Asks if you've stopped. Yes and no, you say.

    Meaning?
    I'm just smoking my last.
    Good.

    She asks you to call her in a week if you've still stopped. The deal stands.

72. That evening you have a cup of tea and a joint, go to bed early. You can't sleep. Get up. Have another cup of tea, another joint. In bed. You wake to find your mattress on fire, heave it out the window, crash on the couch. You dream of Maddy, smoking.

MOVIE MUSIC

by Charlotte Carter

Lying on my back this way is so familiar. But I'm not a prostitute, exactly.

Tears are running into my ears. But I'm not exactly sobbing. I'm streaming. A thin, steady pumping like the blood beating out of my cut finger a little while ago.

It's going to stop any minute, I kept thinking. It wasn't geyserlike, erupting. Nothing to make me throw on a sweater and cab to St. Vincent's. On the other hand, I certainly wasn't going to keep standing there chopping carrots, either. Like the credit that always gives my heart a little kick, Words and Music by Lacy Freeman, the blood and the tears can also be chalked up to nobody but me, I guess.

As a college student I lived in a rented room in the large South Side apartment of an older woman. She had a wonderful figure for a woman in her late 50s, but her skirts were always a little too tight. Her lover was a skinny guitarist in his 20s who sometimes went out on the road with Ray Charles. My landlady usually spent Sunday nights at his place, and occasionally she traveled with the band. I had insomnia every Sunday there in the chilly blue confines of my room, convinced that the only light in all of Chicago was the cutting glare from my black and white portable TV, one of the first items I'd bought with my earnings from a part-time job at a downtown sheet music store. I waited out the night, the lousy westerns, the public service announcements, the local station editorials, and in the early hours, gray morning rolling in through the French doors of the landlady's sittingroom and painting nasty spots on my sheets, I'd be rewarded with *Insight*. That program was a dramatic series produced by a Paulist priest, Father Ellwood B. Kieser, and I never missed it.

The voice (years later I realized that the voice belonged to TV actor Joseph Campanella) in the lead-in to the show described the series as "the dramatization of man's search for God and peace in a changing world." Or something to that effect. The half hour vignettes dramatized how the confused and lonely found their path with the aid of loving family and friends. In the stories, alienated youths were converted to parent-venerating sons, straying housewives returned to Godly domesticity, and alcoholic businessmen sobered up and, before the credits rolled, stooped to help a child. I cried at the end of every episode, not quite knowing why, finally falling into dark sleep and as often as not waking too late the next day for 9 o'clock class.

At around age 10 I'd talked my mother into taking me out of the public school and enrolling me in the one at the local Catholic church, where lay, I convinced her, my only chance at a superior education. It was the next best thing to the place I really wanted to be: boarding school. The sound of those two words never failed to sit me up straighter in my chair. I yearned for austerity. I wanted to be cloistered in some New England town, lost in the rigors of scholarship and piety. So I embarked on instructions to become a Catholic. It turned out, however, that I never made the journey, because I was terrified out of my fantasy of the religious life by the grim and unfathomably ill tempered nuns at St. Albans. A year later, just short of Communion, I was back in public school, and as the nation fell under the Kennedy spell I graduated eighth grade along with a group of classmates none of whom I was ever to see again. But I suppose I can safely suppose they went on to bear out-of-wedlock children, to become biology teachers, to serve prison terms for grotesque crimes, to die in Vietnam.

Just before I got into the tub tonight Win called. This time, I was already streaming even before the phone rang. I couldn't believe his pathetic attempt at sounding hale-fellow-all's-right-with-the-world.

"Lace," he said, laughing nervously, "what's up? Writing a song for me?"

"You bet, asshole. It's a song for you and Alice. I call it 'Losers in Love.'"

I hung up.

Never been able to do that before. It wasn't that hard. What a long, long road. Over. Never been able to say that before. It was pretty hard.

Why does he do that, anyway—when you pick up the receiver he just starts talking. He doesn't identify himself, he doesn't say "Hello" or anything. He just starts talking, as though he's already in the middle of a conversation, as though you'd called and interrupted *him* while he was talking to someone else.

He rang again. I unplugged the phone.

I was in rare form that last time we went to bed. One zinger after another. My delivery didn't exactly stink either. Anyway, I was pretty funny and he was pretty mad. I took my time dressing.

"Who do you think you are, Lacy? Still think you're Dorothy Parker?" And he gave me an awful look I can't stand thinking about. "Well, you're not. Niggers can't be Dorothy Parker."

"Oh," said I, finding my shoe. "Can I be Charlie Parker?"

I thought he was going to get up and hit me, actually.

"Go write another song about hope," he said.

I found a new bath gel. It's called Amber, imported from Italy, exclusive to the bath shop where I spend a deal of time. The woman who owns the store complimented me on my selection, said the fragrance was going to be featured in the next *Vogue* and it was amazing how I went to it instinctively. Amber, I'm here to testify, has absolutely no power against a fountain of tears.

I'm trying to be careful to keep my bandaged finger out of the water.

I watched so much television after my mother died. She didn't live to see me win the scholarship to boarding school. My first year's stipend left me enough money to purchase a little television—that one had a yellow plastic housing. It was at the Shipley School, not at all a punishing Dickensian institution but an ultraliberal prep school in suburban Michigan, that I first discovered *Insight*, adding it to my then-favorite show, *Naked City*.

Coming back to me now is one NC episode where a cop was having a mental breakdown and couldn't stop crying. His wife (played by the great Geraldine Fitzgerald) was sour and vituperative and unyielding as a nun, a devout, driven Catholic harridan. I'm half remembering something else, too—the profile of a man who has just swallowed a lethal number of sleeping pills and is washing them down with Jack Daniels. I see clearly the hollow of his cheek as he sucks the neck of a quart bottle. Where does that one come from? Was it an *Insight*? Or something big budget? A male nurse I met at one of my agent Vera's do's was saying how Seconal and Stolichnaya was the way to go. "S and S," I dubbed it, and we did a riff on going into some very decorous bar like Bemelmans and ordering that. *An S and S, please... No olive.* A few feet away, on the piano bench, Win sat looking at us, unsmiling. That crying cop was a Catholic and he was burned out. He was trying to make enough money working overtime to buy a new suit for his son's first Communion. That actor—what's his name?—has a big face, a big square jaw, and huge watery eyes. John Larch, that's his name. This means I'm about to crack, too—right? It means I'm losing it like one of those brittle Parker girls. We read her books at Shipley and I loved them. I'd pick up her stories for fun when music theory got to be too much. Pretty easy to ridicule them now. Fuck me, as the studio guys say, I ain't laughing now. What goes around, comes around.

Win had the nerve to be pissed off at me. After the party, as we walked downtown, he said I'm too socially graceful to be trusted.

Trying to contain my hiccups, I close my eyes against the growing coolness of the water, white bubbles turning to gray scum. Why the curve of that man's face? Why Jack Daniels? Suicides can't all be bourbon drinkers. With me in the bathroom I have the next to the last bottle of the quite decent, as Theo called it, St. Emilion I found at the liquor store that was going out of business, along with a pretty nice looking plastic wineglass, a pack of Camel Lights, and my father's old Zippo. I've never had a Seconal in my life. I get hiccups when emotionally taxed, like in the seafood restaurant where Roger asked me to marry him. It was our second date and I'd only been in the City a couple of years then. Ginger had fixed me up with him, sensing my tolerance for impossible men. And in spite of this I went on to help make her wealthy; she lives handsomely off those numberless records which contain so many of my tunes. Roger went on to start his own label, forgetting me, presumably, and doing well for a time before his company folded at the end of the disco era. I still get regular hysterical calls from Ginger—she's *got* to go on tour, she's *got* to have a new song, she's *got* to have this or that. Write it now, Lacy. Do it now, Lacy. Come over now, Lacy. Fix it now. So this year she wants to be more "soulful." She wants songs that sound "blacker." Silly bitch thinks she's Chaka Khan this year.

Things would have been incalculably different if only I'd been born with any kind of a voice myself. Adore voices, hate singers. But of course that is in no way true. Theo and I caught Abbey Lincoln, Margaret Whiting, and Carmen McRae all in the same night, impeccable martinis fueling us between locations. Win had never heard of Johnny Hartman before he met me, but now he thinks all he has to do is play that Hartman-Coltrane tape and I'll just melt, forget. Men shouldn't have voices unless they sound like Johnny Hartman. Theo came close. I'm melodramatic, I admit it, but the truth is, I meant it when I said I didn't think I wanted to go on living without Theo. Yet here I am. Clinging to life, as they used to say on the soaps my mother loved.

The Jack Daniels man is receding and now I have a hugely funny—

if unlikely—image of my father crying as he paints an enormous office building lobby, working long into the night to buy a Communion dress for me, sobbing and tripping over his ladder, his tears plopping into the turpentine. I have to invent the details of Daddy Zippo's face, though, because I don't remember the man very well. He split quite a few years before what would have been my Communion, somewhere in there between *Romper Room* and *Playhouse 90*.

Alice, basically, is ugly. As far as I know, Win and I met her on the same night, at Vera's reception for Stevie Wonder. I was chatting with a guy who kept humming something he said he couldn't place, and I tried to tell him it was the break in *The High and the Mighty*. Except another guy insisted it was the theme from *The Unforgiven*. Then the two of them got to congratulating themselves about how many times they'd seen *The Searchers* and the argument was never settled. Vera had told me I might be up for this movie score—an "independent film" was how the Vassar type on my answering machine referred to it—and I should meet these people. In the end the job went to a snotty kid fresh out of Bard— you know, mix a little Tangerine Dream with a hint of Ry Cooder, the stuff that Grammy's are made of. Anyway, Alice is the harrowingly thin discarded wife of some producer. And Win, Mister High Standards Even If You Make Money You Can't Take Yourself Seriously Lacy Until You Compose in a More Authentic Idiom, is going off with her to Berlin. It's just my absolute favorite. I sleep with one other man and I never hear the end of it; I spend ten days *by myself* in Provincetown and he starts the abandonment bullshit; hold one opinion contradictory to his and we're back to the black bourgeoisie-private school girl rap. But who is he shtupping? Alimony Alice, whose favorite charity is Louis Vuitton. Funny. Over. Let it bleed.

Russian Tea Room. Ginger thinks I'm depressed because I don't eat enough roughage, while Vera chalks it up to my not working. (I haven't, in weeks.)

Has it occurred to anyone that Theo's dead, I ask.

Now, there's an idea for a fragrance: Russian Tea Room. Lots of ylang ylang with a topnote of paprika. I'd better get right over to the bath shop. So I excuse myself and leave them eating sour cream.

Since I've unplugged the phone, there can't be any eleventh hour phone call from a savior—why did I say "savior?" I meant "stranger." You, the faithless sinner, have the pistol in your mouth (or you're dancing with Mr. Daniels), trembling, praying, crying, thumb on the trigger, and...BbbRRing! A wrong number saves your life, talking you down, giving you hope. That kind person is a symbol, though. You won't find that person's name in the telephone book. Time for Father Kieser to close the program with a few inspirational words. Lord, maybe Win's right, maybe my only idiom is sloppy TV drama from the so-called Golden Age. Restrained, gracious, pressed down, sewed up, cultured, bubble bath Lady Lacy, how about if tasteful old you makes an S and S special and winds up in the *Daily News?* BOARDING SCHOOL NEGRO DISEASE CLAIMS ANOTHER VICTIM—FROM BERLIN, FORMER COMPANION SAYS SONGWRITER WAS CULTURALLY CONFUSED, DEPRESSED OVER DEATH OF HOMOSEXUAL ESCORT.

Vera says the best thing in the world for me would be to finish the song I started for Theo. Somehow, I just can't.

And this bulletin just in: Musician Lacy Freeman was found dead at her lower Manhattan home last night. Authorities list the cause of death as lack of an idiom.

I let the water out and fill the tub anew. The Amber is slimy on my skin until the bubbles reappear. Keep Lacy in mind, Vera said as she introduced me to the genius piloting the career of a dirty pop idol about to go legit on Broadway. Everyone admires her style, she said. Ummmm, Vera's new companion agrees, Lacy's fabulous. Well, I'm not, I'm just not. What I am is a born nerd who took a strange turn somewhere. Everybody admires my style, sure, everybody except Win, who says my manners are just a cover for rage, my grace a sickness. And what of my killer wit, Win? How about I'm just trying to be nice, asshole?

A Jamaican woman takes care of Win's place. I never worry if I lose an earring over there; I always find it the next time on a shelf in the medicine chest, where Mathilde leaves it. The sheets I buy him are all very dark—murky navies, bitter chocolates, midnight blues with burgundy stripes. He keeps the air conditioner running all year and I sleep close to him, trying to get warm.

"I hate it that I don't have great legs," I said to him once.

He shrugged. "Your legs are okay."

"I know they're 'okay.' They just aren't long and beautiful enough. Well, they're long enough, but they aren't especially beautiful. I always wanted people to gasp when I got out of the back of a cab in high heels."

"Boo hoo hoo." He rubbed at his eyes. "Lacy's not perfect. Lacy'll have to wear boots for the rest of her life."

He didn't understand.

His hands made their way all the way down my thigh, over the calf and the ankle, and then he took my foot and held it. "Come on, your legs are okay. Really. I like touching them... Oh, baby, what happened to your toe?"

"Told you before. I smashed it when I moved to 12th Street, in 1979."

He slid the gnarled thing into his mouth then, sucking it, eyes closed. I lay there, wanting him again.

"You like the way I make love to you, don't you?" he said finally, fingers walking up the leg, across the belly.

Nearly choking, I nodded yes.

"And what about Chris Herbert?" He smiled a little. "Did you like that better?" The sonofabitch still had his eyes closed.

"Jesus, you make me tired, Win. I thought we were finished with the Chris Herbert number."

He said nothing.

"Remember, Win? You said, Let's take a couple of steps back. And I said, Oh, okey-doke. And then you didn't know my name for six weeks. And then you showed up at Vera's Christmas dinner and made a fool of yourself. And then I spent the next week in this apartment, blowing a job in the process. And then..."

"Enough with the calendar, Lacy."

"I'm just bringing us up to date here, Win. Spring is here, pal."

I did not, in point of fact, go to bed with Chris Herbert. And I know it's hateful to let Win go on thinking I did. I know that. But tough shit. Let him writhe in it. One of my favorite *Naked City* episodes was called "Torment Him Much and Hold Him Long," starring Robert Duvall as a sensitive guy who had been raised in an orphanage. He was troubled, psychically damaged, and bitterly lonely, but I can't remember what he did about it. Duvall must've done at least five *Naked City's*; Jack Klugman maybe eight or ten of them. Talk about damaged—with the collection of losers he portrayed on that show, I thought dumpy Jack Klugman was a really interesting actor in those days. I imagine that's quite a key to my sick little personality, having spent my adolescence sitting in dark rooms thinking it would be *intense* to do it with Jack Klugman. Pathetic.

Pathetic, Pathetic, Pathetic.

Chris Herbert is a Brit who directs rap videos. Win loathes him, of course. Win has a conspiracy theory about MTV, in his opinion the singular evil of the 1980s. I sort of have to give him that one. Why don't they all just die. Why don't I just get out of the tub and write a rap song—about Catholic school, perhaps. Get Vera to give Madonna a call.

I once told Theo about the crying cop segment of *Naked City*. A couple of weeks later he came over with a *TV Guide* for that week in 1963. It said the title of that episode was "Today the Man Who Kills the Ants Is Coming." We kind of wrote a tune and gave it that title. "Sounds like something Monk would come up with," Theo said, crashing crazily up and down the keyboard. He had another drink and then he sat down next to me and scatted the shit out of "Straight No Chaser," while I did my best imitation of Ellis Larkin. We did in two bottles of Veuve Cliquot and slept in each other's arms on the sofa. I guess Win was giving me the devil at the time, don't recall what about, and I asked Theo why a person can't just quit a person even though the first person knows the second is utter jive. "Heigh-ho," he arched his eyebrow like Noel Coward, "if jive were all." That's what I mean about Theo.

"I'll quit him now," I say here now, aloud. "Come back and see if I don't, Tee." But I already have quit him, haven't I? Or vice versa. Whatever. Theo. I'll finish your song if you come back, I'll stop smoking, forgive old man Zippo. Come back and keep me company for one night and I'll fucking die for you, buddy. How's that for being good? Giving everything you've got, that's what it's all about, right, Sweetheart? Money where your mouth is.

Okay, one of those hack TV directors is saying. Okay. Cry. Slap at the water. More tears. More rage. Rolling! Beautiful. Heartbreaking.

It is a juicy pink dawn in the naked city and we see Beautiful Sister Timothy (that's me in a short-lived fantasy of myself as a nun) seated at the piano in the late Theo's divine old Armani, eating a raw carrot and picking out "I Should Care" with her good hand. Title of this episode: No more dying, no more lying, no more crying, just for tonight, Sister Timothy. The search for peace in a changing world.

"Goddamnit, Win, spring is here, pal. What are you going to do about it?"

He grabbed me up then, kissing me till I shook. And we went through the whole vaudeville, no music in the background, lights on, for real. Well, fuck it, I thought, rocketing off somewhere.

I left him sleeping, looking like a crime victim, and I walked all the way home, smelly and done in. Maybe this isn't the last time, I remember thinking, but every time after now is just going to be for drill, anyway; and I wasn't wrong; I knew. On Amsterdam and 81st I passed a guy I could swear was Rip Torn, and I remembered "A Case Study of Two Savages," the *Naked* he'd done. He and Tuesday Weld played two murdering rednecks in the big city. They shot him down like a dog.

I've ordered in some mu shu shrimp and have to be careful not to spill on Tee's favorite jacket.

He must have spent the whole afternoon dressing. Except for the fact that he moved more slowly than before, he looked great almost right up to the end. We caught each other preening in the foyer mirror as the *maitre d'* led us into the Whiting gig.

"Don't worry, Girlfriend," he whispered, popping his fingers. "We look fabulous."

"Right," I said back. "So how come nobody wants to fuck us?"

I CAN SPEAK!™

by George Saunders

Ms. Ruth Faniglia
216 Lester Way
Rochester, NY, 14623

Dear Ms. Faniglia,

We were very sorry to receive your letter of 23 Feb, which accompanied the I CAN SPEAK!™ you returned, much to our disappointment. We here at KidLuv believe that the I CAN SPEAK!™ is an innovative and essential educational tool that, used with proper parental guidance, offers a rare early development opportunity for babies and toddlers alike. And so I thought I would take some of my personal time and try to address some of the questions you raised in your letter, which is here in front of me on my (cluttered!) desk.

First, may I be so bold as to suggest that some of your disappointment may stem from your own, perhaps unreasonable, expectations? Because in your letter, what you indicated, when I read it? Was that you think and/or thought that somehow the product can read your baby's mind? Our product cannot read your baby's mind, Mrs Faniglia. No one can read a baby's mind. At least not yet. Although we are probably working on it! What the I CAN SPEAK!™ can do, is *recognize familiar aural patterns* and respond to these patterns in a way that makes *baby seem older*. Say baby sees a peach. If you or Mr Faniglia (I hope I do not presume) were to loudly say something like: "What a delicious peach!" the I CAN SPEAK!™ hearing this, through that hole, that little slotted hole near the neck, might respond by saying something like: I LIKE PEACH. Or: I WANT PEACH. Or, if you had chosen the ICS2000 (which you did not, you chose the ICS1900, which is fine, perfectly good for most babies) the I CAN SPEAK!™ might even respond by saying something like: FRUIT, ISN'T THAT ONE OF THE MAJOR FOOD GROUPS?

Which would be pretty good, for a six-month-old, don't you think, which my Warranty Response shows is the age of your son Derek, Derek Faniglia?

But here I must reiterate: That would not in reality be Derek speaking. Derek would not in reality know that a peach is fruit, or that fruit is a major food group. The I CAN SPEAK!™ knows it, however, and, from its position on Derek's face, gives the illusion that Derek knows it, by giving the illusion that Derek is speaking out of its twin moving SimuLips™. But that is it. That is all we claim. That is all our advertising claims.

Furthermore, in your letter, Mrs Faniglia, you claim that the I CAN SPEAK!™ "mask" (your terminology) takes on a "stressed-out look when talking that is not what a real baby's talking face appears like but is more like some nervous middle-aged woman." Well maybe that is so but with all due respect (and I say this with affection), you try it! You try making a latex face look and talk and move like the real face of an actual live baby! Inside are over *5000 separate circuits and 390 moving parts*. And as far as looking like a middle-aged woman, we beg to differ, we do not feel that a middle-aged stressed-out woman has 1) no hair on head and 2) chubby cheeks and 3) fine downy facial hair. The ICS1900 unit is definitely the face of a baby, Mrs Faniglia, we took over 2500 photos of different babies and using a computer combined them to make this face on your unit, and on everybody else's unit, the face we call Male Composite 37 or affectionately "Little Roger." But what you possibly seem to be unhappy about is the fact that Little Roger's face is not Derek's face? To be frank, Mrs Faniglia, many of you, our customers, have found it disconcerting that their baby looks different with the I CAN SPEAK!™ *on* than he or she looks with the I CAN SPEAK!™ *off*. Which is why we came up with the ICS2100. With the ICS2100, your baby *looks just like your baby*. And, because we do not like anyone to be unhappy with us, we would like to make you the gift of a complimentary ICS2100 upgrade! We would like to come to your house on Lester Way and make a personalized plaster cast of Derek's real actual face! And soon, via FedEx, here will come Derek's face in a box, and when you slip that ICS2100 over Derek's head and Velcro the Velcro, he will look nearly exactly like himself, plus we have another free surprise, which is that, while at your house, we will tape his actual voice and use this voice to make the phrases Derek will subsequently say. So not only will he look like himself, he will *sound like himself*, as he moves around your home appearing to speak!

Plus we will throw in several personalizing options.

Say you call Derek "Lovemeister." (I am using this example from my own personal home, as my wife Ann and I call our son Bill "Lovemeister," because he is so sweet). With the ICS2100, you might choose to have Derek say, or appear to say, upon crawling into a room, HERE COMES THE LOVEMEISTER! or STOP TALKING DIRTY, THE LOVEMEISTER HAS ARRIVED! How we do this is, laser beams coming out of the earlobes, which sense the doorframe! From its position on the head of Derek, the I CAN SPEAK!™ knows it has just entered a room! And also you will have over 100 Discretionary Phrases to more highly personalize Derek. You might choose to have Derek say, on his birthday, for example, MOMMY AND DADDY, REMEMBER THAT TIME YOU CONCEIVED ME IN ARUBA? Although probably you did not in fact conceive Derek in Aruba. That we do not know. Our research is not that extensive. Or say your dog comes up and gives

Derek a lick? You can make him say (if your dog's name is Queenie, which our dog's name is Queenie): QUEENIE, GIVE IT A REST! Which, you know what? Makes you love him more. Because suddenly he is articulate. Suddenly he is not just sitting there going glub glub glub while examining a piece of his own feces on his own thumb, which is something we recently found Billy doing. Sometimes we have felt that our childless friends think less of us for having a kid who just goes glub glub glub in the corner while looking at his feces on his thumb. But now when childless friends are over, what we have found, my wife Ann and I, is that there is something great about having your kid say something witty and self-possessed years before he or she would actually in reality be able to say something witty or self-possessed. The bottom-line is, it's just *fun*, when you and your childless friends are playing cards, and your baby suddenly blurts out (in his *very own probable future voice*): IT IS VERY POSSIBLE THAT WE STILL DON'T FULLY UNDERSTAND THE IMPORT OF ALL OF EINSTEIN'S FINDINGS!

Here I must admit that we have several times seen a sort of softening in the eyes of our resolute childless friends, as if they too would like to suddenly have a baby.

And as far as what you said, about Derek sort of flinching whenever that voice issues forth from him? When that speaker near his mouth sort of buzzes his lips? May I say this is not unusual? May I say that our Billy also had that reaction? What we did, what I suggest? Try putting the ICS on Derek for a short time at first, maybe ten minutes a day, then gradually building up his Wearing Time. That is what we did. And it worked super. Now Billy wears his even while sleeping. In fact, if we forget to put it back on after his bath, he pitches a fit. Sort of begs for it! He starts to say, you know, Mak! Mak! Which we think is his word for mask. And when we put the mask on and Velcro the Velcro, he says, or it says rather, the ICS2100 says: GUTEN MORGEN PAPA! because we have installed the German Learning module. Or, for example if his pants are not yet on, he'll say: HOW ABOUT SLAPPING ON MY ROMPERS SO I CAN GET ON WITH MY DAY! (I wrote that one, having done a little stand-up in my younger days.)

My point is, with the ICS2100, Billy is much, much cleverer than he ever was with the ICS1900. He has recently learned, for example, that if he dribbles a little milk out of his mouth, down his chin, his SimuLips™ will issue a MOO sound. Which he really seems to get a kick out of! I'll be in the living room doing a little evening paperwork and from the kitchen I'll hear, you know, "MOO! MOO! MOO!" And I'll rush in and there'll be this sort of lake of milk on the floor. And there'll be Billy, dribbling milk out of his mouth down his chin, until I yank the bottle away, at which time he bellows: "DON'T FENCE ME IN!" (Ann's contribution—she was raised in Wyoming!)

Mrs Faniglia, I for one, do not believe that any baby wants to sit around all day going glub glub glub. My feeling is that a baby, sitting in its diaper, thinks to itself, albeit in some crude nonverbal way: What the heck is wrong with me, why am I the only one saying glub glub glub while all these other folks are talking in whole complete sentences? And hence, possibly, lifelong psychological damage may result. Now, am I saying that Derek runs the risk of feeling bad about himself as a grown-up because as a baby he felt he didn't know how to talk very good? It is not for me to say, Mrs Faniglia, I am only in Sales, but I will say that I am certainly not taking any chances with Billy. My belief is that when Billy hears a competent, intelligent voice issuing from the area near his real actual mouth, that makes him feel excellent about himself. And I feel excellent about him. Not that I didn't feel excellent about him before. But now we can actually have a sort of conversation! And also—and most importantly—when that voice issues from his SimuLips™, he learns something invaluable, namely that, when he finally does begin speaking, he should plan on speaking via using his mouth.

Now Mrs Faniglia, you may be thinking: Hold on a sec, of course this guy loves his I CAN SPEAK!™, he probably got his for free. But no, Mrs Faniglia, I got mine for two grand, just like you. We get no discounts, so much in demand is the I CAN SPEAK!™, and in addition, our management strongly encourages us, in fact you might say they even sort of *require* us, to purchase and use the I CAN SPEAK!™ at home, on our own kids. (Or even, in one case, the case of one Product Service Representative who has no kids, on his elderly senile mom! And although, yes, she looks sort of funny with that Little Roger face on her frail stooped frame, the family has really enjoyed hearing all the witty things she has to say, so much like her old self!) And although we are strongly encouraged/required to use the ICS system, please don't think I wouldn't otherwise. Believe me, I would. Since we upgraded to the ICS2100, Billy says such wonderful things, and looks so very identical to himself, and is not nearly so, you know, boring as before, when we just had the ICS1900, which (frankly) says some rather predictable things, which I expect is why you were so unhappy with it, Mrs Faniglia, you seem like a very intelligent woman. When people come over now, sometimes we just gather around Billy and wait for his next howler, and just last weekend my supervisor, Mr Ted Ames, stopped over (a super guy, he has really given me support, please let him know if you've found this letter at all helpful) and did we all crack up laughing, and did Mr Ames ever start scribbling approving notes in his little green notebook, when Billy began rubbing his face very rapidly across the carpet, in order to make his ICS2100 shout: FRICTION IS A COMMON AND USEFUL SOURCE OF HEAT!

Mrs Faniglia, it is nearing the end of my lunch, and I must wrap this up, but I hope I have been of service. On a personal note, I did not have the greatest of pasts when I came here, having been in a few scrapes and even rehab situations, but now the commissions roll in, and I have made a nice life for me and Ann and Billy. Not that the possible loss of my commission is the reason for my concern. Please do not think so. While it is true that, if you decline my upgrade offer and persist in your desire to return your ICS 1900, my commission must be refunded, by me, to Mr Ames, that is no big deal, I have certainly refunded commissions to Mr Ames before, especially lately. But my recent bad luck is not your concern, Mrs Faniglia, your concern is Derek. My real reason for writing this letter, on my lunch break, is that, as hard as we all work at KidLuv to provide innovative and essential development tools for families like yours, Mrs Faniglia, it is always sort of a heartbreak when our products are misapprehended. Please do accept our offer of a free ICS2100 upgrade. We at KidLuv really love what kids are, Mrs Faniglia, which is why we want them to become something better as soon as possible. Baby's early years are so precious, and must not be wasted, as we are finding out, as our Billy grows and grows, learning new skills every day.

Sincerely yours,
Rick Sminks
Product Service Representative
KidLuv Inc.

THE RUSSIANS

by Lewis Warsh

The two Russian women were in the kitchen of their apartment when Eddie Perez came in through the window with a gun. One of the women, her blue eyes shielded by tiny gold-rimmed glasses, was standing in front of an ironing board in her underwear. It was ninety degrees outside, hotter inside the apartment. The other woman was sitting at the kitchen table with her back to the window drinking coffee. The two women were in their early twenties. Marina, the woman in the nightgown at the table, had emigrated to the United States five years before. The other woman, in bra and panties at the ironing board, had arrived several months ago. They had been friends in Odessa; now they were roommates in New York City. It had been Marina's job, since she had studied English at the university in Odessa and could speak English fluently, to come to the United States first and find an apartment. The plan was for Irene, her friend, to follow once she had settled in. The fact that five years passed before she arrived was another story.

The man named Eddie Perez had just killed a policeman in the stairwell of a building in the housing projects on Avenue D. There were at least a hundred policemen in the neighborhood looking for him. He had escaped to the tenement rooftops, even though there was a helicopter overhead, and had climbed down a fire escape along the side of the building where the Russian women shared an apartment on the top floor. The policemen in the street below assumed he was holding someone hostage in the apartment. The two women were slow to react when he came in the window. Irene simply put down her iron and stared at the man with her mouth open while Marina turned a slow half-circle in her chair, sandwich in hand.

"Don't say anything, not a word," the man said. He rotated the gun, pointing it first at Irene, then at Marina.

One of the policemen, possibly the police commissioner, was shouting up at him through a bullhorn, asking him to surrender. Pleading with him, really. Where before there had been the animated noise of people talking, the rise and fall of distant sirens, now there was silence, nothing but the voice of the cop. He was repeating the same phrase— "come out with your hands up"—like the refrain of a song echoing down the sides of a canyon.

"Eddie," he was saying, "if you hear this, come out of the building with your hands in the air."

Eddie Perez could hear the cop's words. The whole scene made him want to laugh. He went to the kitchen sink, turned on the cold water and splashed it over his face. The two women were numb with the heat. He waved his gun in their faces and muttered to himself, interspersing Spanish cursewords with English. The two women believed him when he said he would kill them if they didn't follow his instructions. They had learned to anticipate the unexpected in a new country and now it was happening. A baby-faced young man was pointing a gun at them at eleven o'clock on a morning in August. He had entered their apartment. "You," he said, pointing to Marina, "give me some tape. And some rope."

He ordered the woman who was wearing only her underwear to lie face down on the floor. Cops with rifles were stationed on the roof across the street. They were special cops, trained at shooting people from a distance. The guns were aimed at the windows of the apartment where the two Russian women lived. While Irene was on the floor, Eddie

Perez strapped Marina to the chair and pasted a strip of masking tape over her mouth.

"Get up," he said to Irene, pulling at her arm with his free hand. "Where's the bedroom?"

It was Marina who told the police what had happened. How the man with the gun had entered the apartment and tied her to the chair. How he led her half-naked friend into the bedroom.

There were people in the street who were shouting Eddie's name: "Edd-ie, Edd-ie." There were people leaning out their windows chanting the syllables of his name as if he were a war hero or an astronaut or some athlete who earned ten million dollars a year. There was no love lost between the cops and the residents of Avenue D. Eddie had been born in the projects facing the East River Drive. They considered him a kind of folk-hero for wounding a cop who had caught him robbing a grocery on the Upper East Side a few days before. Nothing wrong with robbing a store in a neighborhood where rich people lived. That's why the cops were looking for him in the first place, and that's why he had to kill one of them in a stairwell on Avenue D.

The cop in charge of the case, Harry Cray, decided to lead a team of men up the stairway and break down the door of the apartment, but first he had to try to coax the bastard into taking responsibility for what he had done. He sensed that as he stood in the street doing nothing something horrible was happening inside the apartment. The sharp-shooters across the street couldn't detect any sign of life. Not even the curtains at the window were moving.

Find someone who can talk to the guy in Spanish. Find his mother.

Marina, tied to the chair, said she heard nothing from behind the bedroom door. She assumed that her friend was being raped. Or that he had killed her first. He had killed one cop, wounded another. What did he have to lose? Too bad for the two Russian women who were sitting innocently in their apartment.

A woman who looked as old as Harry Cray's grandmother stepped forth from the crowd.

"I'm Eddie's mother," she said, in English. "Let me speak to him."

Marina assumed that after he killed Irene he would come out and kill her, as well.

Harry Cray handed Eddie's mother the bullhorn and she shouted into it as if she had been preparing for this moment all her life. Harry could see the air vibrate, as if the woman was breathing underwater. All the cops were crouching like stick figures near their cars. The sunlight was baking the roofs of the cars the color of lava and Harry Cray could see every drop of sweat on the face of Eddie Perez's mother as she shouted to her son in Spanish.

Harry knew that the words she used wouldn't be strong enough to convince her son to give himself up. Her voice was raspy and hoarse and she kept repeating the word "Dios, Dios" as if that was going to make any difference. Eddie had gone too far this time. And maybe this woman wasn't even Eddie's mother, but someone playing the part in a movie about cops he had rented from a video store years before, or a movie yet to be made, a pilot for a new TV series about detectives and their girlfriends and wives.

It was Marina, of course, after it was over, who filled in the blanks. How when his mother was shouting at him through the bullhorn Eddie Perez was in the back bedroom with Irene and Marina was in the kitchen, tied to her chair, listening to it all. Her friend crying in the other room and the old woman shouting in the street. It was her turn next. Marina was certain he would kill both of them.

Harry Cray decided that Eddie Perez's mother was only making things worse. He decided that the best plan was to storm the apartment. The point was to take Eddie alive, if possible, but also to insure the safety of whoever he had taken hostage. No one knew if he was alone in the apartment. No one knew about the two women.

Marina, tied to her chair, knew that her friend was dead. There was a period of maybe thirty seconds where the silence was overwhelming. The silence in the bedroom and the silence outside. Even the helicopter circling the scene seemed to have stalled in mid-air. And then, Marina told Harry Cray, after it was over, I heard your footsteps on the stairs.

He had seen her face, when he entered the apartment, the strip of tape over her mouth. He had seen her eyes. They said *in there*. They pointed him towards the bedroom door. He had walked past her, followed by five men in uniform, and they had stood on either side of the door. He could feel her watching him, her neck muscles bulging beneath her skin, her taut breasts swelling outwards, the sweat pouring down the sides of her face. Her hair was sculpted like braided ivy, the color of fire. There was the moment when he had to make a choice, signaling to one of the cops to knock down the door, while at the same time wanting to comfort the young woman in the chair, to kneel at her feet and untie her hands. Rub them between his own to get the blood flowing.

Irene was dead. Eddie was holding her upright in a corner of the room with a gun pressed to the side of her head. The woman was a half-head taller than Eddie and kept slipping from his grasp like a broken mannequin. Harry couldn't believe that Eddie would use a dead body as a hostage.

"Put the gun down, Eddie," he said. "It's over."

The woman had a vague smile on her face, a streak of blood across her forehead.

"I want out of here," Eddie said, tightening his grip on the dead woman. "Get me a car to the airport."

"No chance," Harry Cray said. "You've seen too many movies. It's over."

"It's never over," Eddie said.

And those were his last words.

It was Marina who warned me about Dimitri's wife. "If Natasha ever finds out you're sleeping with her husband, she'll kill you." I had met Dimitri at a party. Marina had introduced us and I guess she felt partially responsible for what might happen. For what did happen. The last thing she expected was that I'd end up with Dimitri. She had invited me to a million parties and introduced me to a million guys. I was often the only non-Russian woman at the party so I always drew a crowd of potential suitors. It was my bad luck that I should end up with the one guy who was married. Not only that: Natasha's brother was a gangster. One of the new breed of hoodlums who collected protection money from the Russian store owners in Brighton Beach, the neighborhood of choice for the Russian immigrants. If Natasha's brother found out about me and Dimitri, Marina went on, we'd both be dead.

Twice a week, Dimitri visited me in my apartment. The only time we spent a night together was the night we met. Natasha and their three kids were out of town, so it was possible for Dimitri to sleep over at my apartment without anyone finding out. After that night, any time we wanted to see one another, he had to lie to Natasha, who was suspicious by nature, and made him account for every moment he was out of the house. It was only a matter of time before she asked her brother Boris to ask one of his flunkies to follow Dimitri when he left work. He had told Natasha that he was taking an English course at one of the ESL schools near Penn Station. He even bought a textbook and did the homework assignments. It was a half-truth, at best, since he wanted to learn English, and was actually improving his English by spending time with me, though we hardly talked at all.

What did we do together? Dimitri wanted to know about all my ex-lovers. Why someone like me wasn't married. I was almost thirty, after all, and by the time Natasha was thirty she already had three children. They had met in college in Odessa, where they were born, and where their grandparents still lived. They had been together ten years. I was the first woman Dimitri had slept with since he met Natasha, or so he said. His first affair.

"What's he like?" Marina asked. We were eating lunch on a bench on the promenade in Brooklyn Heights. We went there every afternoon, weather permitting, on our break.

Marina's boyfriend, Ivan, had just got out of jail, and as a consequence I saw less of her. We still went to parties together. All the

Russian guys got drunk and took turns dancing with me. Eventually, one of them would get too drunk and start a fight with the others. Marina danced only with Ivan, who had a bad temper, apparently, and had a fit of jealousy if she even talked to another guy.

"Da," Dimitri said, and I repeated it back to him, "da." He was trying to teach me Russian. What we did together was teach each other things. He told me about Russian history. About the Romanovs. Peter the Great. All the tsars with names like Alexander and Nicholas. He told me about Trotsky and Lenin. And I tried to teach him English, though he knew more English than I knew Russian. Twice a week I took Russian lessons from a retired professor on the Upper West Side, a man in his early seventies whose wife had recently died, and whose daughter—"you remind me of my daughter," he said, when we first met—lived in California. We would sit in the living room of his apartment, at a large table facing a window with a view of the Hudson River and the smokestacks on the Jersey shore. He would serve me coffee on a gold tray which he said had belonged to his parents in Odessa. That's where he had grown up. His father, he said, had known Lenin.

"Kafye," he said. "And chay."

"What does chay mean?"

"Chay means tea. Repeat after me."

"Kafye," I said, "and chay."

His name was Roshenko, but he told me to call him Karl. That's what his wife used to call him. She had been a ballerina in Russia, before they came here, but she had broken her leg in a bicycle accident and could no longer dance. She had a dream of opening her own dance school but it had never happened. Before she died, she worked in a bridal shop on 5th Avenue, selling wedding gowns to people who never had to worry about money.

I was in the backseat of a car with two Russians and we were all drunk. Marina was in the front seat with her boyfriend Ivan. It was early summer and the windows on either side were wide open. Ivan, who was driving, shouted something to some black guys in a passing car. They were all talking Russian and the guys in the back were laughing, pointing their fingers at the black guys in the car which had stopped alongside us. Sometimes Marina translated for me but this time she didn't and I wondered, as I often did, whether they were talking about me. We were riding down the Belt Parkway, on our way from a party in the West Village to another party in Brighton Beach, where most of the Russians lived, Marina included. I was taking turns kissing the two guys. One of them lifted my skirt and put his hand between my legs while the other began fumbling, like a young schoolboy, with the buttons of my blouse. Both of them were too drunk to wonder whether I wanted them to touch me or not and for the moment I lacked the energy to push them away. All I knew about them were that they were friends of Ivan's. He had introduced me to them at the first party but I didn't remember their names.

Marina said that her parents named her after Marina Tsveteva, the great Russian poet who hung herself because she was too poor to feed her children. Because no one cared about her poetry. Because she didn't care about it herself. Is that the story? Most of the Russians I met could recite poetry by heart. It would happen at every party, someone would get drunk and began reciting Pasternak, a poem that all Russians memorized when they were kids.

We met at school, Marina and I, the private school in Brooklyn Heights where we both taught, mostly white kids with a lot of money and black and Hispanic kids on scholarship. I taught English, *The Great Gatsby*, *As I Lay Dying*, *The Grapes of Wrath*, to high school students, and Marina, who was a painter and a collagist, taught art—art history, drawing, introduction to painting. Once a week she and Dimitri attended the same drawing class, that's how they met and that's how (eventually) I met Dimitri. That's how all the trouble started. Marina spoke with an accent. I asked her where she came from and she said "Where do you think?" I had to admit that for a long time I had a crush on her myself and I think she knew this and was frightened of me (this was my theory) because she had no interest in sleeping with women, or she had an interest (wishful thinking) but refused to admit it.

She told me that she once shared an apartment with a Russian friend on 11th Street and Avenue C and that one morning an escaped convict named Eddie Perez climbed in through the window and held them both hostage and even raped and murdered her friend Irene while Marina, tied to a chair, listened to it all from the other room. She said: "I was having breakfast, Irene was ironing a blouse, when this guy came in the window with a gun in his hand." She said that he threatened to kill them if they didn't do what he told them. The cops were downstairs, apparently he had killed a cop earlier in the week, or the same day, I can't remember, and someone—the police commissioner, perhaps—was telling him to surrender, shouting the words through a bullhorn from the sidewalk. "He kept telling us that he had nothing to lose. That he was going to spend the rest of his life in jail. That he had already killed someone and that killing us wouldn't make a difference." I wanted him to choose me, not Irene, Marina said, but he tied me to a chair instead. He said he was twenty-five, but looked younger, really a kid, with a mop of black hair over his forehead. He pointed the gun at Irene and said, "You—get inside." I sat in my chair listening to her crying and the guy telling her to keep quiet. "And then," she said, "they were both quiet. And then the cops came and killed him."

After that, she moved to Brighton Beach, where she lived when she first came to the states. It was the only neighborhood where she felt safe.

I want to concentrate on the Russians, what I know, what I learned. Everything you don't learn in school I learned from my relationships with Dimitri and Marina. The only way to learn anything, possibly, is to experience it first-hand, this goes without saying. I want to focus on the time I spent with the Russians. I was a California girl, so to speak, though I had been living in New York for five years, escaping a bad marriage back home, bad parents who had split up when I was ten. The phase of my life that involved the Russians only lasted a few years, but whenever someone mentions "Odessa" I feel like I've been there.

Something else happened during this time that only indirectly involves my life with the Russians. I still have his name in my address book: Harry Cray. Next to his address there are two numbers, his home phone and the precinct where he worked. Harry Cray was a cop. The woman in the apartment below me, a prostitute named Yvonne de Marco, had been murdered, and late one Sunday night Harry Cray and his partner Ricardo knocked on my door. I had just gotten out of the shower and was wearing the blue terry cloth robe which Dimitri had bought me for Christmas when I heard the footsteps on the staircase, followed by the knock. And in answer to my question: Who is it? one of them—it must have been Harry—said: the cops. It's the cops.

One thing I know about are cops. My father was a cop. My first lover was a cop. There had even been talk, when I was growing up, that I was going to become a cop. I'm an only child—my mother nearly died giving birth to me and didn't want to risk having more kids—and it was the tradition in my father's family that the children follow in their father's footsteps. Every male in my father's line had been a cop since I don't know when. The Civil War maybe. Every son went into the army. My father had been in Vietnam. He was in Vietnam when I was born and didn't hear that my mother almost died giving birth to me until he returned home for a week's leave. I didn't see much of my father when I was growing up. I call him on his birthday and he calls me on Christmas. He calls me when he knows he's coming to New York, which is about once a year, and we eat dinner together. He says: "You choose a restaurant" and I say "What do you like to eat?" I have almost no memory of sitting around a dinner table with my parents when I was a kid. My mother hated to cook. When my father was in Vietnam my mother took a job as a real estate agent. We were living in a small town along the coast about an hour north of San Francisco. My mother sold houses to rich ex-hippies. She made love to her boss. She hired a baby-sitter to take care of me. Every time the phone rang she assumed it was someone from the army informing her that her husband had died in the line of duty or was missing in action. She dreamed that a coffin containing his body parts had been left on the front porch. She told her lover, Joe Griffiths, the real estate mogul who became my step-father, that it was wishful thinking. "Even if he came back in a wheelchair I wouldn't let him in the front door."

The cops introduced themselves. The tall shifty-eyed one with the chalky complexion who did most of the talking—that was Harry. The smaller, younger guy with the bald spot was Ricardo. Harry, staring at a point a few inches above the top of my head, said that the woman who lived below me had been murdered that morning. A friend of hers who had keys to the apartment discovered the body at four in the afternoon. There was a pause as if they were waiting to see how I would react. The tall guy ("my name is Harry Cray, I'm a detective at the Ninth precinct") asked me if I'd been home earlier that morning, or the night before, and if so whether I'd heard any suspicious noises, voices, an argument. Did I know the woman downstairs? This was Ricardo talking.

I shook my head.

"Does that mean 'yes'?" Harry asked.

"It means 'I can't believe it,'" I said.

I told the detectives that I'd been living in the building for two years and that Yvonne was living here when I moved in. They didn't ask me for this information but I thought it was important to give some background before I got to the point. Ricardo nodded and wrote down the information on a pad, or pretended to. He unclipped a cheap ball-point and balanced a small notepad in the palm of his hand. They were both standing up, Harry leaning against the sink, Ricardo against the front door. I was sitting in a chair in my blue robe with my legs crossed, smoking a cigarette.

"Did you know that your neighbor was a prostitute?"

"We said hello on the staircase, that's all. Once she asked if I wanted to come by for coffee but I had to go somewhere else and she said whenever I wanted to just knock on her door. It's something people say who live in the same building without really meaning it and of course I never went. I should have, I guess, or invited her up here. We didn't seem to be on the same schedule. Occasionally I heard music from down below. Jazz. Some uncomplicated sounding mood music that didn't bother me at all."

A few days later I was sitting with Marina on the promenade, eating lunch. I told her about the two cops, the murder of the prostitute/porn star in the apartment below. The way I found out she was a porn star was in the newspaper. The cops on the case—the newspaper didn't use their names—said there were tapes in the apartment, porno movies, and magazines with her pictures in it. Marina, nibbling the edge of her sandwich, seemed distracted, like she was only half-listening. She didn't pick up on the fact that I was interested in the detective, Harry Cray. I didn't even know his name. What I was conveying in the story had nothing to do with Yvonne de Marco, my dead neighbor, or even the porn star angle, but my interest in the cop. Marina was thinking of something else.

"We want to see you again," she said.

I had spent the night—the night Yvonne de Marco was murdered—over at Ivan and Marina's. The three of us had slept together for the first time, Ivan in the middle. At some point he rolled on top of me while Marina leaned on her elbow and watched. When Harry Cray asked whether I'd heard anything in Yvonne's apartment I stared at my feet and said that I wasn't home, that I'd slept over at a friend's house. Harry looked disappointed. I thought he might be jealous since maybe he thought I was saying (indirectly) that I'd slept at my boyfriend's house. That I was unavailable. Was that what I was saying? Or maybe he was disappointed because I hadn't heard anything, that I didn't know anything, that I wasn't going to be any help. Maybe I was just imagining that he was attracted to me and that he was pretending not to be because he was with his partner. Or maybe he was just simply disappointed about being alive, the dwindling possibilities now that he was forty. Was that how old he was? The disappointment in his eyes, along with the deep furrows that rippled across his forehead when he was thinking (what was be thinking about?) made him look older.

It was only in my mind, in a thought that lasted a micro-second, that I imagined I was falling in love. That Harry Cray and I were falling in love. That we'd live together forever. It was the illusion that everything happened by accident and that you had to be prepared for every encounter. That you had to be open to the possibility. Most people walk down the street with their eyes glued to the pavement. No contact, not even a faint possibility. And they complain about being alienated, how New York is such "a lonely place", that you have to protect yourself, that there are too many different types of people, not racial types but people who are brain damaged, neurotic, schizophrenic, murderous. Angry. There are too many angry people here, that's what everyone thinks. I was angry about something, the defendant explains to his permanently disabled victim, and I took it out on you. That's what people do in the city, they vent their rage on innocent bystanders. They get caught in the crossfire.

I was tempted to tell Marina that I'd only sleep with her and Ivan if she let me make love to her as well. I hoped that if I went along with her I'd be rewarded for my patience. I wasn't sure what she was getting out of it all: watching me and Ivan from the side of the bed. Looking bored, as if she was just waiting for it to be over. As if she was doing it all ("he's been in jail for a year") for him, to please him. Because she liked the idea of people she loved getting together. Her boyfriend, Ivan, and me, her best friend.

"Didn't you have fun the other night?"

Now we had something to talk about.

"And Dimitri. Are you still seeing him?"

She had no interest in hearing about the dead prostitute and the two cops who had come to my apartment.

It was February 1997. Twice a week Dimitri visited me. Once a week I went uptown to see Professor Roshkenko. Every other week, I spent the night with Marina and Ivan. Dimitri, of course, didn't know I was sleeping with someone else. The Russians are a jealous race, prone to extreme solutions to simple problems, especially when they're drunk. Dimitri always asked me if I had other lovers, couldn't believe that I didn't. I was trying to convince him that it was possible for him to change his life. I was naive to think that Natasha couldn't force him to stay. Dimitri shook his head. He'd do anything, he said, to get away from her. Even if it meant giving up the kids. She'd never let me have the kids. Then he shook his head again, as if the thought was inconceivable. Marina had once told me that she thought Dimitri was too passive. That was one theory. The other theory was that Natasha had too much power. Whenever there was a murder in Brighton Beach the cops went directly to Natasha's brother. Maybe he had some information? Marina was certain that Natasha's brother was paying off the cops as well.

"If Natasha ever finds out..." Marina shook her head and suggested I carry a gun. Ivan could get one for her, easily. Ivan, a part-time gangster himself, had been arrested for selling drugs out of a storefront on Brighton Avenue. He had been put in jail not so much for the severity of the crime but because he refused to name names, one of whom would be Natasha's brother. When he got out of jail he promised Marina that he would never work for Boris again, but of course it was Boris who had found him his present job at a print shop in Sheepshead Bay. Nothing illegal about that. The owner of the shop owed Boris a favor, that was all. All the shop owners in Little Odessa, as the Russian neighborhood was called, owed Boris something. The only person to whom Boris owed anything was his sister.

Professor Roshenko, my Russian teacher, had been with Trotsky in Mexico. There was a framed photograph on his mantelpiece: Trotsky, other members of his staff, a young version of the professor standing next to his hero. Trotsky's hand on his shoulder. Another photograph of Trotsky and Frieda Kahlo, another of Trotsky and Diego Rivera, another of the three of them together. Another of Trotsky with his wife, Natalia. It was like a little shrine. One of the brightest moments in my life, the professor said. Especially when the trials began. Stalin had indicted Trotsky and it was up to Trotsky to respond, long distance.

Every newspaper in the world carried the story. It was Professor Roshenko's job to talk to reporters. We worked for eighteen hours a day. We had one focus, one goal. Except for the early years with my wife, this was the most exciting time for me.

The next time Dimitri and I made love I thought of Harry Cray. What we would do together if he came to my apartment alone to ask me more questions (this was his excuse for visiting me) about the dead porn star downstairs. Of course I never told Dimitri that when I was making love to him I was thinking of someone else. Thinking about something is the same as doing it. According to St. Augustine, thoughts are as sinful as actions. The only way I can come when I'm making love is to imagine that I'm making love to someone else. There's a knock on my apartment door and the voice says: It's the police. I remember him, of course, from the other day, when he came by with his partner Ricardo. One might imagine making love to both Harry and his partner simultaneously—I've never made love to two guys at the same time—as Yvonne de Marco did in all her movies. And then after they were done there were two more guys, it went on forever, until the cocks moving in and out of her body resembled the pistons in a car, close up of a car's inner workings, a training film for fledgling auto mechanics: this is how it's done.

One afternoon, on our lunch break, Marina told me she thought that Ivan was falling in love with me. She said that Ivan, who wanted to be a film director, was writing a film script and had told Marina that I would be perfect for the lead role. They invited me over for dinner and we watched movies together in the living room. Me and Marina on the living room rug, her head in my stomach, while Ivan sat in a chair close to the screen. Often we watched movies that Ivan had seen before. He was writing the script for a movie and was planning to send it to a movie producer named Dean Holmstrom who he had met through Boris. He was in Boris's good graces ever since he went to jail without incriminating anyone. He had served his time, without complaining, and this was his reward.

He told us of a party he went to at Dean Holmstrom's house. Elizabeth Taylor had been there. She had just come out of the hospital and spent most of the time sitting in a chair in the corner. Everyone at the party paid homage to her. Everyone at the party was aware that she was there. Ivan was amazed at her body, especially her breasts. He had expected her to be heavyset and somewhat grotesque. It was easy to see how she had often been described as "the most beautiful woman in the world." When he went to shake her hand, or kiss her hand, she leaned forward so that he could see down the front of her dress. It was a very low cut evening gown, ankle-length, since her legs were the least attractive part of her body. It was like being in the room with some ancient deity. Something to tell your grandchildren. Apparently, Dean Holmstrom's wife had given him a tour of the house, a brownstone in the east sixties. She asked him about his script and he told her it was about two Russian women who came to New York and what happened. She promised him more than once that she would make sure Dean read it.

"Did you sleep with her?" Marina asked. It was hard to know from her tone whether she was serious or not and for a moment I wasn't sure who she was referring to. Elizabeth Taylor? The director's wife?

I was worried what would happen to our friendship if I continued to make love to Ivan. The unspoken rule was that we would never get together when Marina wasn't around. Sometimes he called me in the evenings and made me promise never to tell her that we had talked. What he wanted to tell me about was his script. It was based on the Eddie Perez story. The guy who had killed the two cops as well as Marina's friend Irene. He wanted me to play Irene. Marina, of course, would play herself. He was thinking of us when he was writing even though I wasn't Russian. He was waiting to hear from Dean Holmstrom. He had left a first draft of the script at his house the night of the party at which he had met Elizabeth Taylor.

Marina and I no longer ate lunch together every day. She had too much work, she said, but I didn't believe her. Instead, she ate her lunch in her small office at school. I didn't know how long she could endure the idea that I was sleeping with her lover. She had thought that anything was possible, that she would do anything to make Ivan happy, but the way I see it she was getting burned by her own fire. Ivan told me on the phone that he and Marina were no longer having sex. He asked me whether I was seeing someone else and I lied, I said "no," even though it seemed possible that Marina had already told him I was sleeping with Dimitri. The only time Marina and I talked, these days, was when she called to make arrangements for me to come over. When I complained—"I never see you anymore"—she apologized and said that she was busy. I wanted to ask her whether she and Ivan were having problems. I wanted to tell her that I was in love with her, that it was she I wanted to sleep with, not Ivan, but I didn't say anything. "Can you come over Friday?" And then silence, as if she wanted to get off the phone. As if someone was listening on the other end.

Sometimes Dimitri called to cancel our appointment.

"I can't make it," he said. "I'm sorry."

I was getting sick of the deception that involved having an affair with him but it was too late. I'd had an affair with a married man once before, one of my professors in college (when I was in California) and it had ended badly. Dimitri was in love with me, or so he said. Whenever I acted distant he promised to leave Natasha. "I can't live without you," he would say. He didn't have to tell me why he couldn't come over. It was understood that it had something to do with Natasha. The Russians lived in a small community, everyone knew everyone else's business, and I assumed it was just a matter of time before Natasha found out that I was sleeping with her husband, or that Dimitri found out that I was sleeping with Ivan.

I assumed that Ivan knew about Dimitri and that he didn't care. He had no right to care. If he wanted to cause trouble, if his jealousy took the upper hand, he could make sure Natasha found out that her husband was having an affair, and with who. I could imagine a scenario in the future where Ivan felt possessive about me as well. "I want to leave

Marina and be with you," I could hear him say.

I guess you could say that a good part of my life involved my deal-
ings with the Russians. I was sleeping with two Russian men, Dimitri
and Ivan. My best friend was Russian. Twice a week I went uptown to
Professor Roshenko's apartment where I studied Russian, talked to him
in Russian, converted my thoughts into a different language. In my
spare time I read books in English by Russian writers. I watched
Russian movies. My favorite Russian movie was *Solaris*, a science fiction
movie about people on a spaceship whose memories are somehow
encapsulated by the ocean enabling people who are dead to return to
life. It was a beautiful, languorous movie, that was also a love story. The
person who returned by way of the ocean knew he or she was dead. The
movie was filled with longing for something that was lost. When I told
Ivan that I liked *Solaris* he asked me if I'd seen other movies by
Tarkofsky and when I said that I hadn't he said he would get a different one on tape and that we could all watch it the next time I came over.

It was early April and I had begun thinking that when summer came
I would change my life. I would stop seeing Dimitri. I would extricate
myself from the relationship with Ivan. I would travel to California or
to Mexico and when I returned to New York I would change jobs so
that I wouldn't have to see Marina everyday. I had studied enough
Russian so that if I ever decided to go there I could engage in simple
conversations. When I was in Brighton Beach I always impressed
myself by being able to read the odd looking lettering on the canopies
and windows of the shops. I had wanted to recreate my own identity as
a way of getting closer to Marina. But I didn't want to be her sister, that
wasn't the point, and it was no longer possible to deny what I was really
feeling. It occurred to me that I wouldn't be unhappy if I never saw any
of these people again.

Marina felt grateful to Harry Cray for saving her life. After the Eddie
Perez incident, after she moved to her own apartment in Brighton
Beach, they talked on the phone once or twice a week, and occasionally

went out for dinner together. She asked him questions about his life, about his marriage, why it had ended, why he had decided to become a cop, how he felt when he entered the apartment and saw her sitting in the chair, what it felt like to kill someone. She had thought, more than once, of returning to Russia after Irene was murdered, at least for a visit, and until her boyfriend Ivan was released from jail, but she decided that moving in a backwards direction was a way of admitting defeat.

"I'll make dinner for you," she told Harry over the phone. She gave him directions to her apartment, a one-bedroom in a building near the ocean.

She wanted to make love to him as a way of repaying him for saving her life. She thought that it might be possible to sleep with him a few times, not get involved, really, make it clear to him that she was involved with someone else, but that she felt drawn to him because of what he had done. She knew that once they made love it would be difficult to extricate herself from the relationship after Ivan returned. It was hard to gauge another person's feelings, especially after you made love to them, how everything changed once that happened, but the fact that you couldn't predict what might happen was what made it exciting in the first place. She felt drawn to Harry Cray, to the sense of danger surrounding him, and to the fact that he had never showed any interest in making love to her, that he treated her more like a daughter than a potential lover. He gave her the impression, though he was over forty, that he hadn't had much experience with women.

They were sitting on the small sofa in her living room looking through photograph albums. She showed him a photograph of Irene, the day they graduated from the university in Odessa. She told him that Irene had had a baby when she was eighteen, that the baby had died when he was six months old, but that otherwise Irene had been one of the happiest people she had ever known. As she talked she put her hand on Harry Cray's knee, wanting him to respond. They sat very close together on the sofa, their thighs touching. She thought that if she touched him first he would take the cue that he could do anything he wanted with her, that she would let him do anything. She kept her hand on his thigh as he turned the pages of the photo album.

She was frightened that if she acted too aggressively he would leave. It had been three months since her friend had been murdered and she was still in a state of shock. She had never slept with an American before. It was interesting the way feeling gratitude to someone translated into a feeling of love. Harry Cray wasn't her type, really, she wasn't fixed on older men. She felt like she wanted to give him something, that he needed something, but she wasn't sure what. It was hard for her to imagine that he wouldn't want to make love to her. She had never had any trouble attracting men.

He was lying on his back on the sofa and she was kneeling on the floor, her head between his legs. She unfastened the buckle of his belt and pulled his pants down along his thighs. She was wearing an old Indian skirt with bells on the hem which she had bought at the Salvation Army. A string of beads which extended down to her waist. She had the feeling that Harry Cray might come too quickly if she continued and she wanted him inside her. Her hair hung down the side of her face and brushed against his skin. She lifted her blouse and he reached out and put his hand on her breast. She had the feeling that he hadn't made love to anyone in a long time. She thought that she might get pregnant if he came inside her but she would take her chances.

It was after the first time that he became more aggressive. She was making it easy for him. Lying on the living room carpet, pulling him down on top of her. She said something in Russian to him that meant "go slowly" and he said "What? What did you say?" and she remembered that she wasn't making love to Ivan and she didn't bother translating as he went for her hair, tugging at it gently at first and then harder as they exchanged places and she climbed on top of him. So this is what he was like, really, this was the danger. This was what a guy who could murder someone was like in bed. This was where gratitude ended: she was on her knees and he was coming at her from behind. He was remembering what it was like during the first years with his wife, when they made love every night in a different position. Everything he knew about sex he had learned from his wife Sara who was a few years older than he was and infinitely more experienced. Marina thought of saying "you can hit me if you want" because it occurred to her that that's what he wanted to do without realizing it. She wanted to do something with him that he had never done before, that would be a real gift, something for him to remember. She didn't want to come, not yet, his tongue moving between her legs. He was holding her by the waist, her skirt bunched up around her waist, then pulling her hair, then leaning forward to bite the side of her neck. She was glad that she was seeing this part of him and that the feeling of gratitude was what made it possible. He had risked his life for her and she would do anything in return. He had come inside her twice. It was almost midnight and she was going down on him again.

She asked him if he wanted something to drink and she brought him a glass of water. She turned her back to him and he put his arm around her waist and she lifted her leg so that he could come inside her. Then he rubbed her clitoris again, moving slowly, so that he was doing two things at once like Sara had taught him. She began to make noises, breathing heavily, in a way that Sara had done during the first years of their marriage when they made love, when it seemed like all the energy in her life was directed towards pleasing him. He would return home from work exhausted and she would draw him into the bedroom. "I've been waiting for this all day," she would say. Her appetite for sex had worried him but it was only because he was too inexperienced to understand that this was what he wanted to do as well. Instead, he took her for granted, assumed that she would be there when he came home, that she would always want to make love to him with the same intensity, that if he asked her for something she would get it for him. It never occurred to him that she was unsatisfied playing the role of the cop's wife, that she hated lying in bed at night not knowing when he would come home. He always called her if he was coming home late but when the phone rang in the middle of the night she was sure it was someone calling her to tell her that he'd been killed or injured. It never occurred to him that she might have a lover during the time when he was at work. He never asked himself what she did when he was at work and Veronica was in school. When he returned home in the middle of the night—not dead, not injured, but what difference did it make?—she turned away from him when he got into bed. "I'm tired," she said, "let's do it tomorrow." It never occurred to him that she had spent the day in bed with someone else and that she was too sore to make love again.

Marina said, "Don't move—just relax—let me do the work." She wasn't quite sure he understood what she meant. It wasn't the first time she had said this to someone. It was three in the morning. She knelt at his feet at the end of the bed. She took his toes in her mouth, one at a time. "Don't do that," he said. She licked the soles of his feet. "I want to," she said. "Let me."

It took a long time. The only part of him she didn't kiss was his cock. He put his hand out to touch her breast but she pushed him away. It was almost morning. She was on top of him again as the light came in through the curtains. Her cunt was sore, her hair matted with sweat, and she wondered whether he could come again, how long it would go on. She was already thinking of the future, what she would say to him when he called. She sat in a corner of the bed and she touched herself while he watched. There's a mirror at the end of the bed and he can watch himself fucking her from behind, can see her face. They look like people in a funhouse, distorted, a monster with four arms and two heads. They look like the same person. He watched her in the mirror as she knelt on the edge of the bed. She kissed his ankles and his knees. She made a circle with her tongue around his cock without touching it.

"We can do this every night," she says. She doesn't know why she says it. Maybe for a few nights, at best. She had the thought that Ivan had hired someone to watch her, to make sure she didn't sleep with any-one else when he was in jail. He would be out in a few months. Every weekend she visited him, taking the train upstate. He said, "Write to me about sex, tell me what you want to do." All he wanted was to talk to her about sex.

She's thinking in Russian. She wonders about Harry Cray's gun. She asks him about it. "I'd like to see it," she says. It was always possible that someone was spying on her and that Harry would be murdered as a consequence. That no one, least of all Ivan, would realize that her lover was a cop. And she would die too. They would kill them both when they were in bed. She had seen it in the movies. The door opens, the man with the machine gun, the unsuspecting lovers, the bullet holes, the screams. The idea of the danger involved is what made her excited and she was tempted to ask him to show her the gun. She would do anything in gratitude for saving her life. She wondered what he would think if he knew her boyfriend was in jail.

It's Sunday. Neither of them have to be anywhere. Today is the day that she visits Ivan. He'll be expecting her. His family is in Russia and she's the only person who visits him. Harry takes her hand and places it on his cock. It's almost noon and she gets excited thinking about making love to Ivan. They sit up in bed smoking cigarettes. Harry says that he quit a few years ago but he can't resist the temptation. He draws the smoke into his lungs and then reaches across her for the glass of water on the bedside table. He remembers sex and cigarettes with Sara in the early days of their marriage and then he remembers seeing Sara walking in front of him down the street with another man, their arms around each other's waists. It was in the last months of their marriage. The last weeks and days.

"Did you come?" he asks. He isn't sure. It's like a long thread, now, almost continuous, from one orgasm to another. She doesn't want him to stop. She says, "You have to tell me what you want me to do." She begins with his toes, his ankles, his knees, his hipbone, his nipples. She thinks that if she continues he'll come without her touching him but he doesn't and finally he yanks at her hair and pulls her on top of him. He feels tempted to slap her across the face, but doesn't. He wants to go farther inside her, to regain control, so he pushes her on her side. She wonders why he doesn't take his belt from his pants and use it on her like a whip. She gets wet just thinking about it and watches them in the mirror as he pushes against her until she no longer recognizes herself. Then she sees it, the way she looked when she was thirteen or fifteen, when she was still a virgin. That's how she feels now as he comes inside her.

He takes out his gun and presses it against the side of her head. They're lying back on the bed. It's mid-afternoon. There are no bullets in the gun, at least that's what he tells her. "I was only kidding," she said, not knowing whether he was about to turn into a monster. She took the gun in her hand and pointed it at their reflections in the mirror. All she knew was that she never wanted to see him again. She wanted to let it go. Either that or they'd have to stay like this indefinitely. Every time he moved away she grabbed his hand and placed it between her legs. She wondered how often he could come. Twice an hour? There was always the chance that one of Ivan's friends was waiting in the street. She sensed that he was falling in love with her, that he had fallen in love with her the first time he saw her sitting in the chair. He took the gun from her hand and placed it on the floor at the side of the bed. He reached out and touched her cheek, a moment of tenderness as she moved on top of him. She taught him how to touch her clitoris when they were fucking, to put his hand between their bodies. She thought it might be possible for them to come at the same time, but it didn't matter. They were in the shower and she was on her knees again with his cock in her mouth. She was bending over so that he could enter her from behind but it was hard for them to fit. He kept slipping out. He soaped her back, her cunt, put his fingers inside her.

He wanted to ask her if he could spend the night. Possibly they could get something to eat? She was already wondering if she would have to move. She could imagine coming home late at night and Harry would be waiting for her outside her building. Or he would see her with Ivan and know that her boyfriend was a criminal. You can always tell, Ivan once said, whether a person's been in jail. Eventually there would be a confrontation. She was grateful to Harry Cray for saving her life but she didn't want anyone else to die. Irene had died. Eddie Perez had cut her throat. Then Harry Cray shot Eddie through the head. Wasn't that enough?

In the photograph they looked like any other teenage girls. They had their arms around each other, or one of them was behind the other with her head resting on the other's shoulder. Marina was taller so she was often the one who was standing behind Irene. They were inseparable. They were virgins. At fifteen—the time the photo was taken—they had yet to fall in love.

Things began to change when they went to the university in Odessa. Irene was always a bit more advanced than Marina in her relationships with men. She had an agenda which included friendship but there was something else. There was an older man who lived alone around the corner from where she lived with her parents. In his early forties. Irene, at the time, was only seventeen. She began to visit him once or twice a week after school. He had some physical disability, a back problem, that prevented him from working. He did some kind of paperwork for money at his desk. He rarely went out and Irene would bring him food that he liked and even cooked it for him at times. It was at this point that Irene and Marina began to drift apart. Irene's life with the older man was a secret. If her parents ever found out they would kill her. And him too.

It was after Irene became pregnant that things began to change. She moved away from her parents without telling them she was going to have a baby. There was a rumor that her parents knew she was pregnant and asked her to leave. The only person she told was Marina, who was shocked at first, since she had yet to have a lover of her own. She had a different goal, to get out of Odessa, out of Russia. She had decided when she was in high school that she wanted to live in the United States and was studying English so when the moment came she would be ready. That's what she did at night, she sat alone with her books. The only person who mattered to her was Irene, her friend from high school.

When Irene came to her dormitory room and told her she was pregnant, Marina asked "With who?" It seemed like the logical question. "Who's the father?" Irene told her about how she had been spending her weekday afternoons, in bed with the older man with the back injury. A man with scars who didn't know he was about to become a father.

They lived together in a one room apartment not far from the university. Marina had a desk near the window where she did her schoolwork late into the night. Irene had dropped out of school when she learned she was pregnant. There was only one bed and the two young women slept together. Marina tried to deny to herself that she was in love with Irene. It was not something she wanted to think about. She had many men who were interested in her and occasionally she went out on dates with them and allowed them to buy her things. She would press her face against the window of a store and exclaim how much she wanted a particular object and the man she was with would buy it for her in the hope that she would want to sleep with him, but she never did.

The apartment was badly heated and sometimes Irene and Marina slept in each other's arms for warmth. They would fall asleep on separate sides of the bed and wake up, embarrassed, with their arms around each other.

The baby, a boy named Sasha, was born prematurely, and lived less than six months. Irene tried to nurse him but he cried incessantly. He was too small, more like an object you could fit into the palm of your hand, than a living thing. He cried and slept and grew thinner. Reddish spots, the size of dimes, appeared on his cheeks. He sweated constantly. Irene refused to sleep and the doctor insisted that she was contributing to the problem, that she was transferring her anxiety to the baby, that's why the baby wouldn't nurse. "You mean it's my fault that this is happening?" she wailed at the doctor. Marina woke up in the middle of the night and tried to coax her friend into the bed. She was sitting on the floor at the foot of the crib. "It's all my fault," she was saying. It was practically the only thing she ever said. The older man with the scars didn't realize that he had fathered a child. He stood at the window of his room waiting for Irene to appear around a corner and wave to him like she had done before, but she never came.

It was after the baby died that Marina and Irene became lovers. They would spend the entire day in bed studying English, memorizing words and phrases in English, drinking pots of black tea, smoking cigarettes, their long legs intertwined under the blankets and sheets. They would sleep on their backs with their hands between each other's legs. Irene was amused by the fact that Marina was still a virgin. The older man with the scars, Sasha's father, had not been her first lover. Marina would ask her questions about all her lovers, the men who would pick her up on the way home from school. She would stand on a corner and a car would stop and she would get in. She was only sixteen but looked older if she wore makeup. She was never interested in sleeping with men her own age. Once she even slept with the father of a close friend. She saw him watching her out of the corner of her eye and smiled in a way that communicated to him that she was interested in him as well. She had lost count of her lovers. Marina was jealous; compared to her friend, she had lived a sheltered life. All she had done in her short life, or so it seemed, was sit at desk in front of a book, translating from one language to another. Even so, it took her about an hour to read a page of English.

Irene would occasionally wake up in the middle of the night and run to the place where Sasha's crib had been, the corner of the room near the window, and which now contained a little shrine consisting of cheap candles and a picture of Buddha which she had found in a flea market. She would wake up in a cold sweat in the middle of the night and grab for Marina's breasts. She would laugh at anything, a voice on the radio, the way she mispronounced the English phrases, all the English curses like "shit" and "fuck you." Her laughter was like a wave, a tsunami, coming out of nowhere: Anyone who heard her laugh would look at her as if something was wrong. There was a tremor in her voice so it was hard to know whether she was laughing or crying. Her laughter sounded like the cry of the baby who had died.

They made love by the light of a candle at the foot of the bed. They ate black bread and drank tea and cooked old vegetables, pointing to them and addressing them in English as if they were people of different genders until they no longer had to translate the words in their heads. Every other day Marina stood on a line outside a bakery and waited several hours for a loaf of bread. They made plans for the future. They went to the local library and stared at black and white photographs of New York City. They assumed there was a future, that this room with its memories of the dead baby would eventually fade, that they would one day parade down a boardwalk near a mythical ocean, named after the Greek god Atlas, and live in a community of people like themselves.

Marina was frightened of leaving her friend alone. The plan was for Irene to move back to her parents' apartment and wait until Marina found an apartment for them in New York. It was one of many possible plans. Sometimes the future resembled an open door; at other times it was like a small room with the walls caving in. The thought of being separate for more than a few days terrified them. They took turns weeping and comforting one another. They had to force themselves to get out of bed, to eat, to make tea, to buy cigarettes. If it was up to Irene, she would spend the whole day in bed with her friend.

They sat on a bench looking out at the Black Sea. They had a favorite café, in the shadow of the Potemkin Monument, where they went to drink coffee in the late afternoon. They stayed up half the night reading in bed. Marina practiced her English skills by reading novels by popular American authors while Irene read books in Russian: Gogol, Chekhov, Isaac Babel. They wondered if the people they passed on the street knew that they were lovers.

Irene's parents were more sympathetic to her now that she was planning to go to the United States. They assumed that Irene would find an apartment large enough for them as well. They apologized for every infraction, every crime they had committed as a parent. They asked Irene to forgive them for their response to her pregnancy, for not helping her when she needed them. They would get down on their knees and beg for forgiveness if she would help them leave the country. They even began studying English together. They even invited Marina to dinner. The plan was for Marina to fly to New York and find an apartment. Everyone gave her the names of people to contact when she arrived. She had an uncle in Brighton Beach where she could stay until she found a job. The uncle, in fact, would give her a job as a waitress in his restaurant, if she wanted. Now that Irene was in safe hands, at least she wouldn't starve when she stayed with her parents, the plan to move to the United States began to gather momentum. A few days before leaving, Marina moved to Irene's parents house and spent her last nights in Russia in Irene's narrow bed. The parents wandered around the apartment oblivious to what was really going on. They assumed that Marina was sleeping on a mattress on the floor.

Marina met Ivan in the restaurant under the el, her uncle's restaurant where the local gangsters congregated after hours. She had been in New York for three months already and still lived with her uncle, in a kind of basement apartment beneath the apartment where he lived with his family. As part of the agreement—that he would give her a job in the restaurant, that he would help her find her own apartment, that he would buy her clothing—she had to make love to him whenever he wanted. She had realized this on the trip from the airport when he took her hand and placed it on his thigh as he drove. "I'll help you," he said, later that night, "if you do something for me." As he talked, he made a hissing sound in the space between his front teeth. His fingertips were stained with tobacco and his beard scraped her face when he pushed himself against her. She never told him that she was still a virgin and she doubted that he even noticed. Marina thought of Irene while they were making love and some warmth spilled over, spilled out of her, in a sense, and her uncle imagined that he was giving her pleasure. His wife, he complained, refused to make love to him; she had discovered him in bed with another woman a year before and had denied him any pleasure ever since. Forced him to sleep on the couch. "That's where I'm going when I leave here," he said. "The fucking couch."

It was Ivan who saved her, who took her away from her life in the basement. Of course it was necessary to sleep with him as well, to use him in this way in order to make her escape. She had the feeling that Ivan paid her uncle money as a way of releasing her from her obligation. It was a kind of servitude, either way, but Ivan was a more gentle lover than her uncle, and smarter as well. He'd been to college. He was obsessed by movies. That's how they spent their time, at movie theaters or watching movies late into the night on the VCR. Ivan never told her how he earned money, but she assumed he was on the payroll of one of the local gangsters. They went to parties at small mansions overlooking the Long Island Sound. She knew that as long as she continued living with Ivan it would be impossible for Irene to join her. She wrote her friend daily. They had imagined that they would be separate no longer than three months but already a year had passed. Marina had underestimated the amount of money needed to find an apartment in New York. At least, with Ivan, it wasn't necessary for her to work. She went to school at night, taking art history classes and English, until her English was almost perfect and she could get a teaching job. Ivan didn't care whether she worked or not. He was often out of town, doing jobs for Boris, the gangster boss, which was fine with Marina who preferred being alone so she could write letters to Irene, whose parents were dying in Odessa. She told her friend everything: how she lost her virginity with her uncle in the basement and how Ivan stole her away. She told her about the ocean, the endless boardwalk passed Coney Island where she walked every day. She told her about her classes at school, and later her job as a teacher. They talked in their letters about all the things they would do together, imagining the moment of their reunion. It was as if they had never left their bed in the room in Odessa where Irene's baby had died in the middle of the night.

Marina, who worked five days a week in a private school in Brooklyn Heights, was saving her money. She received a Masters in Fine Arts from Hunter College. She had always been a goal-oriented person. Her classmates in Odessa had always hated her for doing well in subjects like chemistry or Latin. The goal, in this case, was Irene, reuniting with her friend. Even if Marina had her own apartment Irene couldn't leave her parents. Her father had Parkinson's and sat in a wheelchair most of the day with his head on his chest. Her mother had had a heart attack and walked with a cane. Irene knew if she went to the United States she would never see them again. She would feel guilty forever. Even though they had banished her from their house when she was pregnant with Sasha, she still felt obliged to accompany them through the final stages of their illnesses. And it was the final stages. Both of them spent more time in the hospital than at home and her father's legs were becoming gangrenous from spending too much time in bed. She sat at the edge of his bed and fed him bits of chocolate but the melted chocolate, which he couldn't swallow, seeped out of the corners of his mouth. Irene wrote to Marina that after a day in the hospital she was tempted to go to the nearest bar and pick up some stranger and go home with him just to forget about everything, but that she managed to control herself and always ended up returning home alone, stopping first at the cafe where she and Marina used to drink their early afternoon cups of hot chocolate. Then she would walk along the desolate embankment looking out over the Black Sea, out into the middle of nowhere with the wind howling in her ears.

The only thing Ivan cared about was that Marina was in bed when he came home in the middle of the night. He would wake her up and force her to make love, even though she had to be up at six in the morning in order to take the subway from Brighton Beach to Brooklyn Heights. Luckily, as a lover, he had simple tastes; for the few minutes that it lasted she could pretend that she was interested, and then fall asleep again while he lounged in bed next to her blowing smoke rings at the ceiling. Some nights he took movies of her lying naked on the bed. From behind the camera he would tell her to assume different positions. She would lie on the edge of the bed with her legs spread and masturbate, thinking of Irene, while Ivan roved around the room with his camera, pretending he was one of his heroes, Jean Luc Godard or Frederico Fellini. Marina had no idea what he did with his movies, whether he sold them to his friends or spliced them into other cheaply made porno movies which were then distributed to video stores in Brooklyn. She wrote to Irene that Ivan preferred movies to sex, that he spent most of his time at home working on one of his many scripts, that he always went to bed long after she was already asleep.

One night, it must have been two in the morning, Marina received a phone call from a man whose voice she didn't recognize. "My name is Boris," the voice said, and Marina remembered meeting the man at one of the parties on Long Island. Ivan had introduced him to her as "my boss." Marina had heard other people talk about him as well. He was everyone's boss, it seemed. Later in the day, when the party at which she was introduced to him was almost over, she noticed him sitting in a lounge chair near the pool with his arms draped around the shoulders of two women in bikinis, girls really, young enough to be his children. "Is this Marina?" the man named Boris said over the phone, and at first she thought that he was going to order her to come and sleep with him, that he had depleted his supply of young women. Not only was he Ivan's boss but he was the boss of Ivan's girlfriend as well. If she didn't sleep with him he would fire Ivan. Or perhaps, if she didn't do what he wanted, both of their bodies would be found floating face down in the East River. She couldn't imagine any other reason why he was calling her at two in the morning.

"I have some news," he said. "Ivan is in jail. Don't ask me any questions. I want you to come to this address tomorrow"—he recited some numbers and she wrote them down—"and ask for a woman named Sheila. She'll give you all the details. Meanwhile"—he said this in Russian—"Ivan sends his love."

There were never any questions and there were never any answers. The woman named Sheila gave her an envelope containing ten thousand dollars. Ivan was in jail, she visited him in jail, he was sentenced to a year in jail in upstate New York. Every weekend she took the bus to visit him. Meanwhile, with the ten thousand dollars, she found a new apartment. That's what the woman named Sheila said: relocate, start a new life. Marina continued to teach art in the private school in Brooklyn Heights. Now she had enough money so she could talk on the phone frequently with Irene, at least once every other day. Both of Irene's parents had died and she was free to visit her friend in New York.

Almost five years had passed since the two women had seen one another and they spent most of their first weekend in bed, just like before. Irene could speak English as fluently as her friend. She had devoted five years to learning the language of her future. She had put her faith in Marina that coming to the United States would be her future. She had prepared herself for this moment. She stepped off the plane and there was her friend waving to her from behind a glass partition. They held hands in the back of the taxi that took them from the airport to the apartment. Irene said: "I know you've slept with many men. I forgive you. I slept with many men before I met you so now we're equal. But I've been faithful to you since you've been gone." Neither of them had ever slept with any other woman. They had learned the art of patience, of waiting. They drank vodka and ate spoonfuls of caviar sitting up in bed. They walked through the apartment naked. They admired themselves in the mirror. They combed each other's hair.

Every morning Marina went to work and when she returned home Irene was sitting at the kitchen table reading a book in English.

"I'm going to read all the books on your shelf," she said.

Marina said: "He's going to be back soon. In a month he'll be out of jail."

She was referring to Ivan, of course. She had skipped her last visit to the prison to spend the weekend with Irene. She had made up an excuse about being sick, not knowing or caring whether Ivan believed her. The question was what to do when Ivan got out of jail. He knew that she had a new apartment and assumed that they would live together when he was released. The two women had enough money to escape, to disappear. Irene was interested in moving to California, a place neither of them had ever been. They could change their names. They could cut their hair. They could become different people. Irene stood at the ironing board in her bra and panties while Marina sat at the kitchen table drinking coffee. It was what they were doing on that August morning when Eddie Perez came in the window.

THE AMERICAN MALADY

by Etel Adnan

{FOR LAÏLA SHAHEED}

I am in Paris, bedridden. My eyes, which are as tired as my soul, try to look at one cloud after another, when there are any. Paris's sky is particularly sealed, in imitation of the iron safes of its banks or the iron curtains which, in little Arab towns, fall on the stores on Fridays and Sundays. The radio is on my left, the door a little further down, also on my left. In front of me there is the window. War is in Beirut. Sorrow is everywhere, beyond borders, like a homing pigeon.

There have not been in Paris spectacular suicides. To the contrary. Arab refugees settle here, or prepare diplomas. In ten years, one Lebanese out of two will have a Ph.D. and one Lebanese out of two will have nothing. But no Lebanese will still have the eyes he or she had before the war. Their eyes, now, express hardness, or the void.

Everything makes "news" nowadays. Newspapers, television, the radio, all follow events the way hunting dogs follow the game and bring back in their muzzle a dying bird. And people have never been as little informed as they are now. Camel caravans were much more reliable lines of communication than the stupid reporting which allows three minutes for an earthquake, a few seconds for the landing of a Saudi king, a minute and a half for the bombing of an Iraqi nuclear center, a bombing which in real time took twenty seconds. The entertainment goes on. On nights when on Channel 4 or 5 nobody dies in Somalia or in El Salvador, children refuse to eat their soup, the parents get all upset and the family meal is spoiled. Television transforms events into dreams and, in their turn, the journalists' dreams become reality.

I am bedridden because of a pain that ceased for quite a while to interest my doctors. I'm reading a book on the Philosophy of History. The carpet is in a dark color and the walls are yellowish. The lighting is poor. I know that in the Arab World they have read all the political theories which originated in Germany, the U.S., or Russia...

Tombs have followed these ideologies, then preceded them, and finally threw them to the sea. But then what are all these friends and visitors who come to my room, enter my somber Parisian life, in the overheated air which I breathe, what are they coming to tell me?

In one way or another they come to tell me that they want to go to America! Did we have to live for years under the passage of made-in-Texas Israeli planes, under their perennial harassment, in order to land our dreams next to the crocodiles that swim in the Gulf of Mexico?

During our era's first centuries Syrian craftsmen used to go to Rome to participate in the building of that imperial capital; Caesar was settling our land, and they had to serve him in his own. And today, what are we doing? We are queuing in front of American Embassies humbly asking for a visa to the New World: When you die in Beirut you resurrect in New York.

Those who left many years ago have the one and only fear of losing their green card, that permanent permit of entry into paradise. And I won't dwell on those immigrants who have become such good citizens of their new country that they have changed their names and imagine that the Arabic language sounds like a lamb's bleating.

Bombs flush out the Lebanese with the regularity of a soft tide. People follow the birds which are bound North-West. Should one submit in Beirut to either slow or instant death, or rather go and live with those that one has accused of all the world's sins?

But then if the people of Beirut think about running away from a cursed destiny, who are these other people who keep coming to Beirut, human crickets in spring, storks in the winter?

War is the most pleasurable of games. You can get drunk with its smell, its color, its rhythms. You can kill with impunity, be decorated for that. Nations living in peace secretly envy those who are engaged in a war. After all, that's where the action is. The most odious among the envious are not the readers of newspapers or the movie-goers, no, they are those real voyeurs, the mercenary image-makers, the militiamen of the camera, the vultures of the battlefields, the war correspondents, the television crews...

Years ago, during a hot summer, in Mexico, I was crossing a desiccated gulch, it was near Los Muertos, a dog was agonizing under the sun while vultures were performing their beauteous dance before zeroing in on its flesh still alive. Now, from the bellies of huge iron-birds we see all kinds of foreign newsmen disembark into Beirut, clasping their cameras. There is always a breeze to greet them at the airport, even in the middle of August. One breathes a mixture of salt water with death, of sand with dried bush, of the craze for departing with the craze for landing. Time in Beirut is always ahead of itself. It is forever hurrying, sucked into the horizon like into a vacuum cleaner. Foreign journalists remain foreign to these matters. They don't know that we vomit in our planes as soon as we enter our country's air-space, because of all the contradictions that are at war within our stomachs. All I can say about these newsmen is that they took interesting views of the Karantina massacre, of Tell Zaatar's siege, of the shelling of Achrafieh, of the turmoil in Zahleh... They have created the particular aesthetics of the Arab-Mediterranean wars... They did a bloody good job. In Nazi Germany everything happened within a grayish zone. In Vietnam the dominant color was green. Here, the sky is blue and blood is red.

Beirut isn't only a privileged laboratory for urban guerrillas but also a darn good movie lab. Hollywood, Italy, Tokyo cannot compete for realism with the picture taken of that Arab body, still wearing its underwear, that a taxicab filled with passengers was carrying on its roof on its way to the morgue. That made a good close-up with no need for a funeral oration. TV journalists know that they drive crazy with envy the most famous movie directors because they are the authors as well as the actors of an ongoing world-wide performance.

In this room where I am lying and which prevents the branches of the courtyard's linden tree from reaching me, there is a TV set. I am watching the Prince of Wales' marriage. I am waiting in the crowd for his carriage to leave Buckingham Palace. The carriage starts to roll. Charles of England is sitting next to his brother, wearing a Navy officer's costume. He suddenly looks at the sky, like Prince Andrei in *War and Peace*. He also has, for a moment, the gaze of Lawrence of Arabia as well as the latter's slightly pink lips.

The prince's retinue, the apparition of the bride carried as a swan on a silver platter, the veil which is hiding her and that will be lifted in the Church, everything is fairy tale, ravishing. My book on the Philosophy of History is put aside. History herself is moving in front of me, riding a horse, personified by a prince and a princess who are authentic. But would Charles become king of England? Isn't Mrs. Thatcher the one who exercises real power in his country? Charles becomes therefore a symbol, a drawing on a page. History does not depend on his will. He plays a role. I am then watching a play. More than a billion spectators are taking part in a game of shadows and lights. The simultaneity of this vision watched from every corner of the planet has abolished time's relativity. The clocks are at zero hour.

I sense that the world is ill, like the sun, like myself, degenerating from the beginning, caught in a process of extinction.

Laïla has just arrived from Beirut. She enters my room, dressed in white and wearing her jewelry. I see in her a Mexican deity. Her eyes are shining although they have around them discernible dark circles due to the war; they are prisms through which I can read History's desperate intensity.

—I am on war leave, she tells me. I have left Beirut for ten days.

—And after?

—I'm going back. Then I'll try to go to New York. Paris is okay but there's such a feeling of emptiness here. Even Beirut as it is nowadays is a better place.

—And our West-Beirut friends, what are they saying?

—Oh well! They would all go to New York if they could. Do you imagine them yearning to go to Moscow? The very idea of it kills them with boredom. You well know how much we Arabs like to be where things are happening. And politically, or for one's safety, it's smarter to be in the U.S. than elsewhere, better be in the tornado's eye than under its path.

—Tell me, what's new in Beirut beside the shellings?

—Schlöndorff came to make a movie

—On Beirut? On the civil war? How is he going to disentangle all the mess we are in. Too many little wars are going on in that single one!

—No, his movie is not on Beirut. His story is set in Beirut but involves only Germans.

He came therefore for the background, the fury, the chaos and the fires, a sadness that no actor can render, the will to live of the people, the burning sea that Germany doesn't have, and those Arab children who become the more beautiful as they get poorer and among whom anyone age seven thinks that he is a football hero. It must be stimulating and cheap to film in Beirut. No "special effects" can compete with the sounds of real war.

—But Schlöndorff did better, says Laïla. He hired "the real thing." He found young men from the warring factions and asked them to stage a battle uniquely for the needs of his film.

—And they accepted?

—They were thrilled. Thus the leaders of the different militias, the rightists as well as the leftists, gave orders to stop the real fighting in the Center of Beirut, for a few days, in order to allow their men to reënact a war scene for the German film.

Before the civil war the downtown plaza was Beirut's heart. Buildings of great symbolic value formed its perimeter: a church and a red-light district, the Ministry for Justice and the city's biggest movie house, jewelry stores and pastry shops. In the heart of that heart there was a monument for the "martyred heroes," the men who at the end of the nineteenth century led an Arab revolt against the Ottoman Empire. Palm trees were lining the square.

From that rectangular city square one was able to leave for Asia. One can also say that Asia stopped there, at half a mile from the sea. One could go from there to Damascus, then Baghdad, then Tehran... Once I took the bus for Afghanistan, in the days when I was traveling.

It is on this square that the divorce of a nation took place. Unattended since the war it has become a garden, enchanted and yet peopled with hostile spirits, the last Mediterranean stronghold of Nature. Banana trees have overtaken it, wild grass, crazy vegetation; an orange tree planted itself in its middle, claimed its space, alongside all kinds of reptiles. This downtown plaza is the Middle East's Vietnam. Our indomitable jungle.

There's something of a Chief of Staff in every movie director, there's always authority in a Westerner who happens to be on an Arab land, and there's something of an actor in any man taking part in a war. All this explains why the Lebanese commanders of the militias said "yes" to the German director who turned a red-hot battlefield into a "theater for operations," and I shall add that we all watched too many war movies for not having lost our sanity.

And, you would ask, what is then the subject matter of Schlöndorff's movie? A one-sided film, a historical saga, a political indictment? Of course not. It is about the translation into film of a novel whose main character is a German journalist who had indeed died in Beirut during the bloody events which feed daily the world's news.

On the square mile which constitutes Beirut's center, itself at

History's heart, a German journalist has died. For him all images ceased to exist. Another German, a movie director, follows his steps and determines to resurrect him, through an actor, among the places and war images that saw him disappear. The Americans produced *Apocalypse Now* about Vietnam... Schlöndorff will create his own version of that tragic opera that armies stage by their very actions in the midst of ruined landscapes. He chose another war in the Third World, the one in Lebanon.

But does anyone know how to portray war, nowadays, in the cinema, without using sunsets, machine guns, and corpses?

Schlöndorff asked that they manufacture for him two or three dozens of corpses in papier-mâché, and these were brought to him and delivered on Saint-Simon Beach, south of Beirut.

"These corpses are so poorly done," said Hassan, one of the extras used in the film, a youngster who was still a child when he witnessed the Karantina massacre. "I can bring you real ones!" he offered.

Two days later the whole German crew was sitting in the Hotel Carlton's hall. It was early afternoon. The Carlton has a view on the sea and the light was reverberating. It is part of that legendary series of hotels in the Arab East where contemporary history was and is still being made: in Damascus, in Cairo, in Palmyra, in Jerusalem, they sheltered the conquerors' dreams and the politicians' betrayals. In Syria Lawrence slept at the Hotel Baron, General Spears slept at the Beirut Saint-Georges, Allenby at the King David, the Kaiser at the Palmyra Hotel... and Schlöndorff at the Carlton!

The thirteen-year old Lebanese youth came in with an enormous burlap bag, emptied it and carefully lined up on the floor, at Schlöndorff's feet and in front of his staff, some fifty skulls and a heap of bones.

—Here they are, he said, I dug them out these last days, washed them carefully, and you can use them. They are yours. How much are you going to pay me for this?

As it was up to the man in charge to speak, Schlöndorff said, after a silence:

—How much do you want?

—Eight hundred pounds, said the boy.

—No, said Schlöndorff, it's too much. It's worth five hundred and I won't give a penny more.

—That's okay, said the boy, after a longer silence.

FROM MANY, ONE

by Colum McCann

I used to love the way she painted quarters. There were many fabulous colors that she could concoct on them. Don't ask me how she got them to stick, because she had big stubby fingers for a little woman, and she must have used a very small paintbrush. But I'd come home from work in the evenings around five or six and she'd be in the back greenhouse, which we had turned into a little studio, and she'd be bent over the table, just all caught up in making these coins look colorful. She never really let me come into the studio. That was her space. There were times that I'd watch her from the kitchen and she would just billow around in her big white apron, past all the flowerpots, like she was being blown around by that big fan. Dallas is hot anyway in the summer, but this was so hot you could fry eggs in there.

I never saw the quarters until one Saturday afternoon when she was out canoeing the Brazos with Jeanie. I was trying to fix her old Karmen Ghia, looking for a screwdriver so I could take the clips off the distributor cap. They were rusted on. So I went into the greenhouse, where I reckoned there were some extra tools, and all these coins were out lying on the table. There were rows and rows of them, all painted.

The eagle sometimes had these weird multi-colored wings. Sometimes there was a small picture—a television, a radio tower, a car—on the eagle's chest. The olive branch was always yellow for some reason. The strangest ones were when you could see into George Washington's cranium. I mean, here's this guy that everyone goes nuts about, father of the country and all that, then all of a sudden he's got a tiny picture of an apple in his brainbox, or weird animals on that big curl of hair at the back, or he's wearing lipstick, or that little tail down the back of his wig looks like a map of Central America. Then there was always these little dots along the year. 1974 had yellow dots, 1989 had green ones, that sort of weird stuff. Then, in all the spaces, there were these psychedelic colors. She colored in the writing, and one of them said, in bright pink, IN 0 WE TRUST, where she didn't color in the G or the D.

I've never been much into modern art or anything. I mean, I like Remington and stuff, but not that other crap. But this wasn't crap, see. This was kind of funny, really. I liked them.

Laura wasn't pleased when she found out that I'd been in there. "That's my studio, for crissake." She said the *my* real loud.

"It's my house," I said.

"It's my work."

"You're my wife."

"And you're my goddamn husband."

We'd been married for three years, and it was around Valentine's Day, but we'd both forgotten. Maybe it was all the work I was doing in the labs—I was a lab assistant to a professor who was building phylogenetic trees of sparrows, breaking down their DNA and grouping them—sometimes ten, twelve hours a day. She liked to draw all the time. She was from a good family, her father was an investment banker in Houston, and I guess she spent a lot of her teenage years doing paintings.

Once I woke up and caught her sitting beside the bed, drawing my face on one of these quarters. She was hunched over the bed with these tiny paintbrushes and a palette, her hair tied back, a real serious look on her face. Boy, did I ever want to see that one. But I looked and looked in the greenhouse, and I never found it. I knew it was around somewhere, because she told me she never spent them. I searched for hours, under the table, in all the plant pots, down under the wrought-iron stand, on the ledges, but it never showed up. I expect maybe she painted me with big black eyes, my hair receding, big jowls and all that sort of thing, even though that's not true.

But I did find some other coins. They were self-portraits, her face painted on top of Washington's, big long mane of red hair running down her back, that one eye all painted with mascara, her lips flaring out. She was pretty, all right. I could see why she did it. She'd always been pretty, right from the day I met her. So, I took one of those quarters and put it in my wallet. I kind of liked to look at it when I was at work. Most of my job was extracting the blood samples.

I came home from work one night and she wasn't there, so I went on down to the bar. We live in a fairly good neighborhood and the nearest bar is down by the highway. It's a dark bar, lots of people hanging out in the corners. You see some strange ones there. But the thing about it is, it's amazing the things you don't know about people. I was sitting there at the bar, talking with the bartender, Paul, and it turns out this guy does computers on the side. There's nobody there hardly, so we talk for a long time, about computer sequencing, research, and things about sparrows and stuff, when all of a sudden he points down at my hand and laughs, then sort of grabs my cheek.

"Doing a little on the side?" he says to me. I look down and realize that I've been fingering this quarter in my hands for the last half hour. It's the portrait of Laura. That face is full of yellows and reds.

I ask him what he's talking about, and he reaches in under the counter and pulls out about twenty of these quarters. They spill through his goddamn fingers. Jefferson with a peace sign on his fore-head, another with the LIBERTY shortened to BERT, the eagle wearing a bra, all sorts of colors everywhere. Says he likes to collect them him-self when customers come from the Rose down the street. Says to me that the guys at the Rose, and sometimes the girls, bring the quarters in. One of the afternoon strippers there makes them.

"They put them in the jukebox," he says, "so at the end of the night they know which quarters are theirs. You see red ones and green ones and blue ones and all sorts. But these are great. This chick is an artist. I'd like to see this chick dance."

I don't know much about things, but I do know that it's amazing, the things we don't know. I went home that evening and wanted to drive that Karmen Ghia right through the greenhouse, plow it right on through, shatter it into pieces. Laura got home, late, and just went straight on out to the greenhouse. She looked awful young and pretty. She swept past me and said: "You look tired, honey." She actually said that. She said "honey." I sat there, in the kitchen, wondering what sort of face she was drawing this time.

PASSAGE TO INDIA

by Dallas Wiebe

Alvin Boneyard couldn't speak dirty to his wife anymore because of his laryngectomy. He could regulate the volume of his amplifier, but he couldn't whisper or coo out his deepest feelings, even when it was raining. When he touched his amplifier to his throat and tried to say something touching, what came out sounded more like goats bleating or like police commands through a bullhorn. To compensate for his deficiency, for the last five years he had sat at home all day. He sat naked in the middle of the floor, his obese legs crossed, his fat face and bald head shining under the bare bulb, and thought of things to say through his amplifier, something to keep life interesting, something he might say to his non-existent children, something to say to his aging wife Alveena when he met her at the door when she returned home in the evening from her job of teaching Education at the University of Cincinnati, something to snarl into her ear as she slept. Something so that when he met her at the door he could take her into his lardy arms, sniff her musky perfume and say, "The voice of the thunder is the morning song of old age." Something so that when Alveena lay and snored away in the dark, he could roll close to her bony back, touch his amplifier to his throat and say into her ear, "Encase your syllogisms in the bark of the sambar." Something so that when she sat up right smart he could laugh through his horn and listen to her whimper in her drowsiness and fright, "Turn off the TV."

After twenty years of marriage, Alvin mostly felt contempt for Alveena. He pointed out to her that she walked and talked like his grandmother. He snapped the dark bags under her eyes with his right index finger and told her her face was falling off. He liked to run his little finger through her downy mustache and tell her that she needed a shave. He pointed out to her that she grew up in Cincinnati, attended a Cincinnati high school, got her B.A., MA. and Ph.D. all from the University of Cincinnati. One night he brought her up real quick out of her blubbering dreams when he growled into her ear, "You are as parochial as an ankle." And then got her an hour later with, "You have all the intelligence of a sandal." He regularly accused Alveena of teaching "Schizoid models for the pursuit of learning." He cheated her when they played "Monopoly" or "Gin." He cheated her when they played "Trivial Pursuit" by giving her wrong answers for her questions. When she lost and complained, he snarled out at full volume, "Your head is a cul de sac and your brain is a speeding oxcart about to hit the wall at the end of the street."

Part of his contempt for her was that they had no children. In the fifteen years of marriage before the amplifier, he whispered and coughed out that it was time for a family, but she said things like, "Later, Al. Later," and "Wait for the monsoon." After the laryngectomy he figured it was the radiation. Alveena said, again and again, that it was because he didn't know how to talk to children, that he didn't know how to be a father. She said, as if it came from the chromosomes themselves, "You can't rear children in unrepeatable babble. Language patterns form the mind, inculcate great thought, deconstruct the will to grossness, make productive citizens out of unformed but malleable gurgling. How could we communicate if we all spoke in the recondite gibberish that leaps from your puny cerebrations? You think children are cockroaches? You think children are putty in the hands of a nincompoop?" When she said to him, "Language creates the parameters of normality," he switched to high and snarled, "Your thighs are like jade elephants."

During the first fifteen years of their marriage, while Dr. Alveena Boneyard lectured on the generation of linguistic concepts and the parameters of language, Alvin sat at home and read books, drank beer and smoked cigarettes. He figured that since he had not gone to high school he would educate himself. For the first five years he sat on the floor his fat belly sticking out, his hair falling out, and read whatever his wife happened to bring home. In the next five years he used the public library. Then he found out he could use the university library and he read "The Waste Land," *The Golden Bough*, *Arabia Deserta*, *The Brothers Karamazov*, *War and Peace*, *The Flowers of Evil*, *Leaves of Grass*, *The Anabasis*, Hesiod's *Theogony*, *The Gilgamesh Epic*, "Genesis." He read anything at hand until he began to dream of going back to where mankind began, back to the Garden of Eden, back to beginnings just as he was, by reading, finding his way back through language. He read about the Tigris and Euphrates Rivers, the Shatt-al-Arab, the Land of Ur. He read all he could find on Mesopotamia, Egypt and the Holy Land.

At night, filled with his readings and his longing to return, he would lie by his tall wife and whisper to her how he longed for her, how lovely her body was, how his passion was beyond all telling. He whispered to her that her hair was like gold thread on a pillow of silver. He said her eyes were like blue peacocks in a valley of green grass. He said her breath was like the western winds that bring the spring rain. He whispered and cooed to her that he wanted to take her to the land of Sheherazade, to the first land, to where we all came from. While Alveena snored and blubbered out her pedagogical nightmares, he sighed and told her that they could go away and discover what they were and how they came to be. He coughed and said that in the beginnings there could be a child. Until the operation and everything changed. Until Alveena told him he was nuts and that she wanted to sleep.

On Friday, December 14, 1984, the jade elephant looked up from her breakfast of oatmeal, two poached eggs, Sanka and chutney and said, "Mr. Boneyard, your cybernetic bombast makes my heart into a graveyard of ineluctable crap. You make my beauty sleep into a tippy-toeing through degeneration." Alvin looked up from the hambone he was gnawing and reached for his amplifier. It was not in his pocket. He looked up again. Alveena wept and pointed to the freezer in the refrigerator. At first he didn't understand. He was confused because he had never seen Alveena weep, not even on their wedding night when he told her that her naked body reminded him of a chicken coop. Not even when he told her that her navel looked like an ashtray. Not even when he told her that she would be for him the vessel of maternity and that he would launch her by cracking a bottle of champagne over her brow, which he tried to do and broke her aquiline nose. Not even then did she weep.

As her tears dropped into her chutney, Alveena told Alvin that she had gone to the doctor the day before. Alvin groped through his pockets for his amplifier. She told him that the doctor told her that she would have to live a different kind of life. She said that the doctor said that at forty-four a woman was no longer a Mt. Everest, which could be climbed over, have junk dumped down her sides, have pictures taken on top of her. She said that the doctor said, "You are no longer young at heart. Your vital systems are going on vacation. They are going on an expedition into uncharted seas, into Terra Incognita, where fire and ice will permeate your deepest proclivities." She wiped her tears, blew her nose. Alvin looked into the deep blue of her eyes and saw black horses dancing through black caves. He saw the horses dying one by one. He saw red acids rot them away until all that was left was a withered old man gnawing on a leg bone. He tried to see who the man was. He tried to see if the man was happy or if he had found satisfaction for his hunger. He felt uncomfortable because he could not see those things. And then he realized that Alveena was not there.

When Alveena came home in the middle of the afternoon, Alvin didn't have his lines ready. He felt flustered. He'd spent most of the day thawing out and warming up his amplifier. Because it hurt his throat to put the cold plastic against his skin he hadn't had time to prepare to welcome home his wrinkled bride. Alveena entered, smiled handsomely and led him to the kitchen table, to the tear-stained chutney, the cold Sanka, the shriveled poached eggs, the dried and cracked oatmeal. She sat him down and, standing across from him, announced that she was going to have a baby. Alvin said, "The stream that flows from the elbow is full of tin fish." "And," she said, "you will not be the father." Alvin said, "The waves that wash the liver circle the earth in the magnitude of their compensatory reverberations, always seeking a piece of the thigh." "Furthermore," she said, "I want twins." "The hair that thrives in the armpit is the garden of fleas that leap at the sound of the trumpet." "And further furthermore, the father will not be an American." "All sound that floods out in the universe turns into flocks of birds that migrate from Mars to Venus and back." "And my pregnancy begins this evening." "Lost handkerchiefs, stolen shoes, misplaced mufflers, all end up in the pockets of the hungry."

Alveena walked to the door and looked back. She wiped a tear from her left eye and said, "Can't you ever say anything common?" Alvin clamped his fist shut and remarked, "The closed suitcase hides the will of congress until separate decrees wail from the Banseri."

Alveena marched into the bathroom. He heard her banging things around. Heard her come out, go into the bedroom and hum herself into her best clothes. He smelled the rush of perfume as she swished by. Heard her say, "Turn off the TV." Heard the door bang as she stomped out. Heard the motor roar as she whisked herself away to become, he imagined, pregnant from some foreign professor who lived in squalor at university expense.

When she was gone, Alvin felt a minor distress. For the first time in five years. It had never occurred to him that what he said was not common. He had come to believe that all language is common, that what we say is acceptable in all instances. A thought of purple fish in a jar of peanut butter was as natural to him as his toes. To say that naturally followed and was not uncommon. To put the words "mulct," "pawky," "epiboly," "tabla" and "Griselda" all in the same sentence seemed as reasonable and common to him as the hair on the back of the hand. Bambi trussed up and dropped from a helicopter into Disneyland was to him a commonplace. To think of a cobra letting the air out of tires on the cars of the FBI was as natural as breathing. What he said was, for him, thoughtless. It seemed to him that some great universal mind was speaking through him. It seemed to him that he was in touch with a force beyond his control. It seemed to him as if what he thought was the leftover reverberations from the Buddha. His language was his nature; it came from first causes, from the first thought that was. It disturbed him that someone thought the first bang was not common.

Alvin got up and went to the refrigerator, got out two slices of rye bread and made a sandwich of sardines, peanut butter, raw oysters, a cabbage leaf and orange marmalade. He poured himself a glass of buttermilk and sat down to eat. He was determined to say something common, to say something to quiet his discomfort, whatever that might be. He wondered why interesting things might not be common. He determined to practice and when Alveena returned, as she surely would, pregnant or not, he would speak lines of perfect commonness. He realized that he would have to think more clearly than he ever had before. So he imagined Alveena, flushed with passion, sneaking into the front door of their house while he hid behind the drapes and practiced common lines. He imagined himself taking her in his arms, dabbing the droplets of sweat from her hot brow, and saying, "You are as beautiful as maggots in sour milk." He suspected right away that if he said that Alveena wouldn't think that common. He tried again. "You are as pretty as a squashed monkey on the freeway." He realized that wouldn't do either. "The third time is a charm," he thought and said, "You are more beautiful than the river that flows from the eyes of dead cows."

The third time wasn't a charm, so Alvin decided to pack it all in and go to bed. He walked into the bathroom and hummed himself into his pink pajamas with the red snails printed all over them. He hummed himself into the bedroom, knelt by the queen-size bed and said, "Oh Lord God, maker, dowse congress with the sweat of peppercorns and lead the president into the foramen magnum of Mahatma Gandhi. Amen." He hummed up from his knees, climbed into bed and covered himself with the glory of his childhood, a comforter tied with bits of green yarn and covered with pictures of snarling tigers.

He fell asleep quickly and dreamed that he was sleeping profoundly. He dreamed that he dreamed about the right stuff, felt cool as a cucumber as he soared like an eagle. A great eagle soaring on the wings of the wind, like an astronaut. When he dreamed that he dreamed that he bailed out of the eagle's mouth, past his claws, past the afterburner, he floated down like a pillow, floating on the wings of song, a song he remembered as beginning, "On the shore dimly seen through the mists of the deep where the foe's haughty host in dread silence reposes." Firmly planting both feet on his mother earth, he ate the parachute ravenously, like a hog at the trough, like an astronaut stepping onto a point in time. On the moon, he dreamed, he awakened and slept like a log, a rock, a tree, a bumblebee, a pterodactyl.

Nightmares came in his dreamed awakening, nightmares of words in piles he tried to sort out. He sweated. He labored like Sinbad. Sweating and working on, he knew that what he was looking for was somewhere in the pile. He didn't know what it was, but he knew perfectly well that it was there. He found: "The bumbershoot is the zygoma of the Eohippus." He found: "A baby's breath is the whirlwind of the hexachlorophenes," "A soul is the path through the junkyard of the stars," "When the cows come home the water fleas cover the earth with spittle." He found: "You need an airhammer to break bread with the whippersnappers," "Slicker than snot on the toe of St. Peter" and "A $60,000 dress is the cocoon of the wrinkle." The word was there. When he found it, he fell to his knees and prayed, "Oh Lord, bless Shakerley Marmion with hemidemisemiquavers" and he dreamed that the nightmares ended. He dreamed that he lay down beside still waters and slept quietly and all dreaming ended.

When Alveena sneaked in the front door at 3:00 A.M., Alvin was sleeping quietly. She carefully closed the door and set her package on the table. She unwrapped it and took out a bullhorn. Removing her sandals, she walked into the bedroom and put the bullhorn on high. She roared into Alvin's left ear, "Your breath smells like the tongue of the water buffalo that lives in a high rise." Alvin jumped up right smart. In his fright and drowsiness, he reached out to turn off the TV. He flipped on the lamp. He saw that Alveena was wearing a pink sari. He saw that she had a red spot in the middle of her forehead. He put his amplifier to his throat and said, "You are as pretty as a picture."

Alveena put down the bullhorn and helped him to rise and stand trembling by the bed. She took him in her skinny arms. She unbuttoned his pajamas and removed them. She hugged him. Alvin heard thunder and heard rain striking the window panes. She kissed him on the spot just above the upper lip and just under the nose. As a faint hint of curry rose into Alvin's nostrils, she said, "Now you are fit to be a father."

THE TELLERS

by Stephen Dixon

Two men come into the bank. One has long hair reaching his shoulders and is carrying a shopping bag. The other has a big beard like a lumberjack and a coat on that practically touches the floor. Both of them I've never seen before, and in this town you get to recognize almost everyone after a while. We have no guard. To reduce payroll costs the bank had a television system installed—three cameras with signs all around saying the cameras are linked up to a private protection service, though two are dummies. The dummies focus on the manager's office and anteroom and on the steps leading to the downstairs vault and time-lock safe. The live camera focuses on the main floor and two teller booths, and I hope the person monitoring the screen now is keeping a close eye on these men.

I knock on the glass separating the two booths. Jane, the other teller, waves for me to hold it a minute till she finishes counting a stack of fives. The bearded man is writing on one of the bank slips at the customer's desk. The other man sits on a bench near the door reading a book. I knock on the glass much harder. "What?" Jane says angrily without my hearing her. Because the booths are totally enclosed with bulletproof glass, Jane and I communicate by exaggerating our lips, face and hand movements without making any sounds.

"You recognize those two men?" I say.

"No."

"Don't they look suspicious to you?"

"No," and she wraps a rubber band around the fives and puts the stack in the drawer.

The bearded man is finished writing. The other man turns a page of his book and then flips back to it as if to reread the bottom lines. There are no other customers on the main floor. Past the low gate to my left is the anteroom where Pati and Darlene, our two secretaries, work. Past them is the office of our manager, who's talking with a woman I've only seen in the bank once.

The bearded man is standing before my window. Jane's busy counting out tens. He points to a withdrawal slip and passbook. The book's one of ours, so I don't know what's been going on in my head about these two men. Maybe I'd recognize him without his beard, or else I wasn't around the time he opened his account. I unhook the disc over the speaker's hole and say through the screen "May I help you, sir?"

"How much can I withdraw from my savings account?"

"As much as you got in it."

"Well this is my bankbook and a withdrawal check for ten thousand."

I switch the revolving tray to his side of the window. "May I see them, please?"

"You'll see them all right—of course you will. But not yet. But you see my friend reading by the door?"

"You came in with him."

"That's right. We're good friends—very close. But my problem is I haven't the ten thousand in my savings I made the check out for."

"Then it's something you'd want to be talking about with the bank manager, Mr. Bayer."

"Mr. Bayer. Good idea. But one more thing. I don't want you to look alarmed. But I have two grenades in my pockets. So I want you to do exactly as I say without showing any emotion, or they go off."

"I thought so. But don't worry. I'll do like you say. But maybe you more than me who can get hurt, as this booth's built to take the concussion of a bomb."

"Your foot's not near the alarm, is it?"

"No."

"Well you're right—I could get hurt. But those office girls will get hurt much worse than you and me put together if the grenades go, and the manager and lady with him too. You see, I'm willing to take the chance. That's because I'm involved with this absolutely insane political group that needs money fast to buy arms. I'm telling you all this so you'll nod and smile back at me. That's right. No, don't overdo it. Fine. Now the only way to get arms is by stealing or buying them. And we've decided, after weighing the risks of both thefts, that there's more chance of getting caught and killed robbing a guarded armory or police station than a small bank patrolled by television set. So continue to look natural. Step back two steps. And in the order I now give you, tell the girl next door not to look alarmed at what you're going to tell her, to step back two steps, and that the bearded man here and the long-hair at the door are well-armed and robbing this bank."

I knock on the glass. Jane, counting twenties, says "What?"

In our silent language I start telling her what the man told me to say.

"Don't mess about," he says. The other man stands and stretches. "Speak so I can hear."

"But she can't hear me from in there. Even my loud knocks sound like taps to her. For her to hear me her speaker hold would have to be open and I'd have to yell out my lungs through mine." Jane knocks on the glass and says "What do you mean don't get alarmed?"

"Joe," the bearded man says.

Joe walks behind the main floor camera, pulls a bench under it, stands on the bench and unsticks a strip of masking tape from his jacket lining and sticks it over the lens. He jumps down, locks the front door, lets down the venetian blinds on the window and door and takes out a grenade and pistol from the shopping bag. Pati and Darlene are still typing. Mr. Bayer reaches over his desk to the woman, who has pushed her chair back and clasped both hands over her mouth. The bearded man tells Jane and I to raise our arms high and Jane to step back two steps. Joe tells Pati and Darlene to can their typing. He opens the office door and orders Mr. Bayer and the woman out and everybody to the middle of the main room.

"Should we get on the floor on our bellies?" Pati says.

"Yes," Joe says, sliding the bench away. "Everyone on the floor on their bellies."

They all get on the floor. The woman is crying hysterically, but stops when Joe tells her to shut up. The bearded man climbs over the gate, goes left along the corridor to my door, and not finding a knob on it, tries pushing it in. I yell to him that I can't open the door without first getting a tick-back from the manager's office.

"What?" he says.

"A tick-back, a tick-back."

Jane is trying to explain to him also. He tries to push in her door.

"Give them everything, Gus and Jane," Mr. Bayer yells from the floor. "For all our sakes—don't be reckless."

I point to the place where in regular doors the knob would be, then to the manager's office. I curl up my left second finger and press my right second finger into the knuckle as if I'm pressing a buzzer.

The bearded man takes a grenade out of his pocket, sticks a second finger through the pin ring and makes jerking movements with his arms to show he's ready to pull the pin.

"Come around," I say, waving him to go around to my window so he can hear me. Joe, keeping his gun pointed at the people on the floor, comes up to my window and says "What's with this stupid tick-back?"

I motion the man at my door to stay there and I'll tell Joe what's wrong.

"What we do when we want out is buzz Mr. Bayer's office," I tell Joe. "Then he ticks back, which electronically releases the door lock. They're on the top right of his desk—top one mine and one below that Jane's."

Joe waves to his friend that everything's all right. He tells the people on the floor to stay put or a live grenade will be rolling their way. He runs to the office and ticks back both our booths. The doors open. The bearded man pulls out two folded shopping bags from his coat and empties my till into one of the bags. Jane comes into the booth and drops the twenties she's been holding into the other bag. He empties both counter drawers of all bills and express checks, tells us to stand in the corridor with our arms raised and goes into Jane's booth. He empties her till and drawers and comes out and takes my wallet and tells us to go round to the front with him and get on the floor with the others. Jane and I lie on the floor next to one another.

"The phone wires," Joe says. He hands the bearded man his grenade, pulls a pair of cutters from his back pocket and runs into the anteroom and manager's office.

The bearded man listens to Mr. Bayer explain why it's impossible for anyone to open the time-lock safe without blowing it up. Someone knocks on the door. The bearded man looks through a slit in the window blinds and opens the door. Mr. Heim, a grocer, walks in and says to the bearded man "How come they closed?"

"On the floor on your face with the others," he says and locks the door. Mr. Heim gets down like the rest of us. Jane says in our silent language "I don't see how they expect to get away with this. They're taking too long."

"Just hope they get caught outside and not in," I say.

"Remember that book which said if a bank isn't robbed within two minutes, the robbers mostly get caught before they leave. That figure was more than nine cases in ten."

"The one with the beard said it's a political cause they're doing it for."

"Political? What's he ever mean?"

"Now be smart and listen to me, folks," the bearded man says. "I've fixed one of the teller alarms with an explosive. So if the alarm's set off, the whole bank goes up. We also have a third man who'll be guarding outside after we're gone, so nobody gets up, nobody leaves. After five minutes he takes off and then you can do what you please."

They tuck some rags into the tops of the shopping bag and leave the bank and lock the door with Mr. Bayer's keys.

"What do we do now, Mr. Bayer?" I say.

"Breathe."

"With a bomb ready to go off in one of the teller booths?" Pati says.

"That was just a con story so we wouldn't set it off," I say. "I was watching the bearded guy filling the shopping bags, and he definitely didn't wire any explosive to the alarms."

"*Fixed* is what he said he did," Pati says.

"Fixed, wired, or anything."

"Oh, you know all about bombs now?" Jane says.

"You saw him. All he did was empty our drawers and tills."

"You still couldn't get me to ring it no matter what you say," Pati says. "And nobody else should either."

"Absolutely," Mr. Bayer says.

The woman customer resumes her hysterical crying.

"Will you please stop that, Miss Frost?" Mr. Bayer says.

She begins weeping quietly.

"This ever happen here before?" Darlene says.

"Never," Mr. Bayer says.

"And what about that great protection service you got rid of the guard for, and their calling the police? Some protection. I bet the one who watches the screen is drunk. Or so dumb he thought we turned the camera off."

"They know there we can't turn it off," Mr. Bayer says.

"Then he thought our electricity went. But something."

"I think it'd be safe getting up now," I say. "After all, there really can't be any third man outside. And if I checked out the alarms and found nothing wrong with them—"

"You stay away from them," Jane says.

"She's right, Gus," Mr. Bayer says. "Let's play it safe and believe everything those men said."

"Listen to your boss," Mr. Heim says.

"But he didn't have time to fix either alarm, I'm telling you. I was standing next to him or watching him from the hall all the time he was in Jane's booth, and he never got near enough to reach the buttons or wires. Now you know I wouldn't be kidding you on that matter."

"Old Hawkeye Gus," Pati says. "Never misses a thing. Okay, so you didn't see him touch it. But I'm still not getting up."

"The police could probably still catch the men if we rang it," Darlene says.

"Are you crazy?" Pati says.

"Nobody gets up or steps on any alarms," Mr. Bayer says. "Now that's an order."

"Good," Jane says.

"Does anyone know how many minutes we've been lying in here?" Mr. Heim says.

"Not five," Mr. Bayer says.

"What I'd like to know is how many minutes those men were in here," Jane says.

"Ten I'd say," Mr. Bayer says.

"More like fifteen," Pati says. "Where do they get the nerve? Not the nerve like it's something wrong they did, which goes without saying. But the physical nerve. Fifteen minutes. By all rightful means more than one person should have been wanting to get in the bank in that time."

"Someone else did knock," Mr. Bayer says. "A couple of minutes after Mr. Heim."

"I didn't hear it," Pati says.

"I did," Darlene says.

"I was on my way to make a safe deposit," Mr. Heim says. "Lucky they didn't take it off me."

"They got my wallet," I say.

"Mine too," Mr. Bayer says. "And my car and home and bank keys."

"My wallet was sitting right on the door shelf," Jane says, "and he didn't touch it. I have more than fifty dollars in it too. I was going to buy a coat after work."

"He didn't get any of Darlene's or my money either," Pati says.

"I'm getting awfully tired in this position," Mr. Heim says.

"Imagine how we feel," Pati says. "We've been lying like this five minutes more than you."

"But my stomach's too big to lie on so long. I'm getting up."

"Please wait the full five minutes," Mr. Bayer says. "Otherwise you'll be jeopardizing the lives of us all."

"I'll turn over then." He turns over.

"Why didn't I think of that?" Pati says. She turns over. So does Darlene, Miss Frost and Jane and I. Mr. Bayer stays on his stomach. The door opens.

"Oh my god," Darlene says.

"We've decided to take a hostage," the bearded man says. "An idea we suddenly got, just so we can get out of the area if we're trapped. You," he says to Mr. Bayer.

"Too much of a squeeze with him," Joe says. "Take one of the girls."

"Not the weepy one," he says. "She'll drive me crazy with those tears."

"All women weep. Take the teller. He's thin enough and he really used his head before."

"Up you go, teller. Everybody else turn over the way we told you. And no stepping on alarms or the bank goes. No getting up for another five minutes or our third friend barges in. No even turning over on your backs again. And when the police come, tell them who we got and not to follow us because your teller here—what's your name?"

"Gus Millis."

"Millis gets killed if they force us into a chase."

"I'll tell them your words," Mr. Bayer says.

We leave. Joe locks the door. We get in a sports car in front of the bank. Mr. Bayer never would have fit. The bearded man sits behind the wheel, Joe in the other bucket seat. I sit between them, my shoulders and thighs touching theirs and the hand brake between my legs.

"Comfortable?" Joe says to me.

"I'll manage."

"Take more of my seat. I still have some room at the door."

We drive out of town, onto the connecting road that leads to the turnpike. Past the junior and high schools I graduated from, the cemetery my parents are buried in, the beer and burger place I've met so many girls at. The bearded man never drives more than five miles over the posted speed limit. A police car is heading toward us in the next lane and Joe tells me "Look natural. Turn your head to me now and when he passes us say 'How is the weather, Joe?'"

I turn to him and say "How is the weather, Joe?" as the police car passes. Through the rearview mirror I see the car continue down the road and out of sight. We get on the turnpike on-ramp going south.

"Where we going?" I say.

"A ways," Joe says. "Don't worry."

"You really going to do something to me if the police give chase?"

"How do we answer that?" Joe says.

"My answer to him is don't try and find out," the bearded man says.

"I won't be any trouble. I'll in fact do everything you want me to to help you escape. And if it does all go right for you, could you later give my wallet back?"

"You'll get it," Joe says. He has a mirror in his lap and is snipping off large chunks of hair with some scissors.

"You don't want to use the wire cutters?" the bearded man says.

"You use them," Joe says.

"And Mr. Bayer's wallet and keys? They're very important to him and the bank."

"Look what he's worried about," Joe says.

"You don't remember those days?" the bearded man says. "Yes sir, no sir, always sucking up to the boss. You're going to go far in the bank business, Gus. Very."

"I only thought," I say. "It's not important."

"You don't have to tell us."

"And that alarm system. You didn't really fix it with an explosive."

"Oh yes I did."

"But you couldn't have. I told them it wasn't."

"Now what the hell you do that for?"

"Because I was watching you in both booths. You never had the time. All you were doing was shoving money in the bags."

"I bent, dumbo. For what do you think—to tie my shoes? I had a gum hold. A miniature E-Z-4. But why am I talking to you like you know what I'm saying? But in the girl's booth. Right after I cleaned out her bottom tray. All I had to do was stick it to the wire and the moment the alarm's touched and vibes start, the bank blows."

"Paul became an expert in explosives in the service," Joe says, still cutting his hair.

"That'll be enough," Paul says.

"I didn't say which service. Not even which country."

"You've said more than enough."

"His names's not Paul," Joe says, throwing his hair out the window. "It doesn't even start with a P."

"All right, Joe. And you, Gus. Let's hope they all know you for the big blowhard you are and my warning sunk in."

"I'm sure they do. I'm sure it did." I pray it did. And that Mr. Bayer's inborn cautious nature and last order about nobody touching the alarm, had swayed the group. The police would find the explosive and know what to do with it after that.

We leave the turnpike twenty miles after we got on it and park behind a new station wagon on a deserted road. Joe, his hair crewcut short, finishes shaving the back of his neck with a dry safety razor and says to me "How do I look? No, really, Gus, how do I?" He gives the razor scissors and mirror to the man he called Paul. He dumps the shopping bags of money into a valise and sticks the valise into the rear of the wagon where there are boxes of food and beer and ten-gallon cans of gas. We get in the wagon. Joe at the wheel, me in the middle again, and drive north on the turnpike past the same places we passed some minutes ago. Paul begins cutting his hair.

"You think we cleared ten thousand?" Joe asks me.

"More like twelve."

"Twelve? What about trying for fourteen, twenty-four, even four hundred thou?"

"No, twelve. There were no big withdrawals or deposits today. And Jane and I usually have about six thousand apiece."

The radio still hasn't mentioned the robbery. Joe says it's because the police don't want to tip us off as to how much they know or don't know. Paul shaved his face clean and now trims his hair. They both look completely different, maybe ten years younger. They're also now wearing conservative sports jackets and white shirts and clip-on ties, though they didn't change their soiled blue jeans.

I awake during the night. Paul's at the wheel. The radio's still on. "There it is," Joe says, turning the volume up when the newscaster leads off the headlines of his report with the explosion bank robbery in my town.

"Oh no," I say.

"Shhh." We stay silent through a minute of commercials before the newscaster returns with the details. Two people were killed, four hurt, one seriously. That's all of them. Twelve thousand stolen, a bank hostage taken, the entire first floor of the bank destroyed. The robbers got away in a red sports car hardtop, no license plate reported and were last seen driving south. They carried shopping bags. My name is given. The robbers are described. The long-haired man was referred to as Joe. The bearded man was called Hank and Frank. His name on the withdrawal check and bankbook was a profanity and apparently a fake. A third might be involved. All are considered highly dangerous and heavily armed. Then another commercial and the next story about the war.

"Twelve thousand," Paul says, whistling. "You hit it on the nose, Gus."

I start crying.

"Look, I don't feel too good about it either. But I warned you about the alarm. You should listen when someone warns you on something like that."

"Maybe it wasn't your friends who got hurt," Joe says. "Maybe it was two police or army men from a defusing squad. It was that complicated a little device."

"No, it was my friends."

"There you go again," Paul says. "Always so sure of yourself. You saw the trouble it got you in before."

Around midnight we reach a national forest reserve. We keep on its narrow rising road a mile till it ends at a twenty-foot high snow drift where the plows must have stopped. We park, keep the motor running, have sandwiches and beer. Joe climbs over the seat to get my wallet out of the valise. Paul runs the radio up and down the band till he picks up the one clear station. A news report comes on. The victims were Jane and the woman customer. I've known Jane since we were kids. We went to school together, both elementary and high. Her age is given as 22, though she's three years older than that. The seriously injured person is Darlene. Darlene is a roomer in the same rooming house as mine. We dated regularly for a few weeks till a month ago when Mr. Bayer got wind of it through an anonymous letter and told us to stop dating or lose our jobs. He was afraid the bank would lose its contract with the agency that bonded us. The newscaster gives my correct age and says federal and state officers are now convinced an accomplice in another car took part in the theft.

"Which ones were Jane Stight and Anna Frost?" Paul says. I tell him and he says "Pity about the teller girl. She seemed like a nice sweet thing and showed lots of courage. The woman with the tears though I think the world's better off without."

"I feel bad about them both," I say.

"Hear, hear," Joe says.

"Of course. So do I. That was an insensitive remark I made about Miss Frost."

"Well, we got to be leaving you," Joe says, handing me my wallet, a blanket, sandwiches, and beer. "There's a hiker's lean-to left past that pine tree. Curl up in the corner of it and you'll survive the night. Then tomorrow early, follow the tracks back to the logging road and go any direction on it and you'll find civilization by the end of day. Oh yeah," and he gives me Mr. Bayer's wallet and keys.

"Won't be needing them as I'm not going back. There's nothing for me there now but a worn-out car, beat-up clothes, and a good chance of a negligence or accessory to murder charge that'll land me in jail for years. I'm going to change my name, grow a mustache, and settle somewhere else. Another kind of job shouldn't be too hard to come by, so long as the hirer doesn't know the damage I caused."

"You'll feel different about it in the morning," Joe says, and they drive off.

But my feeling hasn't changed when I wake up. Back home, if I did get off without being arrested, I'd still always be afraid of running into Jane's family or that woman's, if she has one. And most of all, Darlene's violent alcoholic folks, if she dies. The people there would never let me forget the part I played in destroying the town's only bank and ending those lives. I'd never be able to find a job or get back any of the respect or just plain indifference they once showed me. I'd be known as a fool and murderer for the rest of my life.

I start downhill. At the logging road I go in the opposite direction of where my town lies. After a few hours of walking without seeing anyone, I hear a car approaching from behind. I stick out my thumb. It's a new foreign model, long as a limousine. Inside are Joe and Paul.

"We need your help bad," Joe says.

"Our political movement turned out to be as corrupted as the government we were supposed to overthrow and replace. They were serious enough about buying and using the arms before we robbed the bank. But once they saw the cash, all they could talk about were the cars and dope they were going to buy, the trips and movies they were going to make. They wanted to split it halvsies with us, but it wasn't for their pleasures we'd snitched it for. We tried some associate cells in other cites, but it was the same ride three times around. So, no place to go.

Stuck with a wad we've no use for. We're now going to try and avoid a stiff prison rap and possible death trap by turning the money and ourselves in, exposing the hypocrisy and whereabouts of the various groups, and making sure the police know there never would have been any explosion or deaths if you hadn't told your coworkers to ignore our warnings about the alarm. Hop in."

"I already told you: I can't go back."

They chase me down the road, run out and drag me into the car. Except for gas stops, we make it straight through to my town. My legs and arms bound, they carry me up the police stairs and turn the money and car keys and themselves and me in.

That same day, with the information and addresses Joe and Paul give, many of their organization's headquarters and cells are raided. The attorney general calls it the most successful roundup of political terrorists in the nation's history. He says an attempted armed revolution has been averted that could have cost the country hundreds of lives and millions in property damage. The press and government leaders hail Joe and Paul as reformed anarchists. All charges against them are dismissed.

I'm booked on two charges of manslaughter. But federal officials persuade the state to drop its case against me as it doesn't want to embarrass the country and its new nationally acclaimed patriots—unpunished kidnappers, who would have to be two of the main witnesses against me.

I'm released and go to my rooming house for the night. A note from my landlady is on my bed. "I expected this'd be the first place you'd come running to, which is why I'm staying the night safe with armed friends. Poor Darlene will live, no thanks to you. Though her doctors told me personally she'll be pitiably scarred in the face and mind for life. Your past living here has brought this house sufficient disgrace. Please be gone tomorrow no later than the regular check-out hour—11 A.M."

Next morning I drive through town to the road that leads to the turnpike, the same road I was on with Joe and Paul four days ago. After a mile I get bogged down behind a funeral procession. There are hundreds of cars, all with their lights on it seems and driving very slowly, some with black crepe and cloth tied around their fenders and aerials. Jane, besides being extremely well-liked, once brought fame to our town by winning the state's beauty contest and almost the country's— in front of network television cameras she strutted and sang and came in third.

The opposite lane looks clear all the way to the end of the procession. I get into it and drive past the creeping cars and limousines. Just as I pass the flower cars and hearse, I see a state trooper standing in the middle of the two-lane road signaling me down. I stop. The hearse catches up with my car and makes a left between the trooper and me to enter the cemetery. The flower cars follow and then the lead limousine. Inside are Jane's parents, worn from weeping and shaking their heads sympathetically at me as their car crosses the road and passes through the cemetery gates. Jane's brothers are in the next limousine, enraged, all four of them at the windows shaking their fists at me. And then the rest of the limousines and private cars filled with relatives, neighbors, friends, teachers, bank customers, civic and state officials, people who did business with her dad, young men and women we both went to school with, the man she was going to marry next month, Pati, Mr. Bayer, Mr. Heim, my landlady sitting between Darlene's bawling parents, most either shaking their fists or umbrellas or sticking their fingers up or screaming behind windows or opening the windows and spitting on my car hood or in the direction of my car and yelling obscenities at me and my future children and grandchildren and the memory of my folks who are buried inside. I close my windows and press down all the locks. Finally the last cars pass—people I don't know and who don't recognize me. Then the state trooper turns sideways and waves me on.

BLACK CAESAR'S

by John Williams

The day they were due to finish building the mosque, Kenny Ibadulla was sitting in his front room with the curtains closed, watching the rugby. Wales were playing Ireland at home. Didn't know why he bothered watching it, really. You could just open the back door and, if the wind was blowing the right way, you could hear the roar from the Arms Park.

Always put him in a bad mood too. That's why he didn't like people knowing about it, knowing he still watched it. Everyone knew he used to play; it was part of the Kenny Ibadulla legend—the best outside center Cardiff Boys ever had, at sixteen the biggest, fastest, meanest back the coach had ever seen.

'Course then he'd gone to prison, even if he was only sixteen, and that had been the end of that. And of course he hadn't given a shit, because when he came out he was the man. And he was still the man, fifteen years on. Which was why he didn't specially want people to see him throwing things at the telly when Wales's latest pathetic excuse for a center knocked the ball on one more time.

So he was half furious and half relieved when the phone rang just as they were coming out for the second half. He picked it up and listened for a minute, then said, "Fucking hell, not that thieving cunt. I'll be there in five, all right."

Then he picked up his leatherjacket, XXX Large and it was still pretty snug across his shoulders, ran his hand over the stubble on his head, checking the barber had cropped it evenly, walked through to the kitchen where Melanie was chatting to her mate Lorraine, bent to kiss Melanie on the cheek and told her he was going down the club.

Out on the street he wondered, not for the first time, if building a mosque was really worth the hassle. Seeing as there was a perfectly good one in Butetown already. But then black Muslims and regular Muslims were hardly the same thing, and what Kenny was building was Cardiff's first outpost of Louis Farrakhan's Nation of Islam.

The other worry was whether it was really all right to build your mosque on the ground floor of a nightclub. Still, the club, Black Caesar's, was the only building Kenny owned, and he'd never been able to do much with the downstairs. He'd run it as a wine bar for a bit but Kenny's clientele weren't exactly wine drinkers, and the business types who were down the docks in the daytime never used it either, so he'd given that up. Then he'd tried turning it into a shop selling sportswear and stuff. He'd had the whole Soul II Soul range in but then Soul II Soul had gone down the toilet and so had the shop. Docks boys didn't believe the gear was kosher unless they were buying it down Queen Street from some white man's store.

It had been brooding on this particular question that had led Kenny to his recent spiritual conversion. He'd been up in London, Harlesden way, doing a little bit of business, and the guys he was dealing with had taken him round the Final Call bookshop there. Nearly burst out laughing at first, sight of all these guys standing around in their black suits with the red bow ties, but when they got to talking a bit, it started to make sense. Specially all the stuff about setting up black businesses in black areas.

The way Kenny saw it, he was a community leader, yet he didn't get any credit for it. He had a business already, of course; in fact he had several, but they weren't exactly respectable. That was the way it worked—

people didn't mind a black man selling draw and coke. They could just about handle a black man running a club. But a black man opens a clothes shop, and the punters fuck off up town and buy their gear there. Ignorant fuckers.

So Kenny had come back a bit inspired, like. He'd done his best to explain it all to the boys, and they'd gone along with it. Which wasn't surprising given that most of them were shit scared of him, but still, most of them knew about Minister Farrakhan already, so it wasn't too difficult, once they'd customized the approach for the local conditions.

He'd thought about changing his name, calling himself El Haji Malik or something, but then Melanie had pointed out that he already had a Muslim name. Which was true enough, of course, and his grandad had actually been a Muslim, though his dad hadn't bothered with it, specially not after he met Kenny's mum, who was a fierce bloody Baptist and the one person Kenny was not looking forward to telling about his religious conversion.

Kenny's club, Black Caesar's, was on West Bute Street, right in the old commercial heart of the docks. On a Saturday afternoon, though, the street was almost completely dead. The only faint sign of life Kenny could see came from three of his guys—Col, Neville and Mark—sat in line along the pavement outside the club, holding cans of Carlsberg. Fuckers had been raiding the upstairs bar again.

"So where is he then?" asked Kenny.

Col jerked his thumb towards the building. "Inside, boss. Checking the wiring, he said."

"Fucking hell, Col, you don't want to leave that thieving cunt on his own," said Kenny, and he headed into the club in search of Barry Myers, planning officer of the Docks Development Authority.

He found him downstairs in the back room, now the business part of the mosque, looking at the pulpit.

"Jesus, butt," said Myers as Kenny approached, "looks just like the one they used to have down the Swedish church."

"Hmm," said Kenny.

"Didn't know they had pulpits in mosques, Ken."

"Yeah, it's called the mimbar," said Kenny, and was pleased to see a look of surprise flash across Myers's smug face.

"Oh," said Myers after a moment, "the mimbar, I was wondering where you kept the booze," and he started laughing.

Kenny didn't join in, just stood there wishing he could get away with decking the bastard. But he couldn't, he knew the form and he knew a hint when he heard one. "Fancy a drink then, Barry?"

"Don't mind if I do, Ken, don't mind at all. Just check everything's shipshape down here first."

So the two of them went through the motions of looking around the downstairs and Kenny had to admit his boys had done a decent job. The temple itself was all painted white and was furnished with some pews and the pulpit—mimbar—all of which, as Barry had pointed out, bore a pretty fair resemblance to the fittings in the old Swedish church. Best thing was, the back wall was even facing Mecca. It was just right, Kenny thought. Serious.

The front room still had some of the display cases left over from the clothes shop, but now they held copies of the *Final Call* and a few books on black history, plus a couple of videos of Farrakhan in action, and one of the Million Man March.

There were separate entrances outside for the mosque and the club but Kenny opened a side door and led Myers upstairs. The lights were already on around the bar, and there was the unmistakable smell of draw hanging in the air. The boys had clearly popped up to relax earlier on. Myers sniffed the air too, but didn't say anything. Kenny walked round the bar and dug out a bottle of Glenfiddich, poured a large one and handed it to Myers, then cracked open a Coke for himself.

"Missing the match then, Barry?"

"Oh yes," said the planning officer. "Tell you the truth, Ken, I can't stand the fucking game. When the ball's not stuck in the fucking scrum, they're kicking it into touch. Give me the ice hockey any day. You been down there, see the Devils, Ken?"

Kenny nodded. He'd been a couple of times. Nice to see Cardiff doing well at something. And a lot of young boys now were into it. But far as Kenny was concerned, you were stuck with the sport you grew up with. And suddenly he felt aggrieved that this parasite Myers was dragging him away from watching it. Time to get on with the business.

"So, Barry mate, what can I do for you?" he said, putting his drink down next to Myers and folding his arms, letting a little menace creep into the air.

But Myers didn't seem to register the threat. "Well, Kenny," he said, "I've been studying the records, and this kind of change of use is highly irregular. You have to think about the whole make-up of a neighborhood, and a church—sorry, a mosque—and a nightclub in the same building... Well, there's a lot of ethical issues..."

"How much, Barry?"

Myers looked around, then shrugged, like he figured that there were a lot of things Kenny Ibadulla was capable of, but wearing a wire wasn't one of them.

"Oh, a grand up front and a ton a week should do it."

Kenny just looked at him. The logistics of killing him flashed through his mind. The deed itself would be no problem, whip the baseball bat out from behind the bar, strike one and it would be over. Dump the body in the foundations of one of the building sites his boys were looking after. Perfect. Proper gangster business. Then he sighed inwardly and accepted that wasn't the way things worked down here.

"Fuck the grand, Barry. I've got three hundred here in my pocket. Take it or leave it. You comes back and asks for more, I breaks your fucking legs and I'll laugh while I'm doing it." By the end of this little speech he had his face about three inches from Barry's and that seemed to do the trick.

The weasel didn't piss himself or pass out but the smile certainly disappeared. He stepped back, hacked out a laugh and said, "Yeah, well, Ken, like I say, it'll be a tricky one to get through the committee, but three hundred'll be all right. Long as there's no complaints."

Kenny handed over the money and Myers downed his drink and was out of the club in seconds. Kenny headed past the dance floor and opened the door to his office, turned on the TV just in time to see Wales concede a late try to Ireland and lose a match they should have won comfortably. He switched the TV off again and headed back out to the street, the urge to deck someone growing ever stronger.

He was cheered up, though, when he saw Col halfway up a ladder carefully stenciling in the outlines of the letters prior to painting the words "Nation of Islam" over the door.

"Nice," said Kenny, "gonna be nice. So we'll be ready for tomorrow, then?"

"Yeah, Ken," said Col, not turning around from his painting, "easy. You go on home, give the missis one. See you down the Pilot later, yeah, you can sort out my bonus."

Kenny laughed, said, "Pay your hospital bill more like, you don't get it done," and headed back towards Loudoun Square wondering what else he had to get sorted for tomorrow.

Tomorrow, Sunday, was set to be the mosque's grand opening. Way Kenny saw it, things would kick off about three. Have a couple of stalls and stuff out on the street, bit of music. Open the mosque up for anyone wanted to have a look, stick a video player in there running the Farrakhan tapes. Open the club up and get the disco going around six. Make it a little community dance thing.

Kenny was so wrapped up in thinking through his plans as he cut round the side of the real mosque—as he couldn't help thinking of it— that he didn't notice the noise of movement in the bushes next to him. Then there was a sudden whoop and Kenny spun round. If he hadn't checked himself just in time he would have taken the head off seven-year-old little Mikey, who had launched himself off a tree in the direction of Kenny's broad back.

"Gotcha," said Kenny, catching the little boy and making to throw him back into the undergrowth where a couple of his mates were watching.

"C'mon then," he said to them. "Aren't you lot going to help your mate?" And so seconds later Kenny was buried under a heap of junior-school banditos. He played with the little gang for another five minutes or so before chasing them back in the direction of Mikey senior's flat, and then he carried on home with a positive spring in his step. Feeling well in the mood to do as Col suggested, the second he got indoors with Melanie.

That idea flew out of his head pretty quickly when the first thing Melanie said was that he'd had a phone call. Bloke with an American accent, said he was from the Nation of Islam, and he'd be coming down tomorrow, to the opening.

"Shit," said Kenny, and sat down heavily on the sofa. This he hadn't been expecting. Of course he'd told the people up in London what he was planning. He'd bought all the videos and books and stuff from them. And they'd spoken to head office or whatever in Chicago and got the go-ahead for a new branch. But he'd thought that would have been that. He'd told the London boys about his opening, of course, and if a couple of them had wanted to come down well that would have been no problem. But an American? Fuck.

Kenny started to work through a mental checklist. The mosque was fine, the boys had really done a good job with it. He'd got all the liter-ature and stuff sorted out front. Got a fine-looking sister called Stephanie to work out front too. He'd got security. In fact that had all worked out very well indeed. All the guys who worked on the door for him and stuff already had the black bouncer suits. All he'd needed to do was get a consignment of red bow ties and he'd got the uniform sorted.

Then it hit him. The one thing he didn't have was a minister. He'd been so much in charge of it all that no one had mentioned who was going to be the preacher. Maybe everyone was expecting him to do it. Well, perhaps he could do it, at that.

"Mel," he said, "you reckon I'd make a good minister? For the mosque, like."

Melanie looked at him for a moment, then burst out laughing.

"What's so fucking funny?" said Kenny.

"Kenny," she said, "when did you last say two sentences without the word fuck in them, eh?"

Kenny shook his head, then laughed too. It was true. He'd always had a filthy mouth, and it was worse when he was nervous. And, frankly, the thought of standing up in front of all his people pretending to be some kind of minister scared the shit out of him.

What he needed was someone with a bit of front and a lot of bullshit. It didn't take long for a name to spring to mind. Mikey Thompson. He hadn't spoken to Mikey since he'd heard the little bastard had started doing a bit of freelance dealing for Billy Pinto. But what the hell, Kenny Ibadulla was a big enough man to forgive and forget; he'd give Mikey a chance to redeem himself.

He picked the phone up and called Mikey's number. Tina answered.

"Who wants him?" she asked.

"Me. Kenny."

"Oh, sorry, Ken, he's been out all day. I'll tell him you called, like."

"No, he fucking hasn't," growled Kenny, "I knows he's there. It's fucking *Blind Date* on now, innit? Telling me Mikey's missing his *Blind Date*?"

Tina didn't say anything, just put the phone down and, a few seconds later, Mikey's voice came on the line. "Sorry, Ken, just got in, like. Whassup?"

Kenny laid things out for Mikey. Option one, he signed on as temporary minister in Kenny's mosque. Option two, Kenny broke several of Mikey's bones, just like he should have done months ago when he found out he was freelancing for fucking Billy Pinto. Didn't take Mikey too long to choose option one. So Kenny told him to come down the Pilot around nine, they'd have a chat before the club opened.

Relieved, Kenny put the phone down and went into the kitchen where Melanie was starting to sort out the tea. He put his arms round her and was just letting them start to wander up towards her breasts when the back door blew open and in piled his three little girls and a couple of their mates.

Nine o'clock, Kenny walked up to the club, checked everything was ready for the night, and headed over to the Ship and Pilot. The boys were all there in the pool-room already. Mikey and Col were on the table, laughing and passing a spliff back and forth.

"Mikey," said Kenny, "you still got your suit?"

"Yeah, sure," said Mikey, "You want me on the door tonight, boss?" Mikey loved working the door, perfect chance to check out the talent coming in, and make his mark early. Couple of jokes as he's helping them to the cloakroom, then later in the evening, when most of the blokes are too pissed to function, Mikey leaves the door, comes into the club, and eases on in. Sweet. Once in a while it even worked out.

"Nah," said Kenny, "least I don't think so—check it with Col. No, Mikey, you'll need the suit for the minister number. I'll sort you out with the bow tie and the fez, like."

"Fucking 'ell, Ken, I thought you were joking."

"Wish I was, Mikey, wish I was."

"But why me, Ken? You've got a bunch of boys all into this stuff good and proper. Why can't one of them do it?"

Kenny shook his head. "They're all fucking kids, Mikey. Need a bit of experience for this job." Kenny paused for a moment then decided to give Mikey the full story. "See, thing is, what I need is a bullshitter. There's some Yank coming down tomorrow, from head office, like, in Chicago, wants to see we're doing things right. I need someone can give him a bit of a show."

"Tomorrow, Ken? You're joking."

"Tell you what, Mikey. Best thing, we go over the mosque and I show you the stuff."

And so it was that Mikey ended up spending his evening not hitting on the sweetest young things in Cardiff but closeted in front of the VCR watching Minister Farrakhan in action, and frantically reading back issues of the *Final Call*.

Next day, Sunday, the festivities weren't due to start till three, but the inner circle got together at the club around one. Kenny was a bear with a sore head. Hadn't got to bed till five. Kids had woken him early, and now some fucking Yank was going to come and rain on his parade.

Still, everything seemed to be coming together pretty well. The band had just showed up, on their truck. They were just going to set up in the street outside and play. Brought their own generator and everything. Like Kenny, the boys all had their black suits and red bow ties on; looked damn serious when there was a bunch of you together. Stephanie he'd seen in the front of the mosque, looking absolutely gorgeous. The cleaners had been into the club already and it was looking pretty tidy. Col was busy blowing up balloons and tying them to everything in sight. In fact it all seemed pretty damn kosher, for want of a more appropriate word.

Then the major problem came back to him. "Where's Mikey?" he asked.

"Christ, boss, haven't you seen him?" said Mark. "He's inside the bloody temple pretending to be Malcolm X, like."

And indeed he was. Kenny found Mikey standing at the mimbar waving his hands around and spouting bullshit, wearing a pair of sunglasses so dark that he didn't even notice Kenny coming in. Though, Kenny being the size he was, it didn't take too long for his shadow to register on Mikey's radar. "*Salaam aleikum*, boss," he said, whipping his glasses off.

"*Aleikum salaam*," said Kenny without even thinking about it. It was still a greeting you heard all the time around Butetown. "So, you ready to go, Mikey?"

"I don't know, Ken. I thought I'd just, like, welcome everyone and then read out this introduction, like," he said, waving one of the pamphlets Kenny had brought down.

"Yeah, fine," said Kenny, "just go for it," and he headed upstairs to sort out the music for the disco later on.

By three o'clock there was already a reasonable crowd built up, practically all locals, plus a few social-worker types and a photographer who said she'd try and sell some pictures to the *Echo*.

The band got going a few minutes after, running through a few Bob Marley tunes to warm everybody up. There was a steady stream of people having a look at the mosque, even a few of the elders from the regular mosque, acting like they were just passing by accidentally. The home-made patties and samosas and fruit punch were all starting to tick over nicely and the vibe was just nice, Kenny reckoned, when the limousine drew up.

The limousine was indubitably the business. Some kind of American stretch with tinted windows. It pulled up on the edge of the crowd and double-parked neatly in the middle of the street. The passenger-side front door opened first, shortly to be followed by the two back doors and finally the driver's door. Out of each door emerged a shaven-headed character in an immaculate black suit and a red bow tie. Then, a moment later, a fifth person came out, a slighter figure with the suit and bow tie and also a fez. Evidently the boss-man.

The band kept on playing regardless, chugging through Stevie Wonder's "Isn't She Lovely," but all other activity seemed to stop as everyone stared at the new arrivals.

Kenny nodded his head quickly to a couple of his guys and they followed in his wake as he moved through the crowd towards the out-of-towners.

"*Salaam aleikum*," he said as he approached.

"*Aleikum salaam*," said the guy in the fez, with a pronounced New York accent.

"So you're from, like, head office," said Kenny.

"Kamal al-Mohammed. From Chicago, yes," said the American, cold as anything.

"Well," said Kenny, unaccustomedly nervous in the face of this skinny Yank, "this is the mosque here and, as you can see, we're having a bit of an opening do, like."

Al-Mohammed inclined his head slightly. The four other guys—

bodyguards or whatever they were—didn't say a word. Kenny wasn't sure even whether they were British or American. He waited for the guy to say something and for a few seconds they were just stood there staring at each other. Then the guy shook his head irritably and said, "So. Show me."

"All right, butt," said Kenny and turned to lead the way muttering under his breath, "I'll fucking show you then."

The people parted to let through what was by now quite an impressive Muslim cortège, what with Kenny and his boys and the American's crew. But before they could enter the mosque al-Mohammed stopped, surveyed the crowd and then stared at Kenny before saying, "This is a mixed event."

Kenny didn't know what he was on about for a moment. Thought maybe al-Mohammed meant it ought to be a men-only event. Then he realized it was racial mixing he meant.

"Yeah," he said, "reaching out, you knows what I mean?"

Al-Mohammed didn't look too impressed but he carried on into the front part of the mosque where Stephanie was looking beautiful behind the counter. She should cheer the old sourface up, thought Kenny, but no, not a bit of it. Al-Mohammed took one look at her crop-top and said, "Inappropriate dress for a Muslim woman."

Stephanie just looked at him like she was watching something really unusual on TV. Kenny stayed silent and opened the door into the mosque proper. And he wasn't sure, but he reckoned his face probably fell a mile when the first person he saw in the room, standing by the mimbar, was Mark, looking impeccable in his suit and bow tie, his hair cropped to the bone, but obviously as white as can be.

"Mr Ibadulla," said the American after a brief, painful silence, "have you read any of the Nation's literature?"

Kenny nodded.

"Have you read perhaps our program of belief?"

"Uh," said Kenny, but before he could go on the American cut in.

"Well, I suggest you re-read it."

Kenny felt like he was a kid at school again. Only difference was, none of Kenny's teachers ever dared speak like that to him, at least not after what happened when he was thirteen with that science teacher.

Back out on the street, al-Mohammed took up a position at the back of the crowd looking at the band. Behind him his comrades lined up in a row, all standing with their arms folded in front of them.

When Kenny came up alongside al-Mohammed, the American turned to him and said, "So. When will the educational part of the proceedings start?"

Christ, thought Kenny, realizing it was now up to Mikey to save the day. But he smiled and said, "Yes, indeed, brother Waqar el-Faid will be talking in just a little while, like."

He found Mikey in the shop giving Stephanie the full charm offensive. "C'mon," he said, "you're on."

Kenny climbed up on to the band's truck with Mikey right behind him. They stood on the side of the makeshift stage till the band finished a reggaed-up "Wonderful Tonight," and then Kenny went to the mike.

"Ladies and gentlemen," he said, "and all the rest of you lot. *Salaam aleikum*, and welcome to the opening of Cardiff's first Nation of Islam mosque. I'd also like to welcome our special guest, Mr al-Mohammed from Chicago. And now we're going to have a few words about the Nation of Islam from a man you all knows." Kenny ground to a halt, wondering whether he could get away with introducing Mikey as Waqar el-Faid. He decided against it and just waved his arm in Mikey's direction before jumping off the front of the stage.

Immediately there was a muttering from certain sections of the crowd. No one had quite seen Mikey as a spiritual teacher before. The real trouble, though, it quickly became clear, was that neither had Mikey.

Mikey's speech was basically just a matter of reading out the pamphlet he'd found, but with every sentence it was falling flatter and flatter. Mikey Thompson delivering a lecture on living a clean life and running your own business was just too ridiculous. They might have taken it from an American, but from Mikey? Then he said something about the importance of respecting your women, and a voice shouted, "You should bloody know, Mikey," and suddenly the whole crowd was creased with laughter. Mikey just dried up. For a moment Kenny thought he might be about to burst into tears. But then Mikey started talking again.

"Listen," he said, "like all of you, I'm new to this Muslim bit. But you shouldn't laugh at it just 'cause it's me talking." He paused for another couple of seconds and started again. "I've been thinking about my little boy, little Mikey. He's seven, right, just started junior school. And I was thinking about when I was at junior school, just down the road here, same place as most of you. And I was thinking about how I didn't know I was black then."

A woman laughed.

Mikey put his hand up. "No, I'm not saying I was blind, love, but I didn't know what it meant to be black. Down here, down the docks, it seemed like we were all together, right. Then, when I was eleven, I went to secondary over Fitzalan, and I found out what it meant. Nah mean?"

A rumble of agreement came from the crowd.

"What I found out, right, was that the rest of the people out there think they knows what you are if you come from Butetown. Right. So what I'm saying, and I'm going to shut up now, so don't worry, is that if we're going to make something of our lives, we've got to do it ourselves. And that's why I say that, whatever you think about Kenny here—and I know a lot of you may have had your troubles with Kenny—you've got to respect what he's doing." And with that he too jumped off the stage.

The applause Mikey got wasn't exactly wild, but still, when he came down into the crowd, several people clapped him on the back and said well done. One or two of the sisters gave him *Mikey, I never knew you were so sensitive*-type looks, which he returned with his most sensitive wink. Kenny walked over and clapped him on the back too, then turned round to see what his guests had made of it.

He found them standing in formation once more, this time outside the entrance to the club.

"What's this, brother Ibadulla?" asked al-Mohammed, pointing at the sign saying "Black Caesar's Dancing and Dining."

"It's a club," said Kenny.

Al-Mohammed looked at his coterie and then looked back at Kenny. "You're going to place Allah's temple underneath a nightclub, brother Ibadulla?"

"Well, there are separate entrances," said Kenny, sounding feeble even to himself.

Al-Mohammed shook his head. "Show us inside," he said.

Kenny looked at his watch. Half five. The club was due to open in thirty minutes. That would probably be the last straw for these guys. He had to get them in and out and fast, before people started banging on the doors. So he sighed, opened the door and led the way upstairs into the club. Lloyd the barman was busy washing glasses but otherwise the place was deserted. Al-Mohammed just looked at the bar, shook his head once more and uttered the one word "alcohol" before saying, "Mr Ibadulla, let's go into your office. We have much to discuss."

Kenny shrugged, thinking to himself, this is the thanks you get for trying to put something back into the community. He unlocked the office door, ushering the visitors inside.

The last man in shut the door behind him, and in an instant Kenny found himself looking straight down the barrel of a gun.

Al-Mohammed was the man holding the gun, and once Kenny had registered its presence he started talking again, only this time his voice had no trace of a New York accent. Instead it was pure Brummie.

"All right, Kenny mate. Had you going there, eh!"

Kenny shook his head in absolute and total disbelief. He'd let the Handsworth crew jerk him about like a prize bloody twat.

The Handsworth crew were evidently of the same mind. Two of the bodyguards were shaking with suppressed laughter. "Inappropriate dress for a Muslim woman," said one of them. The other grinned and rolled his eyes and, for a moment, Kenny thought he might have an opening.

The leader, however, kept his gun firmly trained on Kenny and said, "Now, Mr Ibadulla, how about you open your safe and we have a look, see if there's anything we like in there."

Kenny was a pro. He didn't do anything stupid. Just swore under his breath at his gullibility and tried to remember just how much he was holding in the safe. Around seven and a bit, he figured, and sighed as he opened up.

The former al-Mohammed kept his gun steadily on Kenny as his cohorts loaded the contents into a couple of black canvas bags. One of them then stepped behind Kenny, who wondered for a moment whether he was about to die, before a voice said, "*Salaam aleikum*, mate," and unconsciousness hit him like a freight train.

When Kenny came to, ten minutes later, after being given a good shaking by Col and Mikey, he discovered what had happened next. The Brummies had held a gun on Lloyd behind the bar, then knocked him out too. Then they'd walked downstairs and out of the club, back in character, shaking their heads and acting disgusted by what they'd found. The crowd had parted to let them make their way to the limo. A couple of the youth had catcalled them as they drove away, but that was that. The band had launched into Seal's "Crazy" and it had taken a few minutes for anyone to wonder why Kenny hadn't come back down.

"Shit," said Mikey, when Kenny told him what had happened. "Don't know about you, Ken, but I don't think we're cut out for the religious life."

MUAZZEZ

by Mac Wellman

l[Bump]:

They lied to me about the reality of things here on Muazzez. About the foundation of these, their basis, their fundament, the profound bottom of things. I am an Abandoned Cigar Factory (or ACF) groaning in the dunes near the settlement at Culpepper. That alone would be of little interest because there are many abandoned cigar factories near Culpepper. However I am the only one of these many Abandoned Cigar Factories to possess both a telephone booth (nestled handily within the deep recesses of my abandoned tool shed) and also a zygodactyl foot, as of a parrot or vulture.

But they lied to me, when I was a child, small and naïve, and not always able to discern truth from falsehood. Now it is a fact that abandoned cigar factories are, in general, a notoriously gullible bunch; in this regard I am typical of my tribe. But we are also steadfastness incarnate; and surely this steadfastness must be worth something—something more than a brazier's dredge. Our steadfastness has given us abandoned cigar factories—so far as we know, the sole human inhabitants of the wondrous world of Muazzez—a certain fixed and unchangeable constancy, a resolute loyalty to the deep, dark truths of the unreadable three-legged race of a steam engine that is Muazzez; without this steadfastness, we would be as thistles in the wind (whatever "thistles" are; whatever "wind" is).

Now the story of how I came to be lied to revolves in an... what is the word? The human mind? ... like a dead rat in a Simmons Pot. By all accounts, this place, moss-colored Muazzez, ever since the departure of the winged and entitled ones, the High Eulalians I mean, has remained an apolitical postscript. A place whose spindle legs no longer tremble in anticipation of the aroma romantica of the noble ...y... cigar. Of the Eulalians themselves nothing, I presume, is known since if something were to be known surely I would know it, or its rumor at least. All things knowable do possess their attendant rumors, skipping and snapping happily at the heels of whoever the thing known amounts to, and is. But the drift of this thought is not my drift, for there is no drift to my thought. My thought is a rooted thing.

My nearest neighbor, an abandoned cigar factory by the name of Finn, resides there, on the other side of the heavenly ditch known only as Becquerel's Radiant, and is my main man and source of useful information regarding the ways of the world, and its twirl; the ways of the world of Muazzez. Finn has assured me in his deep, deep booming that what most characterizes our world in its primeval yerk and jerk is a primal radial symmetry, as of a series of spokes or spokey type spindles radiating from a deep and frosty central secret; a secret which is in the habit of sitting in the middle, while the rest of us hunch up or hunker down, equally remote, and endure our eternal ignorance seated on the wide circumference of what we all suppose. What we wrongly choose to suppose. Clearly, Finn's rabbit ears are more finely attuned than my tin ones, which on the gradient of things are but a tincal (*tinqkal*) to his fine talcum, tincal being only a crude, unsophisticated borax of Malayan extraction. So I am careful to listen, careful to hear what my wise neighbor tells me regarding the deep, deep things. Finn passes on to me what Finn has heard before, and this is called civilization. Now the immediate problem is, I do not know how to pass on what I know, as there is no man (permit me this humble euphemism) beyond me, noman, nemo; there is none to whom I might in my booming, impart and export the import of my chilly Muazzezian doom. There is simply no room for doom on this part of the world; that is, beyond some tinkers and bong farmers (people without souls) from the titration plants over in Hillsbrother, near the mound of coffee grounds, matchless mounds it should be noted, a topless tower of a mound comparable in airy amplitude to me, or to Finn. Tinkers lost in a tinker's dream that is only an homage to some cosmic Titivillus, lesser god of misprints and perennial fly in the ointment of the Cosmic Text. No more about these, however, and the hideous refrigerator cartons they have a way of setting up near the Pharoanic mass of us; each and every one of us more massy and Pharoanic than the last; all persisting in time's graceful and gradual phase-out beneath the inky skies of moss-colored Muazzez; Muazzez, the only world of all the small worlds (could there be, truly, more small worlds than this?) that has been deserted not only by the High Eulalians but also by the higher concept of tennis. But the higher concept of tennis, tennis with her tendency to bounce, bounce and so on, and thus to elude us, and to escape easy grasp, belongs not to One (Bump) nor to Two (Tilt) but to Three (Laugh it Off). And owing to our pursuit of deep, deep truths—final things, Finn would say—; not to mention our longstanding policy of steadfastness; we have not yet arrived at that third place, that puzzling place of grammatical impasse.

Bumps are another sort of impasse; bumps are the habit of proceeding by jerks and jolts, or by yerk and jerk as is the case on Muazzez where there is no weather, but of a cold so cold it is a frozen bull-roarer and of heat so hot it is of the tribe of bunsen burner; bumps *qua* bumps are bumps. Lumps are often hidden beneath the surface of bumpy things and this is especially true of lumpish, imperfect places like this one, a roundy approximately oblong place resembling, I would suppose, no other. Within my fallen walls and carding tables, my long dank rooms where heaped sheaves of moist Havana hung out to dry, I recollect in aromatic tranquility under the rusted swaying sign of ...y...

Still I differ from all other abandoned cigar factories in one respect, one key respect, at least one, one germane to the Muazzezian narration here deployed. I am referring to my zygodactyl claw which has enabled me to do a little subterranean exploration on my own. I cannot believe any other of the abandoned cigar factories of Muazzez incorporate this useful feature. Even Finn, to whose absolute mastery in matters magisterial and in the molding dish of superior wisdom, I bow or rather lean, is lacking in this respect. As bumps occur, I am able to partially alleviate the force of their impact. Where the bumps come from is beyond mortal reason, that net beyond which lies the realm of what noise, what alien racket, and beyond that and beyond that and beyond that a baseline regressing shot by shot into an infinity even the High Eulalians in the dawn of time knew not the extent, neither by their cunning craft of measuring worm, nor by leap of light's hare, nor by the malign craft of Time's inky wormhole. Bumps are bumps I reckon, and my claw has digged a little deeper during each of them, clutched at each random impact deep down into the fateful stuff of Muazzez, till at long last I begin to perceive a cunning arrangement of layers. I perceive an order in the fundament, just as Finn has asseverated. The more deeply down one delves, Finn declared, the more repetition becomes the rule of the day; the more heavy, inorganic and deeply serious all matters become. The rule of radial symmetry rules all wisdom, even on lumpish, moss-colored Muazzez. As I dig and scratch, scratch blindly and clumsily, as if impelled by a force more basic than mere bumpness, I become convinced like the great geometer Pascal that the riddle of the world's runic confusion resides experientially and experimentally contrived in a vertical grammar only the happy few are capable of deciphering. Happy in my fewness, and in the sparseness of my delight, I would have genuflected to myself, or at least bowed before my image floating like Narcissus on the oily rainwater of Becquerel's Radiant had I not been wary of some structural overstrain in my supporting timbers, long out of service and subject to sprain, rot or worse. It is lonely to be so alone in wonderment; indeed, to be so alone in the wonderment of full knowledge often feels like being alone in the empty cigar box (of course, an ...y... box) of bafflement and ignorance. Total things are radically hinged to the same hub and the same spindly spokes connect grace, purpose, triumph and luck to their opposites both in gravity and degree. Radical symmetry revolves around a mare's nest of darkest centralia, deep and profound.

For instance, in the Marginate Sphere of Bump I encountered first plain old gypsum, then in succession ruddy pangolinite, spongy Uriah stuff, wriggle of lead, and finally pentacle of Ytterbium. In the more rarefied Marinara system I initially scraped and tore through layers of Make Out, Make Shift, Make Ready, only to reach my horny uttermost at a skimpy deposit of Make Mountain out of a Mole-Hill. On the Market Value Sliding Scale System (founded by our nameless predecessors, even before the Eulalians—I am talking about the god-like beings who actually designed and builded the cigar factories—bodies without souls in that void, inenerrable era.) I carefully take note of the following more or less clearly defined substratums: Empathy, Embrangle, Emote, Embowel, and lastly Emission of Admission. Up to this point, regularity and the uniformitarian hypothesis seem to work out much as Finn had indicated it would. Knowledge lay heaped up, like a heap of bottle caps or cigar bands—and the sky? the sky larked about in her mystic absence, larked this way and that, as though dodging the massive fist of sudden infant child death syndrome. All about me lay trisquare, according to Vervier's Law.

2[Tilt]:

I hope you can follow my drift, for try as I might it is almost always elusive to me even though I am present in much of it. Drifts about the self, especially complex and highly evolved selves, selves like abandoned cigar factories, have a way of sliding off into places beyond the beaten path, places like non-self hedges and the hegemony of the self's perfect picture of the world and all things in it. In the best of all possible worlds that perfect picture comes to replace the self, which is a messy, nasty and vile set of arbitrary constructions at best. However, standing as I do, at the very apex of the stepladder of creation, I do not need such a stratagem, as my energies are always perfectly focussed upon their object. Steadfastness, you will recall. But the nightmare alterity of steadfastness is likewise rooted to the same hub; for steadfastness and all her children like the house of stone are also on *sand ybuilded*. That is why bumps of all shapes are drawn to steadfastness as snakes are to sugar-beans, and bears are to honey (what's a "bear"? and what is a "honey"?).

Precept: Bumps are drawn to what is bumpable.

Bumps are drawn to that which is bumpable, and the most bumpable of all objects are those which are mostly steadfast; for those which are most steadfast invariably are the most invariant. I must say if I were a bump I would search high and low for an object of utmost steadfastness to bump upon, because such an object constitutes an ideal target in that regard, as it allows the approaching bump ample time to locate the object squarely in its cross-hairs, and to stamp and clear away all behind and to heighten one's intensity by anticipation of the imagined impact with the steadfast one who for her part reciprocates by not stooping to the low, but all too common resort of the unsteadfast; namely, dodging, ducking, stepping aside or attempting otherwise to frustrate the onrushing bump, now engorged with the pure delight of inescapable collision. But then I don't care for bumps very much. I do not much care for the way they comb their hair. And although I sometimes think it would be a delight, just for once, to get down off my mound of crumbing foundation stones (I surmise those are stones down there) and haul my ruinous ponderation up to the top of a hill, like Mt Sizable Artichoke, there across the far wriggle of Becquerel's Radiant as it disappears over Finn's shoulder across the Great Nguba (Goober) Plain; from whence I would come roaring down upon an unsuspecting campsite of off-season Bumps, Bumps with their wives and children and clotheslines and licorice salad, and give them a taste of their own medicine. Wouldn't that be an unforgettable sight: me, twelve acres of crumbling brick and mortar, thousands of tons of abandoned cigar factory, emerging in full glory out of the elms and sycamores, crested by vines and garlands of blueberry and rosebush; glaring with intense, almost infernal, malevolence before the final, awful, thunderous charge down, down, down upon the squealing bumps below. Still, I know this urge is a low one; it is an impulse that our kind have long ago transcended. But the truth is, bumps even of the lowliest kind, like the bumps accidentally incurred by the tinkers and Bong farmers in their sad drunken revels, are to be taken seriously. For even the most steadfast of the steadfast has somewhere a crack, however faint, flowing waywardly up its massive foundation stone, and a crack, any crack, is a fatal flaw in the steadfast. From cracks flow faults, and from these all manner of dialectical materialism. Bumps lead to tilt, as of the Pisan hypotenuse, and tilt issues forth normally into topple and topple is the lead cause of stop and what stop initiates is as inevitable as the fact that, according to the International System of the Academy of Sciences, the SI unit for inductance is Henry (symbol: H); namely, full stop. Full stop, period. Beyond that terminus no man can go, even if like me, she is an abandoned cigar factory. And what undergirds all this ambulatory frightwig of unappetizing complication is the immootable problem of what prompted all that Radial Symmetry in the first place. Because what this might be can only be, at bottom, a bump, a bump in the night. Finn, I have noticed, never dwells on these topics, at least in any detail. Indeed, Finn does not retail in detail because as the saying goes, God is there (whoever God is) and the spider also.

There, I think I have covered Bump, although again Finn would say I have not done so. In truth Finn would have a puntilla in the regard that in covering bumps I had not covered him, and from a certain disinterested prospect it might just be possible to regard Finn and all his Finnish friends (Tribe of Suomi?), myself among them, all the wild dispersion of abandoned cigar factories near Culpepper and beyond, as a mere bunch of bumps, outsized bumps to be sure, but bumps nevertheless. Bumps, further, disguised bumpishly as ACFs and so totally lacking in ethnic authenticity. Deracinated lumps of bump, trembling in age-old terror beneath a cloth of disguise so habitual it no longer registers as cloth. An unseen mesh or screen, as of the sort the Higher Eulalians would employ to trap fat bumblebees for their feast on Luna, and Bang. Worlds lost to history through the primal loss of the radial symmetry that starts up where the previous start stopped.

Indeed, can one ever be said to have covered Bump? Because a covered bump turns into a lump, and we are back where we began. And this cycle of arid hunches has no further extension in thought, or in the heart's nomenclature, only in the infinite interstices of time. I shudder to think. And so, I do not; instead, I stop.

And so, as I was saying, they lied to me about the profound bottom of things here on Muazzez. But you believe all things when you are small, even when you are a mere lewis (a dovetailed iron tenon made of several parts and designed to fit into a dovetail mortise in a large stone so that it can be lifted by a hoisting apparatus), a mere twinkle that is, in the eye of a sheet bend (a knot in which one rope or piece of yarn is made fast to the bight of another). Now, who did the telling, that I do not know, that I cannot say. It is a mystery, much like the one I mentioned earlier, the problem of not knowing how, precisely, to pass on what I know. Each end of life's road is blocked by a long-handled rake lying dangerous and emblematic, teeth up, across the path destiny seems to have chosen for me. If I proceed with my clumsy lack of feet, my undextrous lower portions rumbling along at their centipede pace; the long hardwood handle of which rake, upon the depression of the row of teeth by my foundation, flies up invariably, and whacks me hard upon the window or doorway of my face. And this consequence follows, follows whether or not I proceed cautiously forward or cautiously back; or incautiously forward or incautiously back. Bear in mind there is scant difference—the merest scintilla of measurable velocity difference between my most rapid progress and my least—so that this variation does not count for much in the matter. In either direction I face an insuperable terminus, and so must rely upon whatever I can glean from my neighbor, Finn. The cycle runs something like this: Finn knows and, possessing no claw, speaks; I listen to what Finn says and think I know, only doubts creep in, and I know that I do not know, I am faking it; besides, there is no one around for me to pass on what I know, what Finn has told me, so I have to sit quietly minding my own business (a thing anathema to human nature); so I grow bored and begin to tap my foot; in this way I discover I possess a foot—I simply did not know before; experimenting with my foot (I possess only one) I begin to move it around a little, this way and that, and come to the realization that this foot is shaped like a crow's foot, or talon; this appendage, I soon discover, is capable of digging, ergo I begin to dig (was it the geometer Pascal who said, when a hammer is the only tool you possess everything begins to look like a nail?); by digging, I discover the joys and wonders of excavation, and thereby come partially to discover my own nature, if an abandoned cigar factory may be said to possess a nature, a nature beyond the obvious.

And if the matter ended there, fine.

And if the matter ended there, one could say the matter ended there, and be done with it. And if the matter ended one could say life on Muazzez resembles that of any normal world, any normal small world (is it not in the nature of a world to be a small world?), endlessly and comfortably repeating the egg and dart motif along a cloudless Muazzezian sky of ever unscrolling ornamental frieze? One could say that, I suppose.

And if the matter ended there I would have no complaint, as there would be nothing radically amiss to complain about, except for the question of a few idle details. Let us not go into the matter of that right now because, as I have mentioned before, Finn does not retail in detail and also God lives there, and the spider too. And I have a horror of both.

But logic is a terrible machine and no one can stay its witless, participial tamboura, tamboura, tamboura. Even on Muazzez, a place I now realize to be a merely accessory being, of no particular importance in the greater, or lesser, or whatever scheme of things. Like a smoke. Smoke, smoke from a time that has passed into memory, and from memory into imagination, and from that into some chronicle of the madness of small worlds.

As I have reported, Muazzez is of the color of moss, or sassy-hued schist and flinkite with flakes of emerald smagdarine. Not terribly attractive, unless the sun, or whatever it is, lies just below the lip of the horizon when you can see refracted—the green light pouring through the stony fibers as though these were living filiamentia—the delicatest nerves of some living things. And the sky of Muazzez, when not obliterated by the dark black of night, attains at noon something of the indescribable hue of a lemon blossom, just as it has unfolded from its bud; or as the sap of the lime, mixed with the juice of the tamarind. And I mention these because, on such occasions there is a sweetness to the air that cuts through even the pungent regret of my dark, nicotine-stained walls; something about such scents that can almost reduce me to tears, though what part of me might be capable of such a powerful sentiment I would not venture to imagine. But everybody knows that old theaters are haunted, so I would not be surprised if there may be spirits lodged deep within my walls, and down under the heavy timbers that crisscross the colossal nave of my interior structure, extending clear from sorting rooms (narthex) to the chancel of my counting room, with deep aisles where patient *trabajadores* sat at desks, rolling patiently my finest Havana while at his pulpit far above, the lector solemnly read from his Cervantes and Shakespeare and Babunin. Peace reigned in the worker's hearts because all knew that each tenth cigar would be his or her own.

But the matter did not end there.

But the matter could not possibly have ended there because, both in visual expanse and vertical drop, the matter seemed endless, or of an extent of some cubic miles at least. The exact nature of this layering, for layering there clearly was, came both to perplex and finally obsess me.

Before too long I had dug my way deep into a hole of investigatory Boogie Woogie. I became overwhelmed by the force of pure curiosity, as if my single thought were to will one thing. To ding some subterranean bell. I sought to examine what lay below, and delve into the issue of the Chthonic. And so I did, all forty-two layers, some more memorable than the rest; a confection whose pure decorative perfection, for a time, took the cake and handed it to me on a silver pladder. Mere utility I despised. The bright core of Radical Symmetry summoned and I knew my mission was to probe that place and reveal what lay there, be it boot or booster cable. To hell with bumps, and all things bumpy; I would go in search of myself, following the pure plumb line of my will, and follow where it led, even to the Koresh hollow of Muazzez's deepest plumbing.

And so, in succession a stratigraphic variorum. First, *bonnyclabber*, the layer of sour, clotted cream; then *brocade*, the candlewax of certain sacred places, places devoted to the placing of jars and the jarring of places, many of them from Cipangu (wherever that is); *bursitis*, a lovely inflammation extending throughout Muazzez's bursa, as it does in the shoulder, tennis elbow (whatever "tennis" is) or knee; *charcoal rot*, an unpleasant stratum, foul and decayed; *a layer composed entirely of clucks and tympanous clucking*, as of a person calling a horse; *cold cuts*, also known as the sandwich layer; *concertina,* a smallish instrument with bellows and buttons—its muffled music may be heard at the bottoms of certain muffled wells; *crème de menthe*, a sticky greenish layer of mint, considered an aphrodisiac among our ignorant tinkers and bong farmers; *decrescendo*, a region of decreasing volume; *demijohn*, an expanse of colored glass supported by an odd wicker thatch; *demisemiquaver*, a thirty-second note pressed like a leaf in the middle of all this; *diffraction grating*, a hunk of glass or metal having a large number or very fine parallel grooves or slits in the surface and used to produce optical spectra by diffraction or reflected light; *dreck*, a thin layer of dung; *ding*, a thick layer of druck; *dry as dust*, a collection of postmodern critical theory, mashed and compressed to form a thin, flat (inedible) flatbread;

ejaculate, a squirt of stuff forcefully expelled; *enflurance*, a nonexplosive anaesthetic, $C^3H^2ClF^5O$; *espresso*, a sludge residue of Espy, the habit of spying upon, a glimpsing or catching sight of Germans; *face down*, to overcome or prevail by a stare or resolute manner; *freaky*, a layer of that which freaks; *hafnium*, a brilliant, silvery metallic element separated from ores of zirconium, and used in nuclear control rods (what's "control"?); *homespun*, a plain, coarse, woolen cloth made of homespun yarn; *integration*, an organization of organic, psychological and social traits and tendencies of a person into a harmonious, if spotty, whole; *loco foco*, a member of a radical faction of the New York Democratic Party, organized in 1835, long missing and presumed dead; *neverneverland*, an imaginary place where all is idyllic or ideal; *new criticism*, a layer of literary criticism that stresses close reading and posits that the facts of an author's life are irrelevant; *paranoia*, a region of non-degenerative, limited psychosis, typified by delusions of persecution; *parasol*, a region of small, light umbrellas; *prosopeia*, various impersonations of absent or imaginary speakers; *roman fleuve*, a long novel in many volumes, mostly flattened; *ruff*, a region of stiffly starched frilled or pleated circular collars of lace, muslin, or other fine fabric, worn by men and women in the 16th and 17th centuries; *scene stealer*, a layer composed of actors who are given to the fine art of drawing attention to oneself when one is not meant to be the focus of attention; *Shick test*, an intracutaneous skin test of susceptibility to Diphtheria; *Schiff's Reagent*, an aqueous layer of solution of rosalind and sulphurous acid used to test for the presence of aldehydes and jeckylhydes; *shinplaster*, paper currency issued privately, and devalued by inflation or lack of backing; *simple closed curve*, a region of Jordan curves; *spackle*, a powder stratum, which when mixed with water is used to fill holes in plaster before painting or papering; *squirting cucumber*, a region of hairy vines; *Ecballium elaterium*, having fruit that when ripe discharges its seeds and juices explosively; *stretch receptor*, a proprioceptor in a muscle or tendon that is stimulated by a stretch; *umpteen*, a stratum of large but indefinite numbers; *Umbrella Bird Land*, a wide layer noted for its population of several tropical American birds;

Cephaloptereus Ornatus, having a retractile black crest and a long, feathered wattle; *vernacular*, a deep stratum of non-standard or substandard speech; upon which I was forced to suspend my excavation owing to what I first perceived, or rather misperceived as a particularly violent bump. The strain of my digging had evidently cleared away a whole mess of underground debris, so much in fact, that tinkers and bong farmers from miles and miles around came with their sledges, flatbeds and dumptrucks to haul away the diverse material I had dug and cleared away behind me, making—predictably—all there a desolation. Even so, the mountain of debris remains to this day a tribute to my folly, Mount Ivy League I named it, because of the fact there were leagues of the stuff, all jumbled together, and because after a few months the prettiest honeysuckle and climbing ivy began to appear, as if by magic, on the attractive, perennially sunlit and positively Floridian, south-east slope. What I did not realize was that in clearing away a great deal of the inner Muazzez, I had inadvertently created a great hole, or vacuum, far below, beneath not only the whole Culpeppper region, but beneath me as well, the tons and tons of my longstanding steadfastness. Now, a hole under the right circumstance becomes, for all practical purposes, a vacuum. And we all know from our high school French that a vacuum is something that nature abhoreth.

That bump, which took me so by surprise, was, you see, no ordinary bump; that bump was a tilt, a full tilt, disguised as a bump. How do I know this? Because shortly thereafter I began to hear bits of song, snatches as of angels singing, and crows and toucans. High-pitched and low-pitched shrills, cries and caws, apparently from the deep interior regions of my fundament. But it is impossible with such cries to discover precisely their origin, just as it is often very easy to mistake a cry of passion and fulfillment with one of futility and hitherto untapped sorrow and regret. The deep emotion of these noises somehow charmed and moved me, moved me in that way an unknown music does, fanning out wide over the dreaming face of a lake in the early evening, shrouded by mists as the willows and Spanish moss, damp with dew, hang low in the waning twilight.

At one point one of the voices I had grown accustomed to suddenly modulated unexpectedly into a strange unhuman creak, as of wooden timbers being twisted and their woody fiber creaking under an intense strain. The whole realm of the unhuman poured into the gap between previous expectation and present realization.

Something about this uncanny transformation penetrated deep into my consciousness, and with it a sudden illumination. The assumption I had made about my own humanity now felt as false and fatuous as that of the tinkers and bong farmers, peoples I had despised and dismissed. What had I overlooked, to be so entirely off the mark? How could I have so entirely misjudged the matter, so that what I had taken for bedrock now seemed sand, or a porous linearization of some talus or heap of slag? But consciousness is double, and how great a mystery to each of us is our own special, inner architecture! But I have always had faith, for I know one day the telephone in my booth will ring, and at that ringing I will rejoice, for I know that that ringing will be a sign, and whatever that sign stands for there will be joy and glad tidings for all; since I am contained in what we refer to when we denominate a group of entities, all; that I shall likewise share in the common celebration; this even though I am unable for obvious reasons to actually answer the phone in the phone-booth that is lodged deep within me. Indeed, were I able somehow through some mechanical Rube Goldberg device to delicately lift the receiver from off the armature where it resides and raise the instrument to the tympanums of my hallways and doorways, and of my ceilings and floorboards, I should not be able to understand what the voice of the other end was saying; and this even if that voice was speaking in a language I could understand, High School French, for instance. I know this in my heart, and even if I am somewhat abashed in the realization I know facts are facts and to suppose otherwise would only amount to a futile exercise in self-delusion. So the ringing of my inner telephone reminds me of the notion of transcendence, just as the creaking of my timbers and floorboards reminds me of the contingent state of human nature itself, at best a double thing possessed of contrary elements forever locked, as mortise and tenon are, in a union that is both perilous and precarious. Even the human face, which we take for granted on the fronts of houses, on the siding of storage bins and warehouses, in the swaying treetops and cumulo-nimbus, even at the bottom of bodies of water, like Lake Tisane over by Rorschach, are but as a meaningless tussle of breezes, idle commotion signifying mere shilly-shally, signification beyond sign-post.

3[Laugh it Off]:

My world and everything within it is formed of pictures; pictures overlapping other pictures, pictures within pictures, pictures simple. I dreamed once that at the end of my foot was not a claw, but an eye. That I see through, at the very tip of my savage appendage. And do all my dreams take place while I am asleep? Who can tell?

But whether asleep or not I know that when I speak, as now, what I am describing primarily is a picture, although what is to be done with this picture, or any of the ones I have pictured here, is far from clear. Of what use are they? Laugh it off, you say; but I cannot laugh it off, for the picture seems to spare us both labor and its cold reversal, levity. It already points to a particular use. This is how it takes us in.

In any event, I notice my entire edifice has begun to tilt, and I begin to swim in the sandy dunes where I had thought to remain perched forever, forever impregnable in my steadfastness. I have begun to sink into the quartz-stuccoed, cavernous interior I have myself dug. The geode of my own strange folly. As I tilt more I begin to break apart and become severally voiced. Olden times speak through my riven hulk. My right triangle topples over so slowly to an irritating Isocelean incline. Between my toes—whose toes are we discussing, my dear?—a long growing filament; I give it a strong tug, and lean over even more precipitously as the banshee voices of my useless, outmoded architecture whine and shriek; whining and wailing what presage? What multivariate termination? As I draw out the single strand and pull, pull, pull, I discover by microscopic examination that it is one long human hair, and I am drawing myself down, inexorably down toward a quicksand vortex where I shall become embalmed forever within the ruby geode of my own excavation. Deep within Muazzez, the redeeming repetition I so much strove to uncover has failed to appear, for at its very core, curled up so tightly, is only hair. A single strand of hair. So tightly wound up one could bat the whole world, the whole small, mad world of Muazzez, like a tennis ball. Face facts, I boom as the quicksand swallows me whole, clear up to my rusty clanking sign, ...y.... Muazzez is a world of hair.

CAVE GIRL

by Deborah Levy

My sister Cass thinks that ice-cubes in the shape of hearts will change her life. Cass is a stone age girl. Does the whole atmosphere business: turns off all the lights in the house and burns up a bargain pack of Tesco night lights. After a while she makes herself a piña colada, lies on the bed and sobs to a CD. It's hard to believe that small silver disc can spin her to the other side and back. Cass wants to be somewhere else. She has been abducted by visions of paradise that are not here, and to punish me for being happy, she twisted her hair into a tight plait and cut the whole lot off. I used to be scared of open spaces until I realized it was indoors that was the most frightening.

At night the satellite dishes on the roofs and walls throw spectral shadows across the tamed gardens. I have grown to love the bronze door knobs in the shape of jungle beasts, a lion's head, a tiger, a snake. These seem to me to be caveman icons on the doors of the bankers and dentists who live here, a clandestine way of keeping in touch with The Divine. Sometimes I lie flat out on the gravel under one of the new shrubs and feel the electricity charge me up. The TV repeats. The CD players and video hires, personal computers, microwaves, dishwashers and hairdryers. It gives me a thrill because I know the world is very old.

At night, I sometimes feel that An Ancient will find me shivering under a stone, clutching a box of fried chicken and chips. He will teach me how to sharpen flint and I won't know what to teach him cos I don't know how to make antibiotics.

And then one night Cass told me her secret. Unburdened her confidence on my white trash shoulders. She said she wants a sex change. What into a man? No, she said, into a woman. But you are a woman. I want to be another kind of woman.

What does that mean Cass?

I want to be light hearted, she begins, and already the worry lines on her forehead come into focus. I want to be airy and indifferent. My sister is whispering this to me under the new shrub in the dark. Her sad girl breath makes me dizzy. She says, I want to have blue eyes for a start, that's the trick. Blue eyes are the gentlest, sexiest, most ambivalent eyes. My blue eyes will cut out, but they will also be very much there. When Cass says "very much there," a thrill jolts through my stomach. She chews her nails for a while and then says, I want to be less real—I want to be more of a simulation of a woman.

I'm glad the gravel is clean and all the cats well fed here. I hate the way butchers display the inside of animals on silver trays. Cass continues talking, her eyes shut tight and the light from the little lamppost chuffing over her shorn black hair. I've found a surgeon to do the op she says in a flat voice. I can already see him drilling a hole in my sister's forehead with a rusty nail. Time to do some press ups and put in the oven chips.

There's been a pile up on the motorway nearby. First there was noise and then there was silence. A collision. Agitation and then calm. Chrome, meat, blood, petrol, glass, skin, tar, hair. Bone and steel. Plastic and plastic. I'm dying for a milk shake.

So this woman walks up the gravel drive, long limbed in sandals even though it's raining. Dragging her bag with limp wrists, smiling under a dirty blond fringe and the bluest eyes, kind of flat eyes, can't get inside em but she's got energy in her body and she says hi bruv.

Cass said "hi bruv" like she's never said it before. There's something about her voice, it just twinkles over me, and she's so cool. Let's sit outside even tho it's raining—she smiles and takes out Swiss cheese from her bag—sets about effortlessly slicing it, and she keeps whooshing her fringe out of her eyes with her long fingers and nibbling at the cheese like she's got a bit of an appetite. She makes a shivering noise and looks at me as if to agree that this is a crazy idea but so what, and we drag our chairs out into the garden, no sun to damage our skin structure and we don't have to talk like we used to.

When Cass speaks it's like she's trailing the tips of her fingers across the surface of a swimming pool, no gloomy silences or deep breaths before saying something truly hideous, and she smells of burnt sugar and antiseptic. She laughs with her eyes and she is all here, but she's also cut out, and she wonders whether we shouldn't plan some pleasure outings, like should we go to the cinema and see something light hearted—what do I think?

This is the unhappiest day of my life. I think I'm in love with my sister. I want to find out who she is. I want to have sex with her and stare into her pretend blue eyes.

There's a pile of bloody feathers on the gravel. A cat has caught, Dickie, the neighbor's budgie, named after the famous cricket umpire. Dickie Bird's eyes have been gouged out and his head chewed up. Bird stuff everywhere. Intestines under the new rose bush.

I tell Cass what's on my mind, and she says, I don't think so. See you are my brother and I am your sister and then she says, you'll find a girlfriend soon, and anyhow why don't we go inside and watch that stoopid sit com we like? I'm frightened to go inside and breath all over the wallpaper.

The man who does the TV weather for the nation, finished his forecast tonight by saying "beware of the chill winds to come." Another thing. The ice in my Pepsi just jumped out of the glass on its own accord. I'm sick with longing for the new Cass. She has become airy. A bird, a hunting bird. When she eats cake, she breaks it up in the palm of her hand, and kind of pecks the crumbs into her mouth. It drives me crazy. I'm also scared that at any moment Cass will morph into her old self. What happened to it anyway? The men around here all make excuses to talk to her when they get back from work. I've noticed how they chat from inside their cars, air conditioning on and the windows down—nothing makes sense. Cass leans in towards them, she is all there, light hearted and smiling.

I ask her why she bothers talking to those men. I know she knows they're boring so what does she get out of it?

I told you, she says, I want to be more of a simulation of a woman. I want to be less real. The surgeon did well. He really fiddled with my controls—she breathes out when she says this, like something amazing has happened to her.

I want An Ancient to find me now. I need to talk to him. I want to ask him if he's scared of the dark and shadows and things lurking in the sea and thunder like I am, and if he ever had a sister who changed herself like Cass did. Her blue eyes took me in, and froze me out.

DAYS OF OR

by Adrian Dannatt

There is something about the Oak Bar at the Plaza as afternoon light starts to dim down into evening that brings reassurance to even the most justifiably agitated. It is as if the setting within and the waning without merge into a solid mood that unites interior and exterior, dark walls and somber skies acting together to neutralize the soul. It is so sad, so redolent of wasted hours, those hours that slowly, mysteriously become wasted months, lives, that it cannot but cheer.

Sherban watched darkness mount and was content. He had just finished lunch and was enjoying a last Armagnac in contemplation of leaving. Not that he actually intended to leave for some while. Dusk came early and he knew from experience coldness and wetness came with it. Here everything was inherently toasty, burnished and agleam as if rubbed down daily by gold bullion wrapped in brown velvet. His host, Marcus Friedman, had left him with a relatively rare Bolivar to smoke and, more importantly, an open tab at the bar. In exchange for paying for everything, Friedman subjected Sherban to a detailed account of the dreary machinations of his job. Marcus hated working for his father, who in return didn't seem much keener on his son's employment. Conversation revolved around whether Marcus should leave, when he should leave, and his incapacity to do so. Clearly this was not very interesting. It was only because of the cruel paradox that Sherban loved the atmosphere and ambiance of expensive restaurants but did not have the means to pay for them that he partook of such talk. How much more entertaining life could have been if Sherban had not been born with a lust for antique paneling, private dining rooms, discreet service. If he had never developed his craving for obscure wines and seasonal truffles he would not have to listen to a whole range of boring things. Oh, for a diet of toasted cheese and the company of those he found amusing. It never occurred to Sherban that he himself might work, make money, save and scrimp and thus afford to buy his own dinner, that perhaps he could even eat alone at his favorite table in the city, with a book propped proud. But between the boredom of a job and the boredom of having to listen to other people he chose to endure that which provided the more immediate form of gratification.

"Another, Professore?" Strange that the barman still thought of him as a distinguished academic—a mix-up over visiting cards stretching back to his days at Yale Law School.

"Grazie, Paolo." He took the glass in his palm, feeling the warm liquid through bowl and stem, letting the acrid flavor haunt his nostrils. Savored like this, one glass could last till nightfall. He assumed Marcus had not set a limit on his tab, yet it would be embarrassing to find out differently. Sherban had nothing in his pockets but a subway token and one very large crisp banknote, sadly of Ukrainian denomination. How he disliked the messiness of attempting to leave a bar and being asked if he could "settle up," having to explain that it had all been taken care of earlier. When you never carried money, like the British Royal Family, every transaction became a minefield of potential hostility. It made you acutely aware of how every deed or venue required a symbolic exchange of cash. Going anywhere, doing anything depended on a series of tiny tithes and small bribes, a network of nodal points at each of which money was required, like medieval town gates. If you tried to get through a day without spending a single coin, the sheer number of these monetary checkpoints—fiscal barriers—became painfully apparent.

Sherban yawned, impressed that he could be almost as boring in his freedom as Marcus was in bondage. Every time they met it was Sherban's role to sympathize about the impossibility of working at Friedman, Friedman & Friedman and to suggest alternatives. He had already come up with an exclusive cabaret on the top floor of the Chrysler Building, a documentary film production company in California, an upstate New York vineyard, and a pleasingly loss-making publishing house. Each time Marcus brimmed with excitement, scribbling strategy on the back of his Hoare's checkbook (a year at Oxford had led him to favor British banking) before going back to his job for another decade. Sherban was quite as aware as Marcus that none of these alternative jobs would ever be realized. Marcus would carry on working for his father and complaining bitterly about it for as long as he, the father, lived. It was just as well these other plans were strictly theoretical, because most of them would have involved Sherban.

He was too polite to refuse any offer of employment. "But would you really be able to come into an office every day, could you see yourself getting in on time in the morning, working late?"

He was always being asked these questions. Every time he reassured Marcus that indeed he relished the prospect of employment, regular hours, a fixed salary; and good Lord, maybe even a health plan.

"I've been lingering in the margin for quite a while now. Actually, not even the damn margin itself, but rather those holes in the margins where the file binder goes. It's time I got back onto the main page, write myself into history, y'know."

Why did he have to pretend he wanted a job when everyone knew it simply wasn't true? Merely his perverse obedience to some archaic law of social obligation. Luckily those weekly offers of screenplay collaborations, book editing, PR positions, and curatorial assistantships, the usual flotsam of the churning cultural machine, always faded away.

Instead he was alone in the luminous gloom of the Oak Bar, among the last of the lunch guests, or was it the first of the evening crowd?

Alone he admired the falling, fallen darkness and skeletal trees of the park, the tone of his Armagnac, and the way it held the very last of any light in the room. Sherban enjoyed his solitude and proud record of unemployment at another day's end. But he was aware sadness lurked right outside the door, the dismal weather of reality, the drizzle of dailiness that would surround him.

The best to hope for was that somebody he knew, a friend of a friend, an acquaintance of an acquaintance, would secure his passage through the rest of the evening. These things were tricky to arrange, the precise mathematics of chronology and cost. He had been at the Plaza since twelve-thirty. Marcus had insisted on an early lunch due to business, leaving for Sherban a tricky gap to be straddled between afternoon and evening sessions, an hour or so during which he would be lost without sponsor, patron, or alibi adrift in this bar awaiting providential synchronicity.

"Are you waiting for someone, Professore?"

The barman was an expert at such delicate issues.

When someone sat in the same place doing nothing, it took decades of waiterly experience to tell the difference between those who wanted to stay and those who wanted to be prodded into action. Paolo remembered the Professore had once performed some amazing card tricks, dropping the pack onto the floor "by mistake" but predicting the order they would land. Moreover, the Professore's guest that evening had been someone of singular importance, both familial and financial, to the hotel. This florid young man of importance, with the red cheeks of a schoolboy and an appropriately enthusiastic manner, had confided in Paolo, drunkenly, "You know this chap is the most extraordinary genius, degrees from every university, Ph.D.s and diplomas pouring out of him, absolute first-rate mind, and never had a job in his life."

Paolo was suitably impressed; he would have been so whatever this man said.

"No job, never! Not a single job. You know how he makes a living?"

Paolo shook his head as required, ready to be awed.

"Card tricks, nothing else!"

For Sherban this had indeed been a brief phase, a sticky patch that lasted no more than four months, though his memory retained the rusty stain of certain tricks. He had met an Iranian backgammon pro who in exchange for lessons in the seduction of American females gave Sherban the ABCs of card feints. All you needed were the standard tricks, a banal repertoire, and then everything else depended on bluff, blarney, and myth. Sherban had been fairly inept at the tricks themselves, but his look had been convincing: seventies Dior tinted glasses, sockless, faux Gucci loafers, a naval blazer with verdigris on the buttons, and a cowboy shirt featuring diamonds and aces.

Such history stood Sherban in good stead with the barman. Thus Paolo happily let him slip down from his barstool without a tip and with a couple of drinks technically not accounted for.

Sherban weaved across the room, expecting at any moment to be brutally shot in the back with a cry of, "Signore? The check!" He was not steering well, being drawn toward occasional tables as if by magnetism, the doors ever distant. He turned to wave goodbye to Paolo with dignified cordiality—a risk—but the good man was back at work polishing glasses, awaiting the evening crowd.

He wandered through the lobbies of the hotel and stopped off in a kiosk to flick through the *New York Review of Books* to see how various acquaintances were doing. He had difficulty concentrating on the contributors' notes. One friend had gained tenure, but Sherban was not in the mood. Academic rituals seemed too distant when he was faced by the cold facts of a winter night, the slush and streets awaiting him. Sherban realized he was shirking, malingering, refusing to confront what lay before him. He felt a chill pass through him, the lightning strike of doubt that he had dreaded for years. He knew how nerve failure began, with the smallest ball of insecurity, and how it spread, paralyzing all one's resources. It was a gray mold, a shadow, that crept up from within and occupied the soul, leaving one with all the tics of bonhomie but incapable of a single smile. As with top salesmen, Sherban had known of legendary installment-plan spielers, fêted country club drageurs who one day, after thirty years of aplomb, find themselves a little reluctant to make even one more cold call. They put it off, don't have the right number, need one more coffee. And when they head back to the phone there is no longer any hiding from the fact that they have lost the confidence they once had. They cannot summon the nerve to make any more such calls, though they have done so every day for decades. One morning like any other and the jig is up, the job is over. Because even when you have plucked up the courage to make that call it will never work as before, because everyone can smell the fear; the greasy anticipation of failure fulfills itself.

Sherban had in the past left the grandest and warmest of hotels with relief, feeling free from the conventions of the toasted muffin brigade, a surge of optimistic intrigue at what might come next; whether better or worse, it would at least be different. Yet now he loitered in the Plaza lobby in a manner that might eventually alert security. And what a truly preposterous hotel to find oneself stuck in, as if the Plaza still retained a shred of mystique with its vulgar Monopoly money status. How long had he been lost in these yellow corridors, a lifetime of prevarication stumbling up and down the rococo dog day looking for exits? It was the shame in even visiting such a hotel, let alone lingering, that drove Sherban to action. He pulled his coat tighter, cupped hands to savor one last time the memory of Armagnac, and strode outside.

It was clearly beastly out by even the most optimistic salesman's estimation. Not exactly sleet or drizzle, but a cruel mixture of the two adjusted specially for single people whose shoes were not well soled, cold wind with a cunning horizontal approach that no umbrella could successfully resist. Dusk for good now. But the steps of the hotel were beautifully lit, proffering a warm welcome, and even though they had so obviously been designed to create a gleaming 3-D advertisement, a blatant, vulgar marketing gambit, they still could not fail to entice. The doormen in their uniforms with big umbrellas, the reflected sheen of water on diamond paving, polished rails, the creak of revolving

doors, how could one have the strength not to return? Plunging his
hands into his pockets, Sherban was delighted to encounter the thumb
stub of a cigar. His luck was changing. He'd forgotten the half Davidoff
Churchill he'd plucked out of an ashtray at the Yale Club last night.
He'd been slightly embarrassed when he realized it was still lit.
Minutes later a man had returned to his armchair with a cognac and,
after adjusting bifocals and finding his place in Gibbon, had reached
blindly, absentmindedly, for his cigar, letting his fingers roam over the
ashtray. Sherban had left the room trailing smoke from the pocket of his
dinner jacket, a jacket that had already seen a great deal of combat over
the years. He now placed the chunky stub of tobacco in his mouth, feeling rich again. Under the awning of the hotel in such tedious meteo-
rology, things were not so bad.

To think this had once been his favorite place. To smoke a cigar
watching the storm bucketing down, the gold statue looming through
the mist like some promise, the prow of a ship of wealth and beauty,
where once he had stood drunk with the potential of this city—a
Noah's Ark of impossible breeds, a freighter weighted full of hope.
Now he was waterlogged, a tramp steamer, stamped teamster, beaten
back to port.

Sherban crossed to the other side of the steps, as if zigzagging back
and forth might grant the courage to launch forward. He approached a
lady of perhaps, just, her twilight fifties under an umbrella decorated
with leaping cats. Her head scarf, tight as a turban, was similarly decorated with prancing felines and she smoked a cigarette with singular
dedication.

"I don't suppose you have a light for my battered old Churchill?"

She glanced at him sideways, a suspicious squint, looked him up
and down.

"My husband knew Churchill, he even went to visit him in
Washington during the war. Something to do with intelligence work,
it was never fully explained."

"Probably encryption. The best minds were set to work on encryption," added Sherban hopefully, taking the cigar from his mouth.

"I don't think my husband was one of the best minds. He was a number cruncher, as they used to call them." She made no indication of reaching for matches.

"They still do. The city is full of number crunchers. They take the best apartments."

There was a sadness in his tone, but he persisted. "Number crunchers did much encryption."

"A Churchill is also the name of a cigar, named after him presumably?"

He agreed and lifted the tip to the flame of her lighter, a veritable petroleum Shiva that danced this way and that in gusts of wind. The demi-Churchill glowed slowly.

"How extraordinary." The woman was staring at Sherban's feet. He shifted them with a certain shyness. Could their odor reach that far?

"My husband, whose wartime record we were just discussing for no apparent reason, had exactly the same pair of shoes. Identical."

"Correspondent?" he ventured, turning them this way and that now with pride.

"Two-tone we called them then. He bought them on one of our trips to Panama and, I have to be honest, I was never quite sure about them. Well, I mean, in his case..."

"No, no." He waved away her blush. "I know exactly what you mean. I've also had my doubts, serious doubts have tortured me some mornings. But they are the only ones I have..."

Sherban immediately regretted this tone of self-pity.

"I mean, of course, the only two-tone shoes I have. The only pair like this."

But the woman was not to be fooled. Her expression was now severe, staring down.

"Show me your right foot again, I just saw something." He obliged.

"There! Stop! Just as I thought. What is that?"

And what was he expected to say? A unique design feature, special aeration?

"It is a hole, isn't it? A huge hole!"

She seemed happy about the whole thing, as if she had just proved something.

"I have a hole in my soul," admitted Sherban.

"A hole in your sole must be repaired."

She stamped out her menthol filter with the determination of a new beginning. "This may sound crazy, but I simply cannot allow you to walk around in the rain with such holes in your shoes. It is my duty to stop you from catching pneumonia, make sure you have adequate shoes."

"That's awfully sweet of you, really..."

She put a hand up to halt him, imperious as a dowager arresting a postillion.

"I should put my glasses on and inspect you properly. One's always hearing these awful stories about serial killers." She adjusted her spectacles and nodded approval.

"Entirely presentable, as I first thought. What are you supposed to be doing now?"

"Doing?" Sherban looked bewildered. "Well, I didn't really have plans as such, I just thought I might saunter around for a bit, get my bearings..."

"You'll be doing no sauntering, young man, not in this weather and those shoes. You're going to come home with me, I'm just a few blocks from here. I'm going to find you a pair of shoes that Saul never wore. What size are you? Nine? I knew it, exactly the same as Saul."

Sherban suggested she had better things to do than look after the shoes of a complete stranger.

"Nonsense, I just had an endlessly dreary tea with the cousins from Dallas. I really shouldn't bother with them at all, and I was just wondering what to do with myself."

The doorman hailed a cab, tipped his cap with a smirk.

"I hope they don't think I'm rustling some young gigolo back to my place," she giggled. "Do you think they noticed the way I picked you up?"

"I don't think anyone would mistake me for a gigolo," Sherban reassured her, a certain poignancy to his tone. "I fear I'm really rather past my sell-by date for such things."

"Nonsense." She looked ahead. "A little battered perhaps, nothing a night's rest won't restore."

They drove in silence and descended outside a large apartment building. Sherban made the shuffle toward his wallet, having long perfected the right rhythm between eagerness and tardiness.

She took hold of Sherban and asked in a whisper; "Are you, by any chance, Jewish?"

He grimaced. "I'm all sorts of things just like that and even more. Not practicing all of them."

"Of course not." She seemed jubilant. "I didn't think you were a Jew, which makes it perfect."

She swept him into the elevator and to the tenth floor. Sherban was insulted at having his putative Semitic heritage so briskly dismissed, but this was how she wanted it and he never took offense. The apartment was everything he had been expecting, serried shelves of knick-knacks, windows clearly not opened for years. Sherban stifled a yawn, so overpoweringly sleepy did it make him. She led him into a storage room and astonished him with the late Saul's shoe collection, a trove of brogues, golfing shoes, and Cuban heels lined up like a Hollywood wardrobe department.

"The only things of his I couldn't bear to throw away. Help yourself, please."

For these were the Days of Awe, the High Holy Days. His hostess, the redoubtable Mrs. Goldstein, believed in the *sefer ha-chaim*, the Book of Life opened for each individual on Rosh Hashanah, closed and sealed on Yom Kippur, and influenced during this interval by acts of contrition, repentance, and forgiveness. Acts of generosity, especially to goyishim, ensured an impressive entry in her book. In her study he found a full-page advertisement placed by followers of Rabbi Menachem

Schneerson. Whilst waiting for Redemption everyone should do everything in their power to bring it about by acts of kindness and charity. There was one paragraph marked with pencil that announced, "Indeed anyone, including you, could be responsible for the one caring act, that special gesture, the charitable gift which tips the scales in our favor and brings Redemption to all mankind." Sherban, it seemed, was the charity case who might tip the balance of the world toward Moshiach, harmony, prosperity, and knowledge. This certainly made him feel better. Not least about Mrs. Goldstein's future phone bill.

It was not disheartening to think that he might be personally responsible for a forthcoming paradise on earth. Bring on the messiah, he muttered, bring him on and let me go home.

BREAKING SUGAR

by A.L. Kennedy

"This bread tastes sweet."

"Mn?"

"This bread, it tastes sweet."

"No, I don't think so. Do you think so?"

"Of course I think so. I wouldn't mention it if I didn't."

Nick bit again, chewed warily. She watched him, also wary, but differently so.

"Sweet?"

"Sweet."

"Probably brushed against something at the baker's—you know."

"Brushed? It was the same last time."

"No, it was brown last time."

"But it was still sweet."

"Really? No, not sweet, surely."

"Yes. The bottom edge. Definitely. Sweet."

"I'll look into it."

"Look into it?"

"With the baker."

She couldn't tell him. He wouldn't understand.

He would fail to see her point. Nick was a clever man and she couldn't doubt that he was good, but they did have to keep their differences, here and there. She no longer saw any purpose in openly rehearsing their odd little shades of thinking and ideas because she would end up having to differ about them and differing was no fun.

What was more, differing simply involved you in saying out loud what you already knew you believed in. Your opposite number did the same. You both, quite inevitably, reinforced each other into deeper lines of difference.

Being experienced with Nick's mind, she could say it was a nice one but also that it clearly wasn't hers—not even close.

Except, of course, on the point of Mr Haskard: there they had been perfectly agreed. He was the right man for them. They were both very lucky in Mr Haskard, very fortunate and blessed.

In the matter of Mr Haskard's skin, which was pale and dry like a powdered bandage or perhaps more like an expensive tablecloth, they were fortunate. Nick's mother had a similar complexion which had once made her greatly sought after, quite apart from her many other, more spiritual, charms. Her glistening lips and the plush interior of her mouth—casually glimpsed—seemed hypnotically moist and intriguing—in comparison, for example, to her dusty chin. Whilst set against her arid cheeks and forehead her eyes were a pure liquefaction of lapping thought, brimming at every available hour of the night and day.

So Nick liked Mr Haskard.

In the matter of Mr Haskard's sociable habits of life which were charming, small and unintrusive, they were blessed. She would watch the corner of his mouth peaceably sucking his pencil's end as he studied his quality broadsheet's crossword and remember all her catalogue of relatives who had not ever left their newspapers properly folded after use and who had not been wise or honest in their responses to even the simplest of crossed words. She had always wanted to be on amicable terms with a man who could unravel puzzles and find delight in harmless, indoor games. Mr Haskard did not chew gum, cough nervously, practice a musical instrument or make immoderate use of alcohol, boot polish, toilet paper, coffee or boiled sweets.

Mr Haskard's beard, she and Nick had both agreed, was glorious. Thick and plump at the mouth; succulent, waggish and probably ticklish in a soft, fine, animal way, it was eminently touchable. Although they didn't dream of touching it, naturally. They only watched and grew used to the modesty of his half-concealed smiles; the sudden, red laughter; the possibilities of hidden bite.

They loved to know that Mr Haskard lived above them slightly like a quiet household god: slim and undemanding; up in the two connecting rooms they were happy he should rent. He patronized the launderette, rather than disturb their washing machine, left the kitchen truly cleaner than he'd found it, and she had never once feared that in the bathroom he might let himself drip astray.

And if she liked Mr Haskard better than Nick could, this was purely because she saw much more of him. Nick's life was increasingly full of lectures and night classes and intensive seminar weekends, while she stayed largely at home, not giving lectures or night classes or even considering seminars. The possibility had always existed, in a theoretical way, that they might both work. They might even have been capable of both holding posts at the same university, but their approaches had been too differing, as had their results. She had slowly found herself unable to relish her teaching or its success. Her life was now the house and its lodger and her research. When her private studies were complete, she intended to write a book. A good, exhaustive, independent book. Nick did not know of these private intentions because they would cause him to differ with her again.

Mr Haskard was in no way cowed by the intellectual atmosphere of his new home. She became oddly used to sitting with him by the window and sharing conversations during which he would offer up the proofs of his own learning.

"Your dress fastens at the back."

"Uh, yes it does. Nick bought it for me."

His left forefinger cradled his mustache and concentration winked behind his eyes. He swallowed, then held his own hands, patient and soft.

"Now I might well advise against that."

"I beg your pardon."

"Against backward fastening. There are three reasons."

"Really."

"Yes. In the first place all popular means of restraint for lunatics tend to fasten and buckle at the back. This is a bad association. In the second place, most clothing designed specifically for the dead, is opened, for postmortem convenience of dressing, at the back. This is a bad association. In the third place, backward fastening disempowers the wearer. Like an invalid or a child, one may not always be able to dress oneself unaided. One becomes dependent."

"Bad association?"

"Indubitably."

"I can see you've given this some thought."

"Some thought, yes. But I intend no offense. The dress is extremely flattering: offering, as it does, little or no distraction between the motion of your form and an observing eye. I do hope it is also comfortable."

"Quite. Thank you."

He perused her kindly, as if she were a well-phrased headline or a foreign stamp.

Nick had conceded that all Mr Haskard's rent money should be hers, to spend as she wished. This was not as good as earning her own money in the course of pursuing a satisfactory career, but it wasn't entirely without its rewards. Mr Haskard always settled promptly in advance with a fold of notes he passed from his hand to hers as if he were returning a happy loan. She never felt like his landlord—or landlady—more like a rediscovered friend.

"Another calendar month, then. Thank you."

"Thank you, Mr Haskard. And, ah, Mr Haskard?"

"Yes."

"Do you like it here?"

"Of course."

"You could pay quarterly, if you wanted to. You have been so reliable."

"Oh, no. No, thank you."

"To pay every month has something temporary about it, even untrusting. And frankly, I'm surprised you don't consider a mortgage—your job... I mean to say, are we going to lose you, Mr Haskard?"

"Well. I don't think so. Not for a while. To explain myself, I am something of a freelance. Systems analysts of my caliber—if I might be permitted to say so—are in constant demand. Mobility is an asset. And I also disapprove of mortgages and the blights of private ownership."

"I see. Thank you for answering so comprehensively."

Curiously, the demands Mr Haskard mentioned meant that she saw a good deal of him during the day. Often, while she was sleeping beside Nick, Mr Haskard's cellular telephone would quietly call him away to pad invisibly down the stairs and out across the city, its dark, geometrical streets and narrow lights. Tight up under her dreams he would search and correct the programs that ran for ever and nowhere within silicon labyrinths. He understood and tasted their atoms' electric shake, admonished the ignorance of their languages, loved and scolded like a father, noted each trace of disease.

Perhaps as she stirred her mid-morning tea, she would hear the open and shut of his door, the bath starting in to fill, the toilet flush. Perhaps she was glad to be aware of his company and to wait for his stepping into her kitchen, his face still slightly softened and colored with washing and sleep.

"Furniture should be taken outside as often as possible."

That morning Mr Haskard had unveiled an especially alarming lack of health within a banking company's patterns of thought and he was in fine spirits. There was almost a growl in his voice, a small wicked note that could make her wonder whether he lifted out all the diseases he found or simply changed their shape and then left them behind to switch and oscillate as signs of his passing.

"You have extremely suitable chairs here; they should be in the sun."

A young summer was blazing, its sunlight pleasantly bitter against the skin, and Mr Haskard pattered along the hallway at her side with a surprising lack of physical reserve.

Within minutes, at his suggestion, she caught herself lifting her kitchen chairs and table out onto the grass at the back of the house. She and Nick had bought the house for its garden—the kind of lazy, unruly expanse that made her imagine English country lunch parties and more money and security than one generation would ever be likely to amass. In fact, their garden wasn't so terribly big as all that, but had enough size to encourage imagination and to accommodate—she now discovered—a considerable range of furnishing.

Mr Haskard loped over the grass, positioning wastepaper baskets, table lamps, a random selection of ornaments. Her belongings looked tired and silly in the sun, too formal and too dull.

"Now you understand." She discovered he had been reading her face, the disappointment. "All of these things, they are really no protection, not in the face of nature. In this country, our surroundings are, currently, gentle; we can imagine they are tamed and patient. But when we take our indoors out of doors we see how dead and insubstantial our achievements and defenses are."

"Yes, Mr Haskard, I suppose we do." She sat down on one of her transplanted chairs and felt it sink into the grass.

"Would you like some pear?"

Mr Haskard had picked out a likely fruit from the bowl near his feet and was cutting it with a little pocket knife.

"Thank you."

In her mouth, the soft wedge of pear was sweet with a tiny shiver of salt where his thumb must have rested against its skin.

The sun dipped late and slowly for them, burning along the chair-

backs and sparking out from the group of cut-glass cream jugs Mr
Haskard had set on the table. Before dark, and before Nick returned,
they knew without telling each other that everything should be back
where it used to be: warmer and scented with grass and the open air,
but back where it used to be.

She walked behind Mr Haskard as he picked up the bread-bin from
close by the hedge. Their shadows darted ahead of them, narrow and the
color of wet earth rather than of darkness.

"Look." Her voice stopped him, held him absolutely, until he could
execute a turn to face back at her. Startled by the obedience of his
expression, she repeated herself, "Look."

"Oh, yes. Our shadows."

"But look at them."

He did so, quietly, neatly, with one hand smoothing at his beard.
"Tell me."

"Well." She wanted to be clear for him, to match his patterns of
expression and then join him inside them. Generally, she had noticed
his sentences felt as comfortable as her own within her mind. "Well, I
see myself there, pulled along through time to something I can't know.
I see how strange and flexible I can be. A little bit of sun can tip me
out in the grass like paint." He had, she noted, half-closed his eyes to
listen. Her voice would be alone with him in the dark. "This makes it
very clear how small I am and how tiny any risk I take could ever be.
Therefore, how easy."

He nodded, appreciating her point, and considered the parallel pro-
gression of the two shapes they cast on the lawn. "I see time." He began
walking towards the house, stopped and without looking back said, "I
always do see time. And I think that I would rather walk this way, with
my back turned on the sun, and see time laid down at my feet, so that
I can understand what I mean. So I have myself in perspective. I like
that. Thank you."

Having given them courteous notice, Mr Haskard would leave them alone for a matter of days every two or three months. In their different ways, they felt his absence, but were surprised at how great an influence he could be even when he was gone.

At these times, she and Nick talked together a little more than they might have done and perhaps, in addition, they genuinely listened to whole sections of what each one said to the other. Nick would come home sharp, rather than spinning out the time around night classes and ultimately returning, sodden with the smell of cigarettes, gin and sweat. He had occasionally given her cause to doubt him. But not now.

"Come on."

"Not here."

"Why not. He's away, come on. We used to do it out of the bedroom all the time."

This was a lie, but an attractive one. She still shook her head, smiling, shrugging out of his arms.

"Why not?"

She backed through the doorway and into the hall, keeping her focus on his eyes, imagining the tilt of his emotions, his likely response. "Not here, upstairs."

"Ach."

"No, right upstairs."

She watched Nick thinking, beginning to smile.

Mr Haskard's rooms were easily opened—she had the spare key. They crept through his dustless, orderly study, vaguely aware of the books he'd added, the small colored pictures he'd hung on his walls. She forced on, pushed back the door to his bedroom, plain and peaceful.

For no reason she could imagine, she sat up on Mr Haskard's naked dressing table and waited for Nick to look at her.

The table was built at an oddly convenient height. Her dress, Nick discovered, fastened and unfastened completely with a number of tiny buttons at the front.

They easily accomplished the necessary act and allowed a degree of unusual passion to overcome them both. She welcomed Nick into her arms and self, closing her eyes and inhaling the brusque, warm scent of Mr Haskard which was, quite naturally, all that filled his rooms.

For some considerable time, she continued her intimate life in much this way. Whenever Mr Haskard left, she found she would take advantage of his living space; would cautiously enjoy his unwitting accommodation.

Nick always remembered to open a window and thoroughly dissipate their tell-tale ghosts of perspiration and she checked they removed any items they might have brought with them and then left to lie.

Whenever Mr Haskard was at home, she continued to enjoy the pleasure of his company and to think—now and then—of her uncovered skin against his door-frame, his wallpaper, his carpet, his dressing table, his wardrobe and his desk.

"Might I ask you something, Mr Haskard?"

"Yes."

"Where do you go to? When you go."

"I'm afraid I don't understand."

"When you leave us; your trips away. If you don't mind my asking. It's really no concern of mine, naturally."

"Ah. Where do I go—that's easy: I go to apologize."

"I'm sorry?"

"No. I am sorry. That's why I go. Will I show you? Yes, I think I will."

He motioned her further along the hallway, smiled and ascended the stairs at a trot. She followed. His door was unlocked, needed only a gentle turn of his wrist, a light push.

"Come in. I was a little fast for you there, I think."

"No, no."

"But you're out of breath."

"Then maybe you were faster than I thought."

"You should exercise."

"I've been taking more lately."

"Good, good. We all have to, don't we. Please. Come in."

She moved inside with him, noting the unfamiliar signs of his occupancy.

"I don't mean to disturb you."

His lamp was set to shine at a soft angle and his cardigan draped easily over a chair. His desk was studiously cluttered with papers and a partly folded map. She felt a stranger here, breathing in the strong new presence of fresh laundry and shaving lotion and warm, unfamiliar skin.

"You're working—I don't want to take up your time."

"You don't. Any more than I want you to. And no one can work all the time. Come here now."

His hand extended smoothly, heavily towards her and she stepped to meet it, to feel the calm pressure of his fingers, the tug in. When she was standing beside him, he released her again and spoke.

"This is where I go."

Because she was looking at his face, she did not at first understand him.

"Here. This is where I go."

He nodded to the pictures on his wall, made a neat smile.

Photographs. Regular, rectangular commonplace photographs of uneven fields and hillsides, strangely insubstantial buildings. Each of his images had a certain emptiness, as if he had arrived too late to catch the heart of it.

"This is only a selection. I travel extensively."

"But there's nothing here."

"I suppose not—not any more—but that's why I go. There, the tower you're looking at, is in York. Built to replace the wooden one, burnt around the city's Jews. Here: torture and execution of Welsh resisters to English occupation. Here: a supremely avoidable mining disaster. Here: murders from the Bloody Assizes. People remember these things, the names and the places can be found out."

"Why?"

"This one is near the place where I was born: the pool where

Witchfinder General Matthew Hopkins was thrown, bound hand and foot. He floated, so they burned him as a witch, like the hundreds he'd condemned. A lovely place. I do go back there, but not as often as I'd like. No time."

"Why are you doing this?"

"Because I know what these places were; I know what happened. I can't be sure how I began to, but now I do know and I disagree. As deeply as I can remember, I disagree, so I drive where I have to and I speak to what people I can and then we all know. I also take photographs and pray."

"Does it do any good?"

"Yes. I make myself content. I hope I may go on to Africa, India, North and South America. There are so many places and so many times, naturally increasing, and no one has ever regretted them formally. I can see I may well be busy until I die. I cannot live in an evil present with any comfort, I constantly feel the harm banked up around me. Perhaps I shall never leave this island. There is so much here to take into account. And perhaps we should go downstairs now. It's such a lovely day, I would hate to miss all of the sun."

She watched him take a chair out into the garden and sit; gently, slowly rolling his shirt-sleeves up on his thin arms, and she thought how strange it was that all the harm and death he must have in his head didn't show. He was only ever peaceful.

The next time she embraced Nick up in Mr Haskard's rooms, she found her eyes ticking aside to the photographs lined near the bed. She considered for a moment the drive he was making that morning, away from her house—the square, where a peaceful crowd was fired on—Glencoe, full of politics and death—two forts of armed occupation—then Inverness and Culloden and more of the ache and the darkness of old blood. Mr Haskard had outlined his route. He had also talked of the beauty he hoped to encounter in the available countryside.

"What's wrong?"

Nick could be remarkably alert, even as he held her, even as he seemed to lose himself in the thought and the reality of her moving reflection in another man's looking-glass.

"Oh, I was thinking of Mr Haskard, how long he would be away."

"Really."

Although her answer had been almost true it seemed to displease Nick. He seemed to have misinterpreted her sense, to have given her a different meaning.

"We don't have to bother with him now."

"No. Of course."

"This is our house."

"His room."

"Oh yes, and his bed."

"No. Nick."

"We gave him a double bed—the poor old bastard doesn't need it. Why not?"

"It's... It would cause problems."

"We can deal with them."

She washed and dried Mr Haskard's sheets, re-made his bed, replaced his folded pajamas under the pillow where they would be safe. He must have another set for when he traveled. Unless he slept naked while he was away from them.

When she held her hands up to her face they smelt of cotton and of night and of her certainty that she would never say what she had done, even though Mr Haskard might well be able to guess.

Nick left to teach his evening class and stayed out late—lost in a discussion too interesting to curtail.

She only realized she had not been waiting for Nick's return when he had settled himself coolly to her left and her restlessness remained.

Three hours later the front door snapped and sighed open. Mr Haskard was home. She lifted herself fully awake and listened for the fast, light movement on the stairs below, beside and then above her, the gentle setting down of a traveling bag. Mr Haskard creaked softly across her ceiling, became silence and almost allowed her to sleep before his descent began again. She could only think he had noticed their intrusion and abandoned his rooms.

The kitchen door was closed when she reached it; a big, numb dark swung out to meet her as she moved inside. She must, after all, have miscalculated, misheard. Mr Haskard must really be sleeping upstairs as usual—only her guilt could have made her think otherwise.

"Do close the door."

She span left and felt her hand bark suddenly against wood.

"I am sorry. I imagined you knew I was here."

"Mr Haskard?"

"Certainly not an intruder. You didn't think I was?"

"No."

"Good." He didn't whisper, his words made one low, even tone. In the absolute blackness, his sound was almost solid. "If you step forward and very slightly right, you'll come to a chair. When you sit I will be beside you. Mind the table."

"It's so dark."

"Yes, I've drawn the blinds and the curtains. It has to be dark."

"For your photographs?"

"Oh, no. I haven't the slightest interest in their manufacture. This is something else. Watch."

She listened as Mr Haskard's hands made a gentle disturbance near her, then felt a minute shudder through the air. Then she heard a soft, sudden impact, saw a splash of violet light. Another stroke fell, more light.

"What are you doing?"

"Breaking sugar."

"No, what are you doing?"

"Breaking sugar, I said. Here—that's it, that's the hammer. Now—" Something slid towards her. "This is your bread-board, feel it?"

"Oh."

"Yes, and that's the sugar and there's a cube I haven't crushed."

"But—"

"Shhh. Check where it is and then move your hand. Hit it. Hit it hard."

She released a faint line of purple sparks where the hammer struck some scattered fragments.

"No, remember where it is. Now."

The tiny explosion flared for a moment and then bleached the dark against her eye.

"I've always loved to do this, since I was a boy. I would look at people stirring their tea and think I knew a secret—that sugar was more than sweet."

"It's not the sugar, its the crystal. The structure. If you crush a crystal, you get light."

"Which makes it even better. A law—under the most extreme pressures, there will be unexpected light. And no one can ignore the laws of nature."

"Mr Haskard, I think you should know—"

"I know." His fingers found her hand, pressed it calmly and lifted away. "I do know and I quite understand." The small push and heat of his words fell against her cheek. She reached into the numb dark and let herself explore the change from the soft hair by his ears to the harshness of whiskers grown over the skin and muscle of his cheek. When he swallowed, the muscle moved. There was a larger motion when Mr Haskard spoke. "That's really quite all right. I know."

She heard herself exhale in one long, live moment and swayed with a lift of weight from under her heart. The matter was very simple now and plain; she and Mr Haskard would break their sugar together and make their sugar dust. It would sweetly coat the floor, the table-top, their hands and clothing, even rise against their faces and flavor their lips. This would be only a small inconvenience, water-soluble and easily removed. A morning after sugar need never differ from a morning after undiluted sleep. They would have no reason to leave involuntary evidence.

"I happen to have some more sugar here, would you like to go on?"

She heard Mr Haskard carefully breathing like a large, close cat and knew she would be quite able to scrub their bread-board and to wash any possible imprint of sweetness away. She also knew she never would.

by Gilbert Sorrentino

A DESK

To make a narrative concerning a number of aspects of what we might agree to be life—a simple enough program, and one that will, perhaps, make us feel closer to the world that we inhabit, more or less, or would prefer to inhabit were things as they should be. By paying strict, even rapt attention to the false world that will deal with certain aspects of life, embroidered, as they must be embroidered, we *may* gain an understanding of, well, real things as they really are. This is how literature works, if "works" is the word. I do not describe narrative, or this narrative, as false so as to mock or denigrate it, but to differentiate it from the real world that exists, despite all, for all of us, outside the narrative. And that is so even if the narrative appears to represent a number of aspects of that real world in, as might be said, moving and well-written prose. This seeming fidelity to the actual, while the actual roars on, unalloyed and unaffected, is one of the gloomy mysteries of fiction, a mystery that remains unsolved to the present day, one, in fact, that deepens with each reader who attempts to order his or her life by means of what can be called fiction. Some also use this latter to educate themselves. There is no telling what a reader may do when alone with a book.

To the narrative, then, or parts of it, of the whole, of that which may ultimately "become" the whole. To that blessed narrative that may almost write itself. Then "control" would seem to be the word, although it is not the precise word, nor, for that matter, is "word." No matter, of course, for all may be corrected, changed, polished, all made clear in revision, the handmaid of "the writing process," for which nobody is too good. Writers often insist that they revise, again and again, everything that they write, for writing must be heartbreakingly difficult to be authentic, heartbreakingly and exhaustingly demanding. Even this small item will be, and has been revised, or is in the process, even as I "speak," revised to a fare-thee-well, an odd phrase, that, but one that comes to mind, another curious phenomenon of writing, the things that come to mind. That such things, or "phrases," are mostly old and warm and as well-worn as an old shoe is part and parcel of that inevitable process, so dear to life, called, well, called something. Perhaps writers don't revise everything, but they do revise a good deal, a lot, actually, if they are to be believed. Even the lacerating yet redemptive personal memoir, chockablock with scenes of guilt-ridden incest and battered puppies must be revised, revised and "touched up" and, well, fucked with, so to speak.

One of the many reasons that the demanding heartbreak of revision is so necessary is its role in making the absolute falsity of the representation of reality more precise; that is, to enable the falsity of the narrative, by dint of laborious revision and the odd polished phrase, to gleam with what seems to be—and why not?—truth. Or at least something that may well be mistaken for it, gleam to a goddamned fucking fare-thee-well, for that matter. So to speak, as it were, after all, in sum, and finally. To insist that the perfection of the false is much closer to the imperfection of the something or other is awkward, yes, but natural and casual. The phrase may be corrected, of course, in revision, or it already has been. Writing takes many drafts, usually, to emerge victorious— well, not precisely victorious—unless the writer is Proust, who was satisfied with one draft, and that a rough one. And, too, there are *Moby*

Dick and *Ellen Finds Out.* Look at them! Book reviewers are often cognizant of such phenomena, but rarely give us the benefit of their profound knowledge, given space restrictions, the demands of commerce and what readers prefer in the way of the good read. They know what makes a good read, else what's a heaven for, and know, too, that good reads make them—and us, always us—feel as if they know the people within the reads and have spent time with them, for instance, Holden Caulfield and others, good pals all. They will not be duped by cheap falsifications of reality, two-dimensional characters lacking not only flesh but blood, and always insist on well-written representations of the real, representations that read as if seeing something or other for the first time. Craft! Well-written craft! That's—or they're—the ticket. Life that throbs is also a big winner in these purlieus. And what of characters who, while throbbing, are redeemed, brought to justice, and speak nothing but the crispest dialogue? Hmm? Take Sarah Orne Jewett. Take Minister Handy. Authors who have made a world that one can reach out and touch, gingerly, to be sure, but touch nonetheless. Living, loving, lolling, losing, and hating. It's not only as good as life, some argue, but better, at least in selected passages. Can the remarks on *Dark Corridors of Wheat*, pointedly made by Patricia Melton Cunningham, be easily forgotten? Huh? Well, this is what one may call, with little fear of contradiction, writing that matters on writing that matters. Consider *The Paris Review*, and other items, if you dare.

So that one evening, sitting at my desk, a comforting pipe glowing near at hand, a hand that seemed to belong to someone else, as did my face, yes, some other face, or, perhaps, the face of the Other, I put the final touches on a letter to a friend, Pat Cunningham, to be precise, a woman who knew the meaning of trust, friendship, logrolling and the lunge for the main chance, when I noticed some impedimenta on the desk, impedimenta that I gazed at as if gazing at it for the first time. Slowly, I came to realize that if I could find a language that permitted these items representation, I could, perhaps, reach out and touch them in all their flesh and blood and flawed humanity. But I had to overcome the terror of the blank page, that famous blank page which all writers confront each and every day that they sit down to cover that blank page with love and laughter, brooding despair and so on and so forth. There is nothing as terrible as the blank page, and so I had informed Pat in my letter, a letter that lay, somewhat forgotten, near the blank page that, too, was slowly in danger of becoming somewhat forgotten. On the other hand, the blank canvas, the blank music paper, the blank notebook are all equally terrifying to the painter, the composer, the notebook-keeper, and there looms, too, the blank stage for the actor, the dancer, the monologist, the hilarious comic. Yet who was it who pointed out that "empty" in such instances would be more precise than "blank"? Good friends are rare, and even rarer are those who pop up just when things are going fairly well. You can count on it, or them.

Could a character be evoked who might evoke the items or disjecta on my desk? A simple noun for each, if properly "handled," might do the job. And yet, what job was it that there was to be done? Lest confusion reign I decided on a handful of nouns, or, as the blank page demanded be uttered, the substantive. Should I show rather than tell, or, better yet, better yet infinitely more difficult, display rather than show? If I could succeed in displaying, or even showing the spondulicks on my desk, *in context*, in picture language, i.e., language that is like a picture, or pictures, lots of them, of course, colorful when needed, it goes without saying, perhaps the reader, ever hungry for actual experience, will be able to reach out and touch them in all their flesh and blood and interesting formal qualities, not to mention all the other things. I know, of course, that awesome powers of revision may abrogate or defer or even occlude, occult, and abort such heady fantasies of literary perfection, yet I feel that I have no choice but to press on. Revision, as noted by Gide, Irving, Bly, Tough, and Epstein is a harsh mistress, finally. Consider the work, the entire opus of the "vagabond prose master" of the Western reaches, or at least the reaches of Los Altos, the town whose motto wisely states, "Our Cars Are O.K.," that wise yet warm penman, Wallace Stegner, of whom his various assistants have noted, *as one*, that even his first drafts were revisions, as were, doubtlessly, his ideas, of which there were plenty. Yet the hot, quick tears kept falling. This was what no-nonsense people called "writing, man."

But how to handle items, memorabilia, flotsam, and the like? How to approach the unforgiving blank page with ideas about such a *pasticcio*, if you'll pardon my French. For instance, is it enough to say "globe," "pen," "letters," or is that not enough? These sound rather haphazard, at best. How about: "Lifting my eyes from the plebeian fastnesses of the worn carpet, I found myself gazing, as if for the first time, at the moon, sailing through the cloudy skies like a bark of yore, like a kind of globe, a globe that had been sketched on the heavens by a ghostly pen, one used not to the demands of art but to the humble task of writing letters." The clock ticks quietly as the fly buzzes against the window globe, the sun warms my letters. All is but a dream.

But what wise man said that the dream is a rebus? And yet, what is the nature of a rebus? Is it flesh, blood, globe, or desk? Or all three? Joseph Cornell knew precisely what a rebus is, but who else knows, or even once knew? Must I return to the beginning, then? To the world of the empty page? Or the blank canvas? The fuckin' shit on my desk yearns for the dignity of representation. Yearns and pines, its blood throbbing as it has throbbed, yes, for aeons and aeons of clanging time gone mad with despair!

I rise and head for the window, gaze out at the winking lights far below on the valley floor. The night is cool, the wind sighs quietly, I feel as if I have walked into the kitchen to avail myself of a cold beverage. I feel as if I have lit a cigarette, filling myself and the house, filling all the crystal-clear air with death! Death that asks no quarter, that laughs with the wild laughter of unbridled love, that laughs and laughs and laughs as if laughing for the first time.

A JOKE

A Jewish matron on a jet from New York to Miami Beach introduces herself to her charming seat companion as Mrs. Moskowitz. After a drink and some light banter about the intrinsic problems of the aporia as it relates to *cutting velvet*, the charming companion comments on the clarity, brilliance, size, and cut of the enormous diamond ring on Mrs. Moskowitz's finger. This might have been Mrs. Cohen, by the by, but that's neither here nor there. And is that the glint of cupidity in the charming seat companion's eye? Mrs. Moskowitz sighs and reports, in a whisper freighted with the sort of fear that suggests the ineffable rebus of life itself that the ring, despite its beauty and obvious worth, has a curse on it, the—Moskowitz curse! The Moskowitz curse? queries the charming seat companion, who has, incidentally, beautiful legs, of the kind highly prized by any number of leering men, many of whom have subjected this young woman to a male gaze, gazing and gazing at her legs as if seeing legs for the first time. Their hot, quick tears fall fast as they chide theirselves for such crudity. The Moskowitz curse? the seat companion queries again, looking up quickly from her copy of *Dark Corridors of Wheat*. What, in heaven's name, is the Moskowitz curse?

Mr. Moskowitz, is the reply.

Or it could be Mr. Cohen, were this another joke. And it had better come out with numbers on it. What are you selling this year, cancer? Everybody's gotta be someplace, yingle, yingle. Max, carry me?

Maurice Bucks, the entertainment bigwig, is so rich, confides Mrs. Moskowitz, that he hires people to count the people who count his money. Ha ha. Or, perhaps, Bucks is so rich that he can find himself in a lather. Has everyone taken note of the fact that he is always immaculately dressed, even on the slopes at Moskowitz Pass? There is, too, that certain Kafkaesque something that he has about him, and even, some say, in him, like bacteria. Many are the nights when Maurice has stared at the blank walls and thought that he might be better off were he still that young actor who wanted nothing more than to direct, nothing more than to be surrounded by the sparkling conversation of the stars. Well, he often sighed.

Schultz is always dead in every joke he's ever lost his virile member in. The charming companion considers this and blushes deeply, rummaging for her biography of Sarah Orne Jewett by Wallace Stegner, the "Prairie Edition," of course.

"Not only is this joke anti-Semitic, misogynistic, and contributory to stereotypes about air travel, it is also, in some as-yet-undefined way, not very nice about the regular family kind of feeling right here in Miami Beach."

Speaking of Miami Beach, I am reminded of a joke, or is it more like a story? It is hard to know what with time, plodding time, clanging outside the window as I write—yet write—what? A man, hired by a rich contractor—a friend, by the way, of Maurice's—as a chauffeur, companion, gin rummy partner, fellow-bettor at divers tracks, both equine and canine, strong-arm, and occasional gunman, finds himself appointed, during those periods when the contractor is away on business, and by the contractor's alcoholic wife, as a dog walker. The boss's wife, Handy Sarah, a lifelong admirer of diamonds and other precious gemstones, is regularly soused by noon. The dogs, two prize boxers named Scotch and Soda, sorely try this rather refined thug's patience, for they demand to be walked at times that are highly inconvenient to his gaming instincts and erotic impulses. Speaking of the latter, he once contracted gonorrhea from a *fille de joie* whose stroll took in some two blocks of Collins Avenue. Encountering the same woman the next year, he remarked, "What are you sellin' this year, cancer?" This man's name was Patsy Buonocore. "Looks like another eyetalian joke, with numbers on it! Some more spaghetti with meat balls, sir?"

One day, upon returning to his employer's mansion on Biscayne Bay, Patsy, sobbing bitterly, reveals that the two dogs have drowned. "It seems that Scotch leaped into the drink to retrieve a little boy's beloved wind chimes, their *yingle-yingle* poignant on the wind, and Soda, seeing that Scotch was encountering some aquatic difficulties, followed. In jig time, both were swept out to sea." Some few months later, both dogs were fished out of a landfill, their brains scattered by .38 caliber slugs.

This is not actually a joke, but an anti-dog story, as mean-spirited as the one about the professors' wives working in the local brothel on their husbands' poker nights. One must admit to problems before one can be helped by those who have already admitted to problems. Look at the recovering alcoholics who can never top off a meal with cherries jubilee, rum baba, or sfogliatelle a la Proust. And yet rarely is there anything less than a wan smile and a chin up! A thousand drinks are never, ever enough, whatever that might mean. "Well, if you won't gimme another fuckin' drink, how about a haircut?"

Max, carry me to the bar? Who does Mrs. Moskowitz have to fuck to get *out* of this job?

Surely, is one of most beautifullest rings ever found on a desk, is it not so? And no more lip about Miami Beach, all right? "I'm not certain about that *jig time*. What kinda phrase is that, an aporia?"

"Come see me at the Fountain Blue, dolling."

A TOMATO

Bill came out of the kitchen, an anxious look on his face. "Say, Charlie, how about a tomato with supper? What do you say?"

I knew that when Bill mentioned supper this early in the evening— it was barely late afternoon—that he had made plans to go downtown to the Jewel Theater to moon over Dolly Rae, the strange, pretty girl who did the cleaning up after the last show. He was trying, I knew, although I wouldn't let on that I knew, to ask her, once again, about her reasons for trying to raise the gleaming white bicycle from the bottom of the swimming pool over at the other motel in town. Dolly Rae Jewett was a determined girl, and her cooking, as the old phrase has it, had won Bill's heart. Well, it was terrific cooking, and her guaglio, matarazzo, and other robust dishes were something to talk about indeed. Bill would have been much better off concentrating on Dolly Rae and her great food and her sweet, pretty face, and forgetting all about the gleaming white bicycle that lay so mysteriously, so silently and symbolically at the bottom of the deep end of that damn pool.

I looked over at him, my mind moving unwillingly to a picture of the two drowned dogs that an old neighbor of mine, Mrs. Moskowitz, used to own. I was twelve at the time, and I'll never forget those dogs being trundled home in a baby carriage, the water leaking out of its sides and bottom. It had been, that memory, a major problem for me for many years, but I'd worked my way through it with the help of a very fine and strong lay therapist, who'd made me realize that I had to admit to the problem before I could even begin to deal with it. "One drink is a lot and a thousand are not too many," she'd say, enigmatically, at the end of each informal session. And, sometimes, she'd tell me of her mentor, Schultz, now dead these many years, and mourned, or so I came to understand, by scores of his students, many of them aspiring poets.

I admired Bill, but it was in his best interest, or so I felt, never to say so, at least not to him. It was better to mention my admiration for him to other people whom I didn't admire at all, but who, or so I learned, admired Bill. He liked to repair cars and trucks and with the money he saved over and above his living expenses he planned on buying a very large, green canvas patio umbrella for his favorite table near the pool in our motel's courtyard. "Let me tell you about another great umbrella I saw in Monkey Ward's yesterday," he'd chuckle.

"Tomato sounds good, Bill," I muttered quietly, looking out at the chipped enamel table by the pool as if seeing it for the first time. "Fresh basil O.K.?" Bill nodded, but it was a distracted nod. He was thinking, I knew, of Dolly Rae and the bicycle that both obsessed and, in some dark, strange way, frightened her. Then he was gone in a swirl of cigarette smoke, and I wondered how many minutes had been taken off my life *this* time.

Six months earlier, when I'd left school to work for a man who made authentic Shaker furniture for people who loved it for its spirit and its subtle hint of the last Shaker colony on Biscayne Bay, I'd met Bill at the Jewel, the only movie house in town. The Jewel showed the kind of offbeat films that you'd never see at the Octiplex out at the Big River Mall, and had a reputation for being cutting edge. It was run by a man called "Chet," who made up in loud brio what he lacked in subtle verve.

Bill had been carrying a bag of what turned out to be ripe tomatoes, and we struck up a conversation almost instantly, although I can't recall a word of it. All I do know is that somehow our shared delight in tomatoes led to an arrangement whereby we moved into the Red Wagon Motel together and split all expenses. So far, it had worked out wonderfully well, but I was beginning to worry about his growing anxiety concerning Dolly Rae and the bicycle. But our first few months together were idyllic, and Bill's pleasure in imagining the green umbrella that would highlight the pool area was my pleasure as well.

As soon as he became aware of Dolly Rae, everything began to change, subtly at first, and then, quite overtly. Dolly Rae, it turned out, not only understood more, much more about Bill's umbrella dream than I ever could, but she had innumerable stories about bicycles and the role that they'd played in the settling—she called it "the gentling"—of the hard-bitten Wheat Corridor back in her home state. Her favorite bicycle color was tomato red, and when Bill discovered this, he was a goner. He'd do anything to impress Dolly Rae, and began making up stories about crawdaddies and drinking bouts and God knows what. And then, one day, Dolly Rae took him over to her motel and showed him, shimmering and blurred at the bottom of their pool, a white bicycle that seemed to glow in the water. He stood and looked at it in silence, and then, suddenly, at the instigation of her little brother, Carver, she jumped into the pool and swam to the bottom. She had her hands on the bicycle and was hauling it to the surface, but although she broke the water with it, it was impossible for her to get it out of the pool. And Bill knew, he just knew, that his help wasn't wanted. As she relinquished her grip on what Bill had decided to call a "symbol," and let it sink, dreamily, to the bottom, Carver whispered to Bill that she'd never get it out, she'd been trying for days, it wasn't going to be pulled out of that darn water!

Each day, often more than once, before her stint at the Jewel or after it, Dolly Rae would plunge fiercely into the pool and wrestle with the white bicycle. And each day, Bill, sullen with despair, would ask her why she needed to *do* this. She would look at him coolly, the kind of look that said she wished she was looking at him for the first time, and ask him to explain, again, what a "symbol" is. It was more and more obvious to me, if not to Bill in his agony of wonder, that life simply goes on and on until, one sad day, it stops.

Some time after that, so Bill told me one night, looking up suddenly from a patio-furniture catalog, Dolly Rae began calling people on the phone at random, baiting them, misrepresenting herself, telling jokes about Schultz and Moskowitz and, afterward, crying bitterly. Bill told me that he thought the calls humanized her, softened her somehow— his phrase was "gentled her," much to my bitter amusement—but that Dolly Rae maintained that they were just as frustrating as trying to haul that bicycle out of the pool. He began to see less of her, and as he grew quieter, I noticed that he had stopped mentioning the green umbrella. It had become, at least for me, a symbol to set against the symbol that he had created for Dolly Rae.

"Be back soon?" I asked, staring into the space above the pool. He nodded, and said, "Sure, where else would I be?"

I smiled and made the gesture of slicing a tomato, then mimed swimming up, through dark, cold water, with a bicycle cradled in my arms, a bicycle that would not, that could not ever reveal its secrets. He laughed, ruefully, and as the sun moved behind the outer cottages, I said, quietly, "Schultz is dead."

"And tomatoes are cheaper," Bill replied.

NOTES

A Desk

[1] The actual, whatever it may look like, does not "roar on."

[2] Many people feel that all the mysteries of fiction have been solved, and a good thing too!

[3] It is probably not a good idea to "fuck with" memoirs in which the victim-protagonist-memoirist has already been fucked with.

[4] Critics and biographers dispute the fact that Proust was satisfied with one draft, despite the discovery of the "Toulouse" notebooks.

[5] Patricia Melton Cunningham's first novel, *Wrenched from Love*, will soon be published by Gusher Books, a subsidiary of Shell Oil Publishers, Ltd.

[6] "Spondulicks" most often refer to quarters and dimes, as in "Drop a spondulick on the bum."

[7] A *pasticcio* may be translated as "a goddamned fucking mess."

[8] Wallace Stegner, although he owned a car, did not actually *like* it.

[9] Death asks no quarter—nor spondulick.

A Joke

[1] It is amazing just how many jokes people know.

[2] "Cut velvet!" is, for instance, the punch line of one of those many jokes.

[3] The male gaze is at its most pernicious in the academic world, for reasons which will soon be made clear.

[4] *Dark Corridors of Wheat* has been out of print for many years, despite a relentless campaign waged by the wheelchair industry to make it available at a reasonable price.

[5] Maurice Bucks is on the record as saying that he "doesn't really care all that much" about money, and after his successful takeover of the Vietnamese government, noted that "it's got very, very little to do with money, and I want people to know that." It has recently been reported that Mr. Bucks has contracted AIDS, which fact has led hundreds—some say thousands—to argue for the existence of God.

[6] The paper used to print the "Prairie Edition" of the Jewett biography is made of acid-free gopher skin, a lame remark, indeed.

[7] "Handy Sarah" is a mistake of the sort regularly attributed to this author, who, it is said, can "really write" if he "puts his mind to it," books that are "wonderfully readable."

[8] People no longer get soused, but, instead, succumb to their addictions, addictions which they cannot triumph over, or "lick," unless they first *admit they have a problem* and then *get help*.

[9] Boxers are excellent swimmers, which should have alerted their owner to the suspicious nature of these two hapless dogs' deaths; of course, the soused Sarah had never admitted that she had a problem and therefore never got help.

[10] The "haircut" joke was a favorite of saloon comedians, who often and anon told it while soused.

[11] "Aporia" is a Greek word that means "who knows?" or, in certain contexts, "what the—?"

A Tomato

[1] A gleaming white bicycle at the bottom of a pool is an example of an aporia—but not in real life.

[2] Spaghetti alla matarazzo is not for everyone.

[3] The author had originally thought to place the gleaming white bicycle in the projection booth of the Jewel theater, pronounced, at least in this story, "thee-*ay*-ter," as if you didn't know.

[4] The baby carriage trundled home to Mrs. Moskowitz was most probably a stroller.

[5] "A thousand drinks are not enough [to pay] for a haircut," or so says the Albanian proverb.

[6] Basil is never used in spaghetti alla matarazzo, save by natives of the Midwest.

[7] The Surgeon General has suggested that the Moskowitz curse is, in all probability, secondhand smoke.

[8] The *green umbrella* by the *motel pool* is a motif that some wag had once thought of donating to Raymond Carver.

[9] "Carver," in this text, has no relation to the late writer (see above).

[10] That the author does not tell us what "tomatoes are cheaper" *than* may be an instance of a free aporia, or, in the parlance of narratology, an ekphrasis.

[11] "Put that in your pipe and smoke it," he laughed.

MADAME REALISM LIES HERE

by Lynne Tillman

Madame Realism awoke with a bad taste in her mouth. All night long she'd thrashed in bed like a trapped animal. The white cotton sheets twisted around her frenetic, sleeping body, and, like hands, nearly strangled her. Madame Realism pounded her pillow, beating it into weird shapes, and when finally she lay her head on it, she smothered her face under the blanket, to muffle the world around her. She wanted to tear herself from the world, but it was tearing at her. She wasn't ever sure if she was sleeping even when she was. Her unconscious escapades exhausted her. All restless night, her dreams plagued her, both too real and too fantastic.

She was in a large auditorium and a work of art spoke for her. Much as she tried, she couldn't control any of its utterances. Everywhere she went, people thought that what it said was the final word about her. When they didn't think it spoke for her, they thought it spoke about them. They objected violently to what it was saying and started fighting with each other—kickboxing, wrestling. The event was televised, and everything was available worldwide. It was also taped, a permanent record of what should have been fleeting. Mortified, Madame Realism fled, escaping with her life.

In another dream, a sculpture she'd made resembled her. It didn't look exactly like her, but it was close enough. Friends and critics didn't notice any significant differences. But she thought it was uglier. Still, what was beauty? ugliness? Maybe she'd done something to herself—a nose job or facelift, her friends speculated. But the statue was much taller—bigger than life, everyone said—with an exaggerated, cartoonish quality. People confused her with it, as if they were identical. Madame Realism kept insisting, We're not the same. But no one listened.

In the last, she took off her clothes repeatedly, and, standing naked in a capacious and stark-white hospital-like room, where experiments and operations might be performed, she lectured on the history of art. To be heard, she told herself, she needed to be naked, to expose herself. Nakedness was honesty, she thought; besides she had nothing to hide. But no one saw that. They just saw her body. And it wasn't even her own. It was kind of generic.

Madame Realism rubbed the sleep out of her eyes. Everything was a test, each morning an examination. She was full of delinquent questions and renegade answers. In her waking life, as in her dreams, she concocted art that confronted ideas about art. So life wasn't easy; few people wanted to be challenged. But Madame Realism had principles and beliefs, though she occasionally tried to disown them, and her vanity made her vulnerable. What if she didn't look good? Still, she didn't want to serve convention, like a craven waiter, or fear being cheap and brazen, either.

Things had no regard for the claims of authors and patrons, and Madame Realism's work wasn't her child. But, inevitably, it was related to her, often unflatteringly. Sometimes she was vilified, as if she were the mother of a bad kid who couldn't tell the truth. But what if art can't tell the truth? What if it lies? Madame Realism did sometimes, shamelessly, recklessly. She remembered some of her lies, and the ones she didn't could return, misshapen, to undo her. Uncomfortable now, she stretched, and the small bones in her neck cracked. The body realigns itself, she'd heard, which comforted her for reasons she didn't entirely understand.

Sometimes, in overwrought moments, in her own mental pictures, where she entertained illusions, she made art—no, life—perform death-defying feats. It wiped out the painful past. Life quit its impetuous movement into unrecognizable territory. She herself brutally punched treacherous impermanence in the nose. In her TV movies, art took an heroic stand, like misguided Custer, defeated criminal mortality, and kept her alive, eternally.

But Madame Realism, like everyone else, knew Custer's fate. So it wasn't surprising that her late-night dates with Morpheus had turned increasingly frantic. She didn't believe in an afterlife, and those who did had never been dead.

What if, Madame Realism mused, finally arising from her messy bed with an acrid, metallic taste in her mouth, what if art was like Frankenstein? Mary Shelley's inspiration for Frankenstein was the golem, which, legend goes, was a creature fashioned from clay by a Rabbi Low in the 17th century. The figure was meant to protect the Jewish people. But once alive, the golem ran amok, turned against its creator, and became destructive. Rabbi Low was forced to destroy the golem.

Madame Realism walked creakily into the kitchen and filled the kettle with water. She put the kettle on the stove. She always did the same thing every morning, but this morning she felt awkward. Then she walked into the bathroom and looked at herself in the mirror. She discovered a terrible sight. What she had dreamed had happened. There was a cartoonish quality to her. All her features were exaggerated. Her breasts had disappeared and her chest tripled in size, her ass was so big she could barely sit on a chair. Her biceps were enormous, and she flexed them. It was strangely thrilling and terrifying.

Madame Realism started to scream, but what came out of her mouth was the first line of a bad joke: "Have you heard the one about the farmer's daughter?" She recited this mechanically, when she really meant to cry: This can't be happening. She tried to collect herself. She could be the temporary product of her own alien imagination. She could be a joke that wasn't meant to be funny.

Tremulous and determined, she walked into her studio—actually shuffled, for with so much new weight on her, she couldn't move as quickly as she once had. Carrying the burden of new thoughts, she reassured herself, was weird and ungainly. Just as soon as she said that to herself, all the art in her studio metamorphosed. It was not hers, but she recognized the impulse to make it. Still, she was shocked. She'd never used rubber or stainless steel before.

Then, like golems, these monstrous pieces—which is what she thought of the invaders—became animated. A large inflatable flower pushed her into a chair. And her ass was so big, she fell on the floor. When she looked up, there was a ceramic double figure staring down at her. It was Michael Jackson and one of his pet monkeys. Michael was crying. She'd never seen him cry before. Then he said:

Call me tasteless, it doesn't matter. What you expect to see is just as tasteless. What is taste? Educated love? Don't you love me? After all this time, don't you know me... aren't we friends?... Don't be surprised—I might be Michaelangelo's David. I am popular and so was David. He protected his people and fought Goliath and won.

Well, Madame Realism heard herself say aloud, do you know the one about... She wanted to say something about ideas, but she couldn't stop kidding around.

Michael Jackson and his beloved monkey became silent, and suddenly she was overcome by a copulating couple. Madame Realism felt embarrassment creep over her new, big body. The lovers disengaged, and the beautiful woman spoke:

Against death, I summon lust and love. Lust is always against death. It is life. Without my freely given consent and with it, totally, I'm driven to mark things out of an existence that will end against its will. It's a death I cannot forge, predict, violate or annihilate. Ineluctable death is always at the center, and like birth the only permanent part of life, central to meaning and meaninglessness. And to this meaning and meaninglessness, I ask, Why shouldn't you look at us in the act of love? What happens to you when you do?

The sculpted male partner nodded in agreement. The couple moved off and threw each other to the ground.

Madame Realism knew the word pornography meant the description of the life and activities of prostitutes, of what was obscene, and that there were drawings of prostitutes' activities in private orgy rooms back in ancient times. Even now, the rooms weren't supposed to be seen. But what shouldn't be seen, and why? Legendary New Yorker Brendan Gill, known as a man of taste, was asked why he watched pornography. He said: Because it gives me pleasure. Pleasure, Madame Realism said aloud, pleasure. Her biceps flexed.

With that, an enormous and brilliant painting appeared on the wall. Unlike the sculptures that had conversed with her, the painting remained mute. But it looked at her, it looked at her with an enormous unblinking eye, and it stared at her as if she were an object. It seemed to be the viewer, so she was being viewed by art. This had never happened before, she thought, with peculiar wonder. She felt naked in a fresh and violent way.

Art was a golem. It had taken over. It had a life of its own, and now she feared it was assessing her. What did it say about her? To be winning, she told it a joke, which more or less popped out of her mouth. But the painted eye kept looking. She followed its gaze and realized the painting wasn't really seeing her. She wanted it to, but it didn't. It stared past her, perhaps into the future or the past. It didn't speak, though maybe it spoke to her. It didn't offer an opinion of her. It said nothing at all about her. Nothing.

Madame Realism swooned and fainted. When she awoke, everything was as it had been in her studio. Her work was back in its place. She was no longer cartoonish.

She thought: My work can't protect me. I will be true to my fantasies, even when I don't recognize them. What I make is not entirely in my power, as conscious as I try to be. It's always in my hands and out of my hands, too. I like to look at things, because they make me feel good, even when they make me feel bad. I'm proud to be melancholic. I like to make things, because they usually make me feel good. I am not satisfied with the world, so I add to it. My desires are on display. What I make I love and hate.

Forever after, and this is strange to report, maybe unbelievable, Madame Realism saw things differently. Like Kafka's "Hunger Artist," who fasted for the carnival public who watched him waste away, until one day, when no one was looking or cared that he was starving, he wasted into nothing and died, she did what she wanted. She made a spectacle of herself from time to time, mostly in her work, trying to tell the truth and finding there's no truth like an untruth. She kept pushing herself to greater and greater joys and deprivations, which were invariably linked. And like any interesting artist, who can't help herself and is in thrall to her own discoveries, Madame Realism shocked herself most, over and over again.

THE READER

by David Gilbert

As I give a public reading, my attention, such as it is, divides, then divides again. I'm functionally unhealthy, split and yet adaptable like one more information device. I suspect in many ways I am just like you. But you don't front for a best-selling author. If I were reading my own work, "my book," I would at this moment be one person, subject to no more than typical lapses of attention. I would not be reading in protest in a smart downtown bookstore, an independent that is fighting the good fight against the chains. With my book I would be reading to my standing auditors as they press against my admirers who came early and took all the chairs. I would be reading to them as if gravity were of a downward cast and at the same time moving bodies toward the reader.

For a number of years I have fronted as a living pseudonym. I am the reader and not the author as the author is commonly defined, a definition my author/employer uses, again and again. Even giving interviews does not grant me author status. I am, as the author likes to call me when we argue, a corporate shill. As I read I loathe the fat, phobic and best-selling cow hiding in our suite of rooms. I loathe our mutual dependence in its conceptual terms and images. Having said that, I do like her early work, the writing I first read in public. Unfortunately, her early writing is not what I'm reading now.

At first, my imposture was very exciting as entry-level celebrity. As the glamorous reader, my face lives in close proximity to her books. I read in good faith for a number of book tours before I came to resent it. I don't know how I've lasted so long as puff pony for the exhausted book lover. I have a stamina that has outlasted common sense.

Consistent with my role, I've come to believe that as a glamorous woman I am more important than the author. What else would you expect? It sounds like the tortured and resenting complaint of a grad student. I admit as much. Yet book by book, interview after interview, I have taken over the writing; I am the hand behind its evolution and genesis, if it has in fact evolved. There is no longer any reason not to think that the publisher hired the cow to provide me with texts to milk in public. God knows she can't be seen. Getting her through a hotel lobby is a major undertaking.

The promise of the arrangement is gone, despite my unflagging Q-rating. To my growing horror the author is no longer writing about my life, rather, she is writing my life as a revenge of the weak against the strong. She resents those who can present themselves in public. Hers is a subversion that I have not as yet been able to counter. I manage only by the smallest of margins to work the writing so it is worthy of presentation. Of necessity I have learned to counter-read the text and at times I have rewritten passages to save me the embarrassment. No one knows. My audiences continue to lean towards me in unsustainable postures, too exhausted to fall.

The book tour is coming to an end at which time I will walk away from our collaboration. Money is no longer a problem, but my contempt is. As I read I know that my gestures and psychological states do not correspond. This fragmentation is part of the charm. The audience might as well have cards to raise at intervals with scrawled guesses— what is she experiencing? Or is she choosing her date for the evening? It's common knowledge that I take someone back to the hotel after a reading. I have admitted as much in interviews. The choosing of my date (with its lurid fantasies) is yet another split that is at work while I read. It is not as clean as multiple images on a screen, nor as simple as a two-headed author in a hotel suite. This is the subject of my book.

As the reading ends, I have decided to take the Stalker back to the hotel. The mad cow does not like him and her judgment is for the most part right on. He has followed me from city to city. He is compliant, appreciative of subtle abuse, and disposable. I like sending him to the lobby to wait all night in a chair. Then, in the morning, if I feel like it, I send for him before I shower. The cow especially hates to hear us when she is having her "working" breakfast. She is especially fond of pastries with her coffee. I think the sweet buttery goo is the source of her out-sized pimples which look like carbuncles on a plumber's ass.

As I pause for water, the Stalker is thumbing through a book from the Eastern Religion section. He is right—enough duality. He also knows that he will go home with me. Had I more energy I might take the admiring blonde in the front row. If she hangs around for the book signing, I'll take it as a sign that she is inexperienced (or not since college) which means admiration, fumbling and dithery breathing. The cow's breathing is enough for the entire floor. The Stalker is so well-conditioned and fit that he hardly breaks a sweat. He is to eroticism what I am to authorship.

My reader will soon make her dutiful yet subordinate entrance to report on the reading. She will boast, bluster—she's doing me a favor, mind you—and put on such a display of the psychologically trivial. I make sure that I'm in bed with as little light as possible. My praise—I am grateful—is an apology that also allows me to patronize and her to forbear our pathetic roles. Contractually, she must give me a report on the reading, which she likes to do immediately upon returning. Then she is free to be serviced by one of her groupies, if she is slumming at the hotel and not out with another author. Imagine a real author thinking that she is also a real author. How stupid we've all become.

Our interaction is so complicated now that I've completely lost myself in it. I simply comply with her need to unburden herself. My

listening goes a long way in keeping a lid on things. She is an opinion-
ated bimbo of the highest order. Her opinions used to amuse me. Now
I have little interest in her analysis of our authorship and her iconic status as the glamorous presenter of my work. She's really a glorified sales
lady selling what she can't afford.

What is more interesting, and at the same time pathetic, is how she
has had an influence on me. How I decided not to be a public persona
is not the story of a woman with great confidence. It is gossip. This
much I will admit. What choice did I have considering market forces?
Her influence is too common and as a result I'm an embarrassment. She
has diabolical auto-suggestive talents which she uses on me daily. My
weight is out of control, bulging around my small features. This change
came about after she accused me of eating tubs of chicken while she was
out reading my novels aloud. The room "smells of KFC" she would say
when she returned. I laughed for a week. Then to gall her and ruin her
partnered masturbation, I began sending out for the worst food, ribs,
chicken, anything as long as it was greasy, smelly and came in
Styrofoam. Now I'm quite happy if there is rib sauce on the sheets or if
I wake the next morning with chicken bones in bed with me. After all,
this is what I do while she's out shopping for clothes. It's shocking how
easily I became the person she imagined.

When I auditioned readers she stood among the other women in
what amounted to a police lineup. She was the only one who made me
cry. I cried behind a screen with the consultants who went on and on
about her potential Q-rating. Now she often comes home to find me
crying. I hate her because she makes me cry and finds me crying. She
takes great delight in consoling me. It wouldn't surprise you to know
that I'm not always sincere. I can cry without sadness just as I eat without appetite. Often my crying is wet hysterical laughing. When I do
this, and I do it often and dismissively, she invariably leaves the room
and joins her date. I'm sure she takes it out on them.

My reader has never accepted, or for that matter, understood that I
write the books and we do better if she simply fronts for me. Her obser-

vation that the books have nothing to do with my life is unworthy of response. They are, though, my books. She is a very good reader. We all have our roles. I attended the readings for several tours taking notes, but it made us both nervous. Who needs it? In the vulgar, I am very wealthy and she is well compensated. It galls her. She has the national disease of nothing ever being enough. One more book and it's over. I'm bored. I'm fat, but I can get help. I had better skin when we simply fought. This can't go on.

I've never returned to our hotel room with two dates. I hope they understand that they have to do all the work. The Stalker is with me and the blonde, who gripped my hand as I signed her book, agreed to return for a drink. She claims to have studied me in college. Does that give her the right to touch me? The Stalker and the blonde eye-ball one another in the elevator. The tension is exciting. They will know each other intimately tonight and they know that. Maybe I'll just watch and work myself into a jealous delirium. The cow will be pissed with an orgy in the suite.

It sounds like she's arrived with an entourage. I supposed her dates are carrying the books she's stolen. Always titles she couldn't possibly read. Books she pretends to be reading while she's working on her abs. I can see her demonstrating gym equipment on an infomercial.

They didn't need much encouragement. I put them to bed and watched for a while. The Stalker is more versatile than I thought and eager for some side action. And if the blonde did or did not experiment with women in college, she's not inhibited now. She probably wrote a paper defending pornography. God knows why I gave my bed away on a night when I'd like nothing more than a hot bath and a good night's sleep.

The cow is waiting for a report on the evening's reading. If only I had a hat full of money to dump on her bed, the evening's take. Invariably, I enter her room while she's studying her financial portfolio on her greasy laptop. A few minutes with her will determine the rest of my evening. My disgust for her does not help my judgment. I could very well end up in bed with my admirers, pummeled between their sweaty bodies.

My reader confesses, she unburdens herself breathlessly as if she had just staggered out of an orgy. She says that she wants to write a book about our experience, a memoir rancid with hurt feelings. As she speaks, I admire her stamina which I always thought a kind of dogged stupidity. I thought she would have tired of being a reader long ago. She's determined to make a damn fool of herself in public. Go ahead. I don't tell her but I've known this would happen for a long time. I've been tightening her garrote book by book. I had no choice just as she has no choice but to expose herself in the most limited way. As a practical matter, I know all about her book. I blessed the project. I've encouraged her editor—no litigation. The only hope for her is to publish her book and read it as herself. She has been more in hiding than I have. In the end she'll want to reconcile. We'll cry together.

They are in bed following my explicit requests as if they were being filmed. If they do what I have asked while I'm reporting to the cow, they are more gullible than is fair. I can't help but hear them as I tell the cow of my plans to publish. My book has a publication date. Of course, I tell her enough to elicit patronizing support. It is patronizing support that has destroyed her talent. She has worked with her material in a disingenuous manner, ruining it. She has a kind of mad cow disease. She's eaten her own brains.

Another lecture. So what if my act as the seducing author is tired. What is lost in my act of self destruction is the phony reader, not the glamour or my book. I have gone to school on her talent. I will dedicate my book to her. When I read for myself, I will return to my hotel alone. Unless I hire her to read for me.

We've gone too far. If it were not melodramatic, I would have shouted this at her and at her spent colleagues gawking in the doorway. But it's all so funny. Who do they think I am? Their eager-to-please faces tell me that they are enjoying themselves on my publisher's tab. Apparently they are waiting for instructions. My reader is uncomfortable now that she has confessed to authorship. She's too tired to join them when they swing again. The gravitas suggests drooping buttocks. Her colleagues are frozen in their preposterous what-next expressions. I offer them ribs. They're all so reticent. They fuck like rabbits but no one will make the first move. I bark at them and they all come at once. The young woman with the small pointy breasts. The stalker with his sticky shorts. And trailing behind is my reader, eyes filled with tears. They make a piquant mess.

When my dates are fed and sent home—I'll give them some cash—I must beg out of my contract. There are only a few dates left. I will grovel. I'll do anything. I can't stop crying. This scares the blonde away. Competing hysterics. I suppose she'll dress in the elevator. It's just too weird for her. I would be happy to be dressing in the elevator with the Stalker. The mad cow is weeping with her amused eyes.

Yes, you may go. I'll read my own work. I'll just stand up there and read without explanation. People will walk out. Just stop crying, I'll pour you a bath. You can be in the audience. We'll acknowledge the deception. It will do wonders for both our books. At the mention of her book she revives and begins undressing, the only thing she does well.

SUNDAY MORNING

by Karl Roeseler

We bought an early edition of the English newspaper's Sunday paper on Saturday afternoon. We also bought a bag of coffee beans and two small loaves of unleavened bread, dusted with powdered sugar and filled with almond paste, so that we had everything we needed. We could sleep as late as we wanted. And when we woke, we'd simply grind our beans and heat our water.

But we forgot milk. We both drink milk in our coffee.

So there it was, Sunday morning, and we'd have to venture out anyway, venture out into the Old City which we were still getting to know.

Our friends from home had warned us. And although we received a few house-warming presents and several letters describing attempts to call us during our first week in residence, we secretly suspected that most had written us off when we insisted on moving to this city with its schizophrenic nature, the disjunctive halves that will never be whole, the Old City and the New.

All our friends from the embassy lived in the New City, where each neighborhood was really a compound of flats reserved for the members of this nation or that tribe.

In the Old City, all were outsiders; refugees might rub shoulders with famous poets and politicians, yet everyone was somehow aligned to the revolution, and the poets were often as famous for their poverty as for their poetry.

We wanted to prepare our Sunday so we wouldn't have to venture out, but we forgot our milk.

So we showered and shaved after all. We left our apartment thinking: There must be a store open in this quarter. There must be.

The stairs were empty—we could hear running water in one apartment, smell baking bread from another, and some voices could be heard from the street but when we got outside there was no one there.

And although it was still early enough to be cool, and the coolness made the air seem moist, we knew that it would soon be hot and arid.

We walked for several blocks and passed a store on nearly every corner, but they were all closed. So eventually we turned around.

We were almost in front of our apartment building again when we heard the sound of yelling and laughing, which seemed to come from the alley beside our building.

A barefoot girl, in blue jeans and a grey sweatshirt, was leaning her back against a baby grand piano, pushing as hard as she could, and laughing, nearly collapsing. A woman from the top floor of our building was yelling down to the girl, then, also laughing, waved her arms to us. She was captivating, an instantly likable blonde of robust friendliness and a sultry world-embracing sensuality. She was old without being old, fleshy without being fat—and even this early in the morning, as she swayed with the heaviness of her breasts, her sensuality stopped us, we were captivated by her body and her spirit—her voice sounded direct, bright, like a mother calling to children.

Without thinking we turned to see if she was smiling and calling to someone behind us. But, of course, there was no one.

We turned back just as two boys, also in jeans and sweatshirts but wearing bright athletic shoes, came out of the building across the alley.

They immediately took their places alongside the girl and started to push the piano.

The woman at the window continued calling to us.

Other people—mostly elderly—opened their windows and began laughing.

The girl and the two boys began to move the piano but it was slow going—they would move ahead a foot or two and then had to stop... the piano was clearly too heavy for them.

The girl looked at us and smiled.

They boys stopped pushing, looked at us as well, their faces blank— only beginning to smile as we walked over and pantomimed our desire to help.

All five of us pushing together were able to move the piano easily, but we couldn't steer very well, and we drifted from side to side of the road as we made our journey. And, although many of the streets in the neighborhood were unpaved, the path we followed began on asphalt and took us to cobblestones. Every once in a while one of the piano's wheels fell into a gap between the stones and suddenly stopped us. Starting again was difficult at first, but we quickly learned the right balance of pushing and tugging necessary to regain our momentum, although this sort of thing made steering even more difficult as we tended to roll toward the smoothest and most-worn sections of the road. The occasional Sunday morning car had to stop while we drifted toward it then veered away.

Finally a man, who could just as easily have been a streetcorner flower vendor as an anarchist, joined us and acted as a kind of helmsman, pulling at the front of the piano and guiding us to the loading dock of the small brick warehouse that was, it turned out, our final destination: we had traveled a distance of only four or five blocks although it seemed much further, possibly because we had spent the last two blocks pushing the piano without the benefit of any shade whatsoever—the day was now so hot and the air so dry that the earlier coolness of the morning seemed like an illusion to us.

We shook hands with our new friends but declined their repeated offers to join them for hot tea. We simply wanted to buy some milk, we said.

The man who might have been a flower vendor showed us the way to a store, located some seven blocks away, just outside our quarter.

As we paid for our milk, the store clerk, perhaps even its owner, a man about our age who, although outwardly friendly, seemed to stare at us, and eventually asked us who we were and where we lived, since he couldn't recall ever having seen us in his store.

We told him we were Americans living in the Old City, just a few blocks away.

He spat. "Those people are all thieves." He dropped our change on the wooden counter and turned his back to us.

There were more people in the street now, and, as we strolled back to our new home, several people nodded to us. Even so, we were glad to finally reach our apartment, and take off our shoes, and resume making our coffee.

We poured milk into our cups as we waited for the water to boil.

Someone knocked at our door.

We almost didn't answer, our little excursion for milk had drained all our energy, but I wanted to see who was knocking so politely, a firm yet gentle rapping, immediately repeated, then a moment later repeated again.

I tiptoed to the door and looked out the peephole: the man standing there wore the uniform of a policeman.

As I opened the door, I noticed that he was about my age, with clear eyes that seemed somehow amused, not unfriendly, but distant also as if preoccupied by some intellectual abstraction.

"One of your neighbors," he said, "has reported the theft of a piano."

THE CONTRIBUTORS

ETEL ADNAN lives in Sausalito and Paris. She is a poet, fiction writer and playwright. In recent years, she has also collaborated with a number of composers, including Gavin Bryars, who features her work on his recent CD, *Cadman Requiem*. Works of fiction include the novel *Sitt Marie Rose* and the collections *There*, *Of Cities & Women (Letters to Fawwaz)* and *Paris When It's Naked*. Works of poetry include *The Arab Apocalypse*, *From A to Z*, *The Spring Flowers Own & The Manifestations of the Voyage* and *The Indian Never Had a Horse*.

CHARLOTTE CARTER lives in New York. She is the author of the novels *Rhode Island Red*, *Coq au Vin*, and *Drumsticks*. She is also the author of a volume of short stories and poetry *Personal Effects*.

ADRIAN DANNATT lives in New York and is Editor-at-Large of *Open City*. His stories have been published in many literary journals. He has also written about art and is the author of *The United States Holocaust Museum*, and edited *Beat Streuli USA 95* and *Wim Delvoye*.

LYDIA DAVIS lives in upstate New York and is the author of the novel *The End of the Story* and the short story collections *Almost No Memory* and *Break It Down*. She is also the translator of Maurice Blanchot, Michel Leiris and Pierre Jean Jouve, and is currently at work on a translation of Marcel Proust's *Swann's Way*.

STEPHEN DIXON lives in Baltimore. He is the author of the novels *Frog*, *Interstate*, *Fall & Rise: A Novel*, *30: Pieces of a Novel*, *Gould: A Novel in Two Novels*, *Too Late*, *Work*, *Tisch* and *Garbage*. He also has many collections of short stories including *Sleep*, *Long Made Short*, *All Gone: 18 Short Stories*, *Love and Will: 20 Stories*, *Friends: More Will & Magna Stories*, *No Relief*, *Fourteen Stories*, *Time to Go*, *The Play & Other Stories*, *Man on Stage: Play Stories*, *Movies: 17 Stories* and *The Stories of Stephen Dixon*.

DAVID GILBERT lives and works in the San Francisco Bay Area. In addition to being the co-editor of this anthology, he is the author of a collection of short stories *I Shot The Hairdresser* and the short novel *Five Happiness*. He also co-edited the previous Trip Street anthology *2000andWhat? Stories about the Turn of the Millennium*.

JAMES KELMAN lives in Glasgow, Scotland, and is the author of the novels *How Late It Was, How Late*, *The Busconductor Hines*, *A Disaffection*, *A Chancer* and *Greyhound for Breakfast*. His short story collections include *The Good Times*, *The Burn*, *Not Not While The Giro*, and *Busted Scotch*, a selection of his stories published in the US. Other publications include a collection of plays *Hardie and Baird & Other Plays*, and a collection of essays *Some Recent Attacks: Essays Cultural and Political*.

A.L. KENNEDY lives in Glasgow. She is the author of the novels *Original Bliss, Everything You Need, So I Am Glad* and *Looking for the Possible Dance*, and the short story collections *Night Geometry and the Garscadden Trains* and *Now That You're Back*. She is also the author of a work of nonfiction *On Bullfighting.*

DEBORAH LEVY lives in London and writes plays, poetry, and fiction. Her plays include *Pax, Clam, The B File, Pushing the Prince into Denmark, MacBeth—False Memories* and *Honey Baby*, collected in *Deborah Levy Plays I*. She is the author of the novels *Billy and Girl, The Unloved, Swallowing Geography*, and *Beautiful Mutants*, a collection of short stories *Orphelia and the Great Idea*, and a collection of poetry *An Amorous Discourse in the Suburbs of Hell*. She is also the editor of the drama anthology *Walks on Water*. See www.deborahlevy.com for more information on Deborah's work.

DAVID LYNN lives in Gambier, Ohio, and is editor of the *Kenyon Review*. He is the author of a collection of short stories *Fortune Telling* and a volume of literary criticism *The Hero's Tale: Narrators in the Early Modern Novel.*

COLUM MCCANN lives in New York. His novels are *Songdogs* and *This Side of Brightness*. His short stories have been collected in *Everything in this Country Must* and in *Fishing the Sloe-Black River.*

ZZ PACKER lives in the San Francisco Bay Area. The story included here will be part of her collection of short stories, forthcoming from Riverhead Books.

KARL ROESELER lives and works in San Francisco. In addition to being the co-editor of this anthology, he is the author of the novel *The Adventures of Gesso Martin* and a book of poems *Last Decade*. He also co-edited the previous Trip Street anthology *2000andWhat? Stories about the Turn of the Millennium.*

GEORGE SAUNDERS lives and works in Syracuse, New York, and is the author of the collections of short fiction *Civilwarland in Bad Decline* and *Pastoralia*. He also collaborated with illustrator Lane Smith on a children's book *The Very Persistent Gappers of Firp.*

GILBERT SORRENTINO lives and works in Stanford, California, and is the author of the novels *Mulligan Stew, Steelwork, Imaginative Qualities of Actual Things, Crystal Vision, The Sky Changes, Odd Number, Rose Theatre, Mysterioso, Under The Shadow, Splendide-Hôtel, Aberration of Starlight, Blue Pastoral* and *Red the Fiend*. Works of poetry include *The Orangery, Corrosive Sublimate, The Darkness Surrounds Us, Selected Poems 1958-1980* and *White Sail*. He is also the author of a volume of criticism *Something Said.*

PHILIP TERRY lives in Exmouth, Devon. He is the author of the lipogrammatic novel *The Book of Bachelors*, which was published as a special issue of *The Review of Contemporary Fiction*. He is also the editor of a recent anthology of stories based on Ovid's *Metamorphosis* called *Ovid Metamorphosed.*

LYNNE TILLMAN lives in New York. She writes fiction and nonfiction. Her novels are *No Lease on Life, Cast in Doubt, Motion Sickness* and *Haunted Houses*. She is also the author of the short story collections *Madame Realism Complex* and *Absence Makes the Heart*. Her nonfiction includes *The Velvet Years: Warhol's Factory 1965-1967* and *Bookstore: The Life and Times of Jeannette Watson and Books & Co.*, as well as a collection of essays *The Broad Picture.*

LEWIS WARSH lives in New York and writes poetry, fiction and autobiography. He is the author of the novels *A Free Man* and *Agnes & Sally*, the collection of short stories *Money Under the Table*, and the volumes of autobiographical writing *Part of My History, The Maharajah's Son* and *Bustin's Island*. His books of poetry include *Avenue of Escape, Private Agenda, Methods of Birth Control, Blue Heaven, Dreaming as One, Information from the Surface of Venus* and *The Corset*.

MAC WELLMAN lives in New York. He writes plays, fiction and poetry. He plays include *Girl Gone, Jennie Richee, Terminal Hip, Bad Penny, 7 Blowjobs, Crowbar, Sincerity Forever, Whirligig, Dracula, Swoop, The Bad Infinity, Softshoe, Harm's Way, The Professional Frenchman, Cleveland, The Self-Begotten, A Murder of Crows* and *The Hyacinth McCaw,* and have been collected in *The Bad Infinity, The Land Beyond the Forest* and *Crowtet I,* as well as in the forthcoming *Cellophane Plays.* He is also the author of the novels *The Fortuneteller: A Jest* and *Annie Salem: An American Tale,* as well as several books of poetry, including *A Shelf in Woop's Clothing, Satires* and *In Praise of Secrecy.* He co-edited (with Douglas Messerli) the anthology *From the Other Side of the Century II: A New American Drama 1960-1995.*

DALLAS WIEBE lives in Cincinnati, Ohio. He is the author of the novels *Our Asian Journey* and *Skyblue the Badass.* His short fiction is collected in *Going to the Mountain, The Transparent Eye-Ball* and *Skyblue's Essays.* He is also the author of a book of poetry *The Kansas Poems.*

JOHN WILLIAMS lives in Cardiff, Wales. He is the author of a novel *Cardiff Dead* and a collection of short stories *Five Pubs, Two Bars and a Nightclub.*

ACKNOWLEDGMENTS

"Black Ceasar's" Copyright ©1999 by John Williams, originally published in the UK in his collection of short stories *Five Pubs, Two Bars and a Nightclub*.

"Muazzez" Copyright ©2001 by Mac Wellman.

"Cave Girl" Copyright ©2001 by Deborah Levy.

"Days of Or" Copyright ©1999 by Adrian Dannatt originally appeared in *Open City*.

"Breaking Sugar" Copyright ©1997 by A.L. Kennedy originally appeared in the British edition of *Original Bliss*, published in 1997 by Jonathan Cape and reissued by Vintage (Random House UK) in 1998. It was also published separately in the magazine *Story*.

"Sample Writing Sample" Copyright ©1997 by Gilbert Sorrentino originally appeared in *Arshile*.

"Madame Realism Lies Here" Copyright ©2001 by Lynne Tillman.

"The Reader" Copyright ©2001 by David Gilbert.

"Sunday Morning" Copyright ©2000 by Karl Roeseler originally appeared in *First Intensity*.

The editors would like to acknowledge the assistance of Mrs. Catherine Trippet, Random House Archive & Library, in obtaining permission to include A.L. Kennedy's story.

The editors also thank Anastazja Siebor for her help with proofreading.

OTHER FICTION BY TRIP STREET PRESS

DOOMSDAY BELLY by Susan Smith Nash
A collection of short stories by the author of *Channel-Surfing the Apocalypse* and *A Paleontologist's Notebook*. Susan Smith Nash possesses the rare ability to write about topical events and issues without being predictable or mundane. Oklahoma will never be the same. "These brilliant, often riveting apocalyptic narratives are so complex, edgy and darkly funny that it is almost a betrayal of them to point out the beauty of their style."
—*Jack Foley*   ISBN: 0-9639192-4-5 $12.00

MONEY UNDER THE TABLE by Lewis Warsh
A collection of short stories from the author of *A Free Man* and *Private Agenda*. "Lewis Warsh's stories are devastatingly good. Fragments of plain unlikely lives are enacted in expertly simple, sinuous prose. Characters evolve in a bewitching and scary realm somewhere between event and insight, at the unnerving center of what we take to be reality. These people are all too convincing—we wouldn't want to be them, but we probably are."
—*Harry Mathews*   ISBN: 0-9639192-3-7 $10.00

THE ADVENTURES OF GESSO MARTIN by Karl Roeseler
A novel by the author of *Last Decade*. "Particle by particle, with glittering clarity, the world of the fortunate Gesso Martin, the gentle chauffeur-cum-philosopher, gradually accumulates around us in an engagingly fantastic tale..." —*Lydia Davis*
                                                               ISBN: 0-9639192-1-0 $8.95

FIVE HAPPINESS by David Gilbert
A short acrostic novel by the author of *I Shot The Hairdresser*. A narrative extravaganza in which characters appear and disappear without warning. Fiction has never been so strange. "Captivating, brilliant prose that may be blinding to the normal eye."—*Kevin Sampsell*
                                                               ISBN: 0-9639192-0-2 $6.95

2000ANDWHAT? STORIES ABOUT THE TURN OF THE MILLENNIUM
A collection of 20 short stories about the turn of the millennium featuring both known and emerging writers of innovative fiction. What unifies these writers is their ability to avoid a predictable response to an inevitable event. Stories by Etel Adnan, Margaret Atwood, Frederick Barthelme, Lydia Davis, David Gilbert, Steve Katz, Kevin Killian, Donna Levreault, Harry Mathews, Ameena Meer, Susan Smith Nash, Niels Nielsen, Karl Roeseler, Teri Roney, Linda Rudolph, Kevin Sampsell, Lynne Tillman, Karen Tei Yamashita, Lewis Warsh and Mac Wellman.   ISBN: 0-9639192-2-9 $12.00

Order from your favorite bookseller or directly from our distributor, Small Press Distribution
1.800.869.7553 or www.spdbooks.com